KING IN TRAINING

MELODY TYDEN

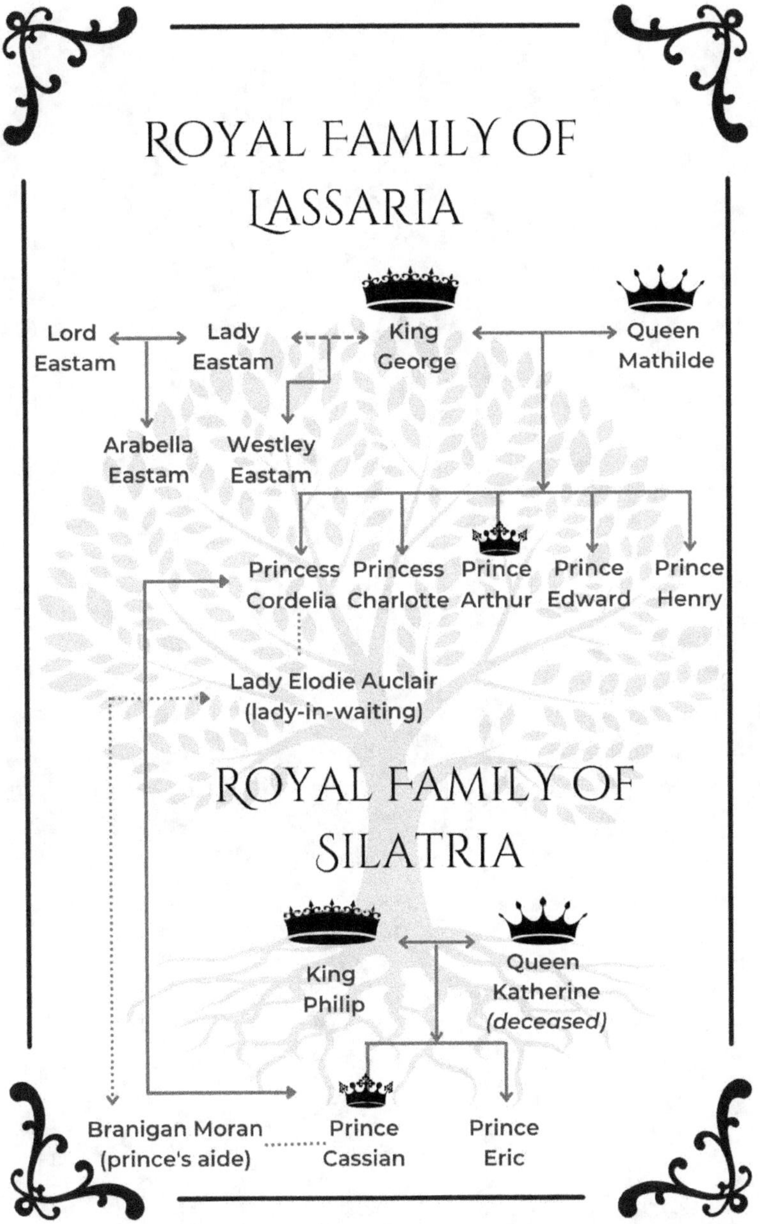

ROYAL FAMILY OF LASSARIA

Lord Eastam

Lady Eastam

King George

Queen Mathilde

Arabella Eastam

Westley Eastam

Princess Cordelia

Princess Charlotte

Prince Arthur

Prince Edward

Prince Henry

Lady Elodie Auclair (lady-in-waiting)

ROYAL FAMILY OF SILATRIA

King Philip

Queen Katherine *(deceased)*

Branigan Moran (prince's aide)

Prince Cassian

Prince Eric

CHAPTER ONE

~Elodie~

Round, lazy raindrops fell silently to the cobbled ground of the castle courtyard as I sat by the open window of the princess' chamber. In the outside space below me, people went about their business, moving food into the castle larders, delivering messages, or arriving or departing for meetings with the king or the prince. Their steps quickened as the rain hit them, trying to get somewhere dry. High above them, I jotted down a few sentences in the book I always kept with me, whilst simultaneously keeping my ears attuned to the one sound I hoped to hear above all others: the sound of horses' hooves, bringing my fiancé, Bran, safely back home.

It had been three weeks since Bran, Arthur, and Eric left to try to track down Her Highness' scheming half-brother Westley Eastam. Three weeks, and yet no matter what else I tried to focus on, my heart remained in that moment when Bran told me he had to go.

It took place here in Princess Cordelia's rooms. If I looked up, I could almost see him as he appeared then, his large frame almost filling the door entirely. I assumed he had come on behalf of the prince, so I bowed to him politely. "I'm afraid Her Highness isn't here. She went to meet with His Majesty a short while ago."

"I know," he replied, looking around rather nervously at the other ladies in the room. "I'm actually here to speak with you, my lady."

Immediately, I understood his meaning and it made my stomach flutter. Whatever he wanted to say to me must be personal in nature.

"Please," I said simply, inviting him into the princess' small study. Her personal space to write letters and carry out whatever duties her husband the prince assigned to her, this room hadn't been put into use yet since we were so recently arrived. It seemed the most private place for us to go.

As soon as the door closed behind us, Bran dropped the air of restraint he had worn in front of the others and took me by the hands instead. My heart soared in anticipation.

Since our very first meeting, I had been drawn to this gentle giant of a man with his unusual red hair and his kind eyes. At the time, he thought I was the Lassarian princess rather than her lady-in-waiting. My mistress Dee, or Princess Cordelia as most people knew her, had insisted that we swap identities for the trip to Silatria where she would marry the crown prince. I had been unable to resist her pleading, as so often happened, and so, even as Bran and I spent more time together and my feelings for him became clearer, he still kept a respectful distance, believing me to be his employer's fiancée.

Eventually, the whole truth came out, not only about Dee being the princess, but that one of the men with Bran, a man we had known as Sean, was actually Prince Cassian, Dee's original fiancé who we had all believed to be dead. The twist of fate amazed us all, but for me, aside from being delighted that my dear friend could marry the man she had fallen for, it also meant that, if he were so inclined, Bran would be allowed to reciprocate my feelings at last.

We were the same, he and I: two people from rather humble beginnings who had a close friendship with our royal masters. With Dee and I living in the Silatrian castle now, nothing prevented Bran and I from pursuing a courtship, if we so desired.

However, he behaved so properly and respectfully at all times that I really hadn't known if he felt our connection the same way I did. I didn't know it for sure until the night before this meeting when he had helped to rescue me after Dee and I were abducted, and made his feelings far clearer than they had previously been by kissing me in front of all the soldiers, and in front of Dee and the prince too.

Although Dee's excitement knew no bounds, I tried not to get carried away. In my head, the happy-ever-after ending had already written itself, but I had to remind myself that Bran had not actually told me how he felt or what he wanted from me. So far, we had only our quiet, week-long friendship and that one unforgettable kiss.

So, when he took me by the hands and I looked up into his deep blue eyes, I couldn't help hoping that this would be the moment I had been waiting for my whole life.

"Elodie, I need to leave for a while."

For a moment, the deep rumble of his voice as he said my name distracted me so much that I completely missed what he actually said. When it finally registered, my lips parted in dismay. "Leave? When? Why? For how long?"

He answered me precisely, in the order I'd asked the questions. "Now, because the prince asked me to. I don't know how long I'll be."

His explanation left a lot unanswered, so I added one more question: "To do what?"

"Cass wants me to go with Arthur and Eric to try to track down Eastam. If we're lucky, it might only be a week or two. If we're not lucky..."

He trailed off, but I didn't need him to explain any further. I understood; if they couldn't find him, it might be months rather than weeks before he returned.

My heart ached at the idea of not seeing him for so long, but I tried to put on a brave face and look on the bright side. That had always been my nature. "The prince trusts you very much to give you such an important job."

Bran nodded in agreement. "He does, which is why I can't let him down, no matter how much I would prefer to stay."

Did he want to stay because of me? The way he looked at me seemed to suggest that might be the case, but he still hadn't actually said so.

"We are subject to the whims of our superiors, both of us," he added, giving me a gentle smile. "Whether it's pretending to be someone we are not, or going somewhere we would rather not go."

"I understand," I assured him, smiling back at him. No one understood that better than I. "I will be wishing you good fortune and praying for your safe return."

"Thank you." A sincere smile of gratitude graced his lips before his eyes slid away from me and a new, nervous expression crossed his face. "And when I get back, perhaps we could... I mean, if it's okay with the prince and the princess, and if you want to... or if you would at least agree to consider it... perhaps we could discuss..."

He had lost me in all the conditions, and I tried to move him along to the point. "We could what?"

He swallowed before forcing the words out. "We could... get married, perhaps?"

It felt like my heart stopped beating for a second. Did he really just ask me to marry him? This sweet, kind, loyal man truly wanted to be mine? Dee had suggested he might want to marry me but I thought she had only exaggerated to make me feel better, as was in *her* nature to do.

"Elodie?" He said my name again, nervously this time, and I realized I hadn't actually answered him yet.

"Yes? I mean, yes. Yes, we could. If you would like to."

"I would," he agreed. "If you would like to."

This could go on all day, I could see, unless one of us took responsibility for the decision, so I limited myself to a two-word response. "I would."

This time, a smile of relief and genuine happiness broke out across his face, but before long, sheepishness replaced it. "I know this isn't the most romantic proposal ever. It's not getting stuck in a cave in the rain together or making a moonlight escape on horseback."

I smiled as he recounted Cass and Dee's adventures. "That's okay," I promised him. "They have their love story; this is ours, and I think it's perfect."

"I think you're perfect," he whispered before pressing his lips gently to mine in only the second kiss of my life. The first one had been a shock, and this one surprised me too, so full of tenderness that it made my heart melt.

I knew being with a man as husband and wife involved more than just kissing. Dee had told me about what she and the prince did together and how she enjoyed it, but I couldn't imagine anything that felt better than this.

When he pulled back from me, both joy and sadness played in his eyes. "I didn't want to go without telling you how I feel, but now, I must leave. I'll return to you as soon as I can."

I believed that with every fibre of my being, and before he went, I gave him my favour, the small linen square embroidered with my initials that every lady in my position kept to gift her knight when he went into battle.

Bran's destination wouldn't be a battle, thank goodness, but he still needed good luck, so I gave him the cloth and my best wishes with it before he took his leave.

"No sign of them today?" Dee's cheerful voice pulled me out of my reminiscence as she walked into the room, a couple of her other attendants trailing after her. She shooed them away with her usual straightforwardness and closed the door behind them, leaving the two of us alone.

I could pretend I had another reason to sit by the window besides listening for the horses, but it seemed pointless. She could read me like a book. "Nothing yet," I told her.

I spoke too soon, though. A moment later, the clatter of horse's hooves reached our ears and we both headed to the window just in time to see two cloaked men dismounting in the wet courtyard below. They pulled their hoods back as they got under cover, and my heart sank at the sight of their dark heads. Neither one could be Bran.

"Never mind," Dee said, trying to cheer me up. "They might have news! Let's go and see."

At her insistence, we headed downstairs to the great hall where the king received petitioners. The guards caught sight of Dee as she entered and escorted her to the front of the room to take a seat next to Prince Cassian. He gave her a curious but affectionate look as she joined him, and she leaned over to whisper something in his ear. The prince's eyes moved to me and he gave me a sympathetic nod and a smile. He knew all about me and Bran.

The men we had seen approach arrived soon afterwards, saying they had a message for the king's ears only. Rising from his throne, the king, the prince and Dee all moved towards the king's private receiving room while my heart sank once again. Although Dee would tell me what they said, I had still hoped to hear it for myself if it had anything to do with Bran.

Just before the door closed, however, Dee's face reappeared and she beckoned to me, indicating I should join them. With a quick glance around, I did just that. It might not be entirely proper, but my curiosity overruled my sense of propriety.

The men were already speaking as I entered, and Dee and I stayed near the door, careful not to draw attention to ourselves.

"We have a message, Your Majesty, from Prince Arthur of Lassaria."

I'd hoped for exactly that, and my heart beat faster with the news. Had they been successful? Were they on the way home? Dee's hands gripped mine as we waited to hear the rest of what they had to say.

"He says they had almost cornered Eastam but the bastard managed to elude them again. Unfortunately, during the skirmish, one of your men went missing. They believe Eastam has taken him."

"Eric?" the king demanded in agitation, wondering if Eastam had managed to capture his own son. Cassian's younger brother had also gone to help in the search.

The messenger shook his head, and I knew deep in my heart what the next words out of his mouth were going to be before he said them. "No, he took one of the prince's men. His Highness said you would know him as Bran."

~Cordelia~

I couldn't tell who looked more upset when my brother's messengers announced that Bran had been captured: my best friend, holding onto me for dear life, or my husband who had sent him away in the first place. Guilt and worry flashed across Cass' handsome face as he pressed the men for more information.

"When did this happen?"

"Three days ago, Your Highness," the man who had delivered the news replied. "Prince Arthur's men are attempting to track him, but Prince Eric thought you would want to know right away."

That was surprisingly considerate of Eric. Perhaps the few weeks he'd been away were already starting to do him some good in terms of thinking of people other than himself. We could only hope.

Cass looked to his father, clearly torn. "I know you don't want Eric and I both gone at the same time..."

"I don't," the king quickly agreed. "You can send a small contingent of soldiers back with these men, but you need to remain here. You still have a lot of work to do."

Cass' lips tightened and I could see how much he wanted to argue, but he held his tongue. He had been working non-stop for the last few weeks, trying to clean up the mess that Westley Eastam had made of the kingdom's army and finances. The work needed to be done, but I knew that in his heart, he wanted to jump on his horse right now and go make sure his best friend was safe and sound.

"Dee?" Elodie whispered my name beside me and I quickly turned my attention to her. "What would Westley want with Bran?"

"I'm not sure." Who could say why Westley did anything he did? My father's illegitimate son had been a thorn in my family's side for as long as I could remember, but only recently did we come to realize the full extent of his scheming. He had infiltrated the Silatrian court, blackmailed the hapless Prince Eric and attempted to kill Cass, all in an attempt to place his half-sister, Arabella, on the Silatrian throne as Eric's bride, enabling him to take over my father's kingdom of Lassaria.

The whole plot felt needlessly complicated, full of treachery and fraud, and only due to the lucky accident of Cass surviving the attempt on his life and coming back to Silatria in disguise had we been able to fully uncover it. However, Westley himself had escaped capture, and continued to do so from the sounds of it.

What *would* he want with Bran? He might try to get information from him, or to hold him for ransom, perhaps. There were many scenarios I could think of and many others I probably couldn't, but sharing any of those with Elodie right now wouldn't be helpful, not when she looked pale with worry and so fragile that a light breeze might blow her over.

"What is she doing in here?" The king had, unfortunately, heard our whispering and noticed Elodie's presence in the room.

"She's with me, Your Majesty," I replied confidently, even though I knew a better reason than that would be required for anyone to be in the king's private receiving room without his permission.

"Then you both can leave," he ordered. Elodie's hands trembled in mine at the king's tone, but I didn't take it personally. His anger and frustration had much more to do with the situation than with us, frustration over the news that Westley hadn't yet been brought to heel. Cass shot me an apologetic look as I led Elodie out of the room and back up the stairs to my own chambers.

Refusing the assistance of my other ladies, Elodie and I barricaded ourselves in my bedroom, as we often did when we wanted a bit of privacy.

"Do you think he'll be okay, Dee?" she asked as we sat down on the bed together, tears pooling in the corner of her eyes. "If something happens to him..."

"Don't fire up your imagination now," I commanded firmly. "He'll be fine. Cass will send his very best men to go and find him, and Bran will be back here with us in no time."

"You don't really believe that, do you." She didn't even phrase it as a question, just a quiet statement, all the more devastating for its simplicity. Usually so optimistic, it pained me to see her lose faith. "Westley is ruthless. He tried to kill His Highness and replace you, and who knows what he would have done to us if we hadn't escaped from him. Perhaps he has already killed Bran."

Two tears spilled over, trailing down her cheeks as I quickly pulled her into a tight hug. "No, we're not thinking that. Bran has been in worse messes than this, Lodee, and he always pulls through. Cass has told me just some of the things the two of them got up to when they were growing up. If he can survive being Cass' friend, he can survive anything."

I hoped to make her laugh, but her lips trembled instead. More tears slipped down her cheeks, faster and faster until I couldn't take it anymore. Elodie was the sweetest, most selfless person I had ever met, and for the first time, she wanted something for herself. I would be damned if Westley Eastam, of all people, would take it away from her.

"Stay here," I told her, grabbing a blanket and wrapping it around her. "Climb into my bed if you want to. I'll be back as soon as I can."

"Dee? Where are you going?" Her tear-stained face broke my heart as she looked up at me.

"To fix this," I promised, jumping to my feet and leaving the room, heading back down the way we came.

The throne in the great hall sat empty, which I took to mean the king and Cass were still in the king's private room. I made my way back there, the guard opening the door for me deferentially as I approached.

They were, indeed, still inside, and alone now, which suited me even better. Both men looked over at me as I walked in, Cass' face softening the way it always did when he saw me.

"How is Lady Elodie?" Cass asked, referring to my lady-in-waiting by her proper title in front of his father.

"Distraught," I replied bluntly and honestly. "And I know that you are too."

He might not be crying about it like Elodie, but I knew how much it must be upsetting him.

His brow lined with concern and frustration. "I wish I could go, Dee. My father and I have just been discussing it, but…"

"The crown prince of Silatria cannot abandon his duties to go look for one man," the king interrupted, addressing his lecture to me as if he expected an argument. "Eric and your brother are responsible for the safety of the men under their command. Cassian must remain here."

"There are no circumstances under which you would allow him to go, even for a short time?" I wanted to be sure I understood exactly what the rules were.

"No," the king insisted. "Not for one man."

"But he came after me when Arabella's men took me," I pointed out.

"That's different. You're his wife, the crown princess. In that case, we could make an exception."

Ah-ha. I could work with that. "Very well," I conceded. "I understand, Your Majesty."

I bowed my head to my father-in-law before turning back to my husband.

"I will see you later, Your Highness."

"Dee?" He gave me a suspicious look, his eyes narrowed. "What's going on?"

He knew me too well. He suspected I had something up my sleeve and he was absolutely right, but if I told him now, it would ruin my plans.

"I will see you later," I repeated, taking my leave and returning back to my own rooms once again to where Elodie waited for me, still wrapped up in the blanket. Her eyes were dry now but still filled with that look of hopelessness. I would drive that feeling from her heart, no matter what it took.

"What happened?" she asked as I walked in, determination in every step.

"We need to pack, Lodee. You and I are taking another trip."

CHAPTER TWO

My men came out of the manor house with doleful, apologetic expressions on their faces. "No sign of him, Your Highness."

I wished I could say it surprised me, but after three weeks of going from estate to estate, following the leads we had about where Westley Eastam might be hiding out, the disappointment had become routine.

The man was like a ghost. We were told we'd find him in one town, but by the time we got there, he'd either just left or had never been there at all. We searched the Eastams' two main properties extensively, but he had dozens of other smaller landholdings across the kingdom. By now, it felt like a never-ending goose chase and everyone in our party had already started to tire of it.

We had a close call three days ago when we came across some men wearing his colours in a local tavern. We hadn't even been looking for them at that point, we were simply searching for a place to rest and eat after a long day's travelling and there they were: not Eastam himself, but certainly the closest we'd come to him.

They scrambled as soon as they caught sight of us and in the melee that followed, we somehow lost Prince Cassian's man, Bran. I had no idea how they captured him, but after over an hour of searching, we had to accept that he must have been taken. Or killed, perhaps, but that seemed less likely. They probably would have left the body behind if that were the case.

I had several reasons to regret his loss. First, I had come to like him in the short time we had spent together. He was a serious man, but kind and thoughtful. Second, his strategizing skills far exceeded those of his prince, Eric. And third, I knew Cassian would not be pleased at all if we couldn't recover him. The last thing I needed right now would be to make an enemy of my new brother-in-law.

Speaking of Eric, he came back from the stables where he and some of the other men in our group had been looking. He just shook his head at me, not bothering to say anything. Since I had already checked the other outbuildings, it looked like we'd reached another dead end.

"Back to the town we passed earlier, then," I suggested wearily. The town had an inn where we could regroup and plan our next move.

An hour later, Eric and I were huddled over a map at one of the tavern tables. Black marks had been made against the places we had already checked, but Westley could easily go back to any of them. He could literally be anywhere, and if we were ever going to find him, we needed better information, getting to us faster. It felt like we were always a step behind.

When we'd decided on a destination for the next day, Eric leaned back in his chair, scanning the room. "Those two serving maids have been eyeing us since we walked in," he told me, raising his eyebrows suggestively. "Which one do you want?"

"This isn't a pleasure trip for me," I replied, not even bothering to look at the women in question. "I'm going to get a good night's rest so I can be ready for tomorrow."

"Suit yourself," Eric replied with a shrug, getting to his feet. "I'll just have them both then."

I rolled my eyes, but as he walked off, I couldn't help watching as he approached them to see what their reaction would be. Surely if he suggested such a thing to them, they would be appalled?

But instead, they all smiled and whispered to each other as one of Eric's hands moved to one woman's waist while his other hand touched the other one's face. Soon, he and one of the women left the room while the other returned to her work, looking far more flushed than before.

How did he do it? In nearly every town where we stopped, he ended up with a woman in his bed. Their rank, or lack thereof, never bothered him, nor did he care if they had another man in the picture. So long as they were clean and willing, he simply took his pleasure and moved on, unbothered by any other considerations.

Perhaps my reticence came from growing up with the constant headache of my illegitimate half-brother, but the idea of bedding a woman who could easily end up with child left me in a cold sweat. As heir to the kingdom, I couldn't simply go around spreading my seed anywhere I felt like it. Knowing what it felt like, I never wanted to put my own son under the threat posed by those who felt they had a rightful claim to his throne.

Eric, however, seemed to have no such worries. Maybe he thought his position as second prince gave him some leeway, or maybe he simply figured that the women who would go with him so easily would do the same for any man, so they wouldn't be able to pinpoint him as the father of any child that might result.

Whatever the reason, he seemed to be having a lot more fun than I was on this trip, or in general, for that matter.

Because the one thing he didn't know and that I would never admit to him? I had never taken a woman to my bed at all.

~Bran~

So far, I couldn't complain about Westley Eastam's treatment of his prisoners. When his men managed to get the jump on me, I truly feared the worst. I didn't fear death; if my time had come, I would meet it bravely, but I couldn't help regretting the idea that I wouldn't get to see Elodie at least once more before I died.

Those thoughts turned out to be unfounded anyway. His men had no intention of harming me. They simply lashed me to one of their horses in such a manner that I had no chance of escape, and brought me here, to the small manor house by the sea where I'd spent the last three days.

I met with Eastam himself once, on my second day here. He came to the small room where they kept me; basic, but not inhospitable. It had a bed and a small privy in one corner which hung out over the side of the house onto the grass below. Food and drink were brought to me twice a day. Besides being bored, the arrangements were otherwise perfectly comfortable. I had endured far worse before.

"So, you're Cassian's man," Westley said as he entered the room flanked by two armed men, just in case I might attempt anything.

I made no reply. I wouldn't give him any information, no matter how basic.

Undeterred by my silence, he continued. "If you join me, I can give anything you could possibly want. Money, power, women? Help me bring down Cassian, and it can all be yours."

I didn't bother to respond to that either. I would never betray Cass, not for anything, and I already had everything I could possibly want waiting for me back in Silatria.

He seemed to have expected my silence in response to his offer. "Very well. I will be using you to bring him to me in any case. If you cooperate, you can reap the rewards. If you don't, you can suffer with him. It's your choice."

When I still said nothing, he left, and I hadn't seen him again since. His threats about luring Cass sounded hollow to me. The king would never let Cass come and look for me, not with Eric already searching for Eastam, so I had no intention of wasting my time fretting about that.

Instead, I spent every minute I could looking for a way out of this room and this house. The room had only one door, barred from the other side and, from what I could hear, guarded at all times. I spent one morning searching every inch of the wall for some kind of hidden passage like those at the Silatrian castle, but every stone stayed securely in place.

Well, all except for one that I managed to pull out, but it led nowhere, simply leaving a small hole that the wind could blow through. My body would never fit through the small privy hole, nor the windows either. I seemed to be well and truly stuck.

The only glimmer of hope came from the twice-daily visits from my jailers when they brought my meals. Usually, two people arrived: one with the food and one additional guard. I paid careful attention to their routine, the way the person brought the tray in for me and set it down on the small table, his back to me. The first day, the guard had his sword drawn, ready for trouble, but by day three, he left it in its scabbard, simply keeping his hand on the hilt.

When they brought the second meal on the third day, I'd made my preparations. As the man brought the tray in, he tripped over the loose stone I had placed in his path and the tray went flying, sending food and liquid everywhere. As the guard went to help him up, letting go of his sword, I grabbed it from him and held it up to them both. "Any noise you make will be your last," I warned them and they both nodded silently as they looked up at me. At times, my size could be a powerful tool in my favour.

Quickly, I left the room, barring it behind me so they couldn't follow, and crept down the empty corridor. There had never been much noise outside my door, so I didn't expect to find many people there now, and thankfully, the hall appeared empty. As stealthily as possible, I moved down the passage, hurrying past each opening until only one open door remained between me and the exit. Voices came from the room, but the exit was close enough that if I ran, even if the people inside saw me, they shouldn't catch me. Then, I just had to hope I could find a horse outside and I would be on my way before anyone could do a thing about it.

Just as my muscles tensed to make my break, a sentence drifted out from the open doorway, stopping me in my tracks. "So, we're agreed: you'll make your approach to Arthur and get the item for me."

There could be no mistaking Westley's voice, and it sounded like he'd hatched some new scheme involving the Lassarian prince. If I knew the details of it, I might be able to warn him, so I held my breath, waiting for the response.

When the reply came, it took me completely by surprise; the words were plain enough, but the voice itself stood out: a woman's voice, in an unusual accent.

"You can count on me, Your Grace. No one will suspect a thing."

My eyes darted to the exit again. I should really leave now, but this could be important information. Indecision tore at me as I struggled over whether I should stay or go.

Smugness permeated Eastam's response. "I trust you. After all, we both know what's at stake for you."

The woman made no reply that I could hear and I leaned closer, straining to pick up anything I might be missing. The next thing I knew, a flash of colour filled my field of vision and I somehow found myself on my knees, the sword taken from my hand.

"It seems you have an eavesdropping problem, Your Grace." The woman's voice came from directly above me as Westley's boots announced each step as he came to join her. I could hear him clearly, but I hadn't heard her move at all.

"How did you...?" Westley muttered at the sight of me before calling for his guards.

"Do you want me to take care of him?" The blade of the sword pressed against my neck as the woman spoke to Westley rather than me. I still hadn't seen her face and I didn't dare look up now. An inch in the wrong direction could mean my end.

"No. I need him alive," Westley replied brusquely. The men he'd called for arrived and he ordered them to take me back to my room and increase my guard. That would make getting away more difficult, but I would keep trying, no matter the odds.

As the men hauled me to my feet, I caught just a glimpse of the woman who had been speaking, and my mouth dropped open in surprise. She wore a blue dress, suited to nobility, with long, dark hair covering her shoulders, and skin that appeared nearly as dark. I had seen paintings of people with skin that colour before, but never anyone in real life.

Where on earth had Westley found her and what, exactly, were the two of them planning?

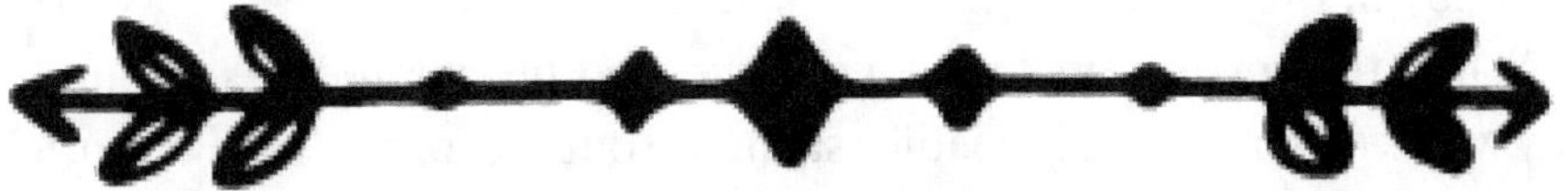

~Cassian~

The longer my father's business dragged on, the more frustrated I became. He received petitioners one day a week, which happened to be today, and he wanted me there with him while he did. Now that I had married, he insisted that I begin to train in earnest to take over from him. Personally, I saw no need for urgency. He had years left ahead of him, a young-ish man still in good health, and I hoped to enjoy those years simply being the crown prince with my beautiful new wife and the family we would hopefully be starting soon, rather than having all the burdens that came with the crown.

Right now, however, I couldn't get my mind off exactly what my wife might be up to.

I knew that look in Dee's eye when she bowed her head to my father in apparent submission. Despite appearances, she hadn't given in, not by a long shot, but exactly what she had in mind, I couldn't begin to guess.

She had it completely right that the news about Bran had upset me. The idea of that bastard Eastam holding him, torturing him or doing God knows what else to him, gnawed away at my stomach. But other than sending a few extra men to try to help track him down, what could I do? Even if I could go myself, what good would it do? I had no more information about where to find Eastam than Arthur did, and the thought of joining the hunt and being away from Dee for weeks held little appeal to me.

We needed to talk about it privately, and I needed to give Lady Elodie my sympathy personally. I could only imagine how worried Elodie must be with this news, but despite the distressing nature of it, I remained optimistic. Knowing Eastam, he probably intended to hold Bran as part of some convoluted new scheme, and as soon as Arthur and Eric tracked him down, Bran could return to us safe and sound.

When the session finally ended, I excused myself and headed up to my wife's rooms where her ladies sat in the outer room, as usual. Neither Dee nor Elodie were among them, but the door to Dee's bedroom was closed, so they must be in there.

I followed proper protocol, asking one of the ladies to make Dee aware of my presence, and the woman obligingly went over to knock on the bedroom door. A few moments went by before she frowned, knocking again, still to no reply.

"Your Highness?" she called through the door. "Lady Elodie?"

Still nothing, and my feeling of foreboding increased. How upset must she be if she ignored her lady? It seemed I would have to take matters into my own hands.

Walking over to the door, I knocked myself. "Cordelia? It's me."

I never called her Cordelia in private, but in front of her ladies, I had to be more proper. Sometimes, I thought back fondly on those days we spent together on her trip here, away from all the trappings of the court, and wished we could have more days like those. I far preferred when we could just be Cass and Dee without having to worry about propriety.

Nothing but silence came from the other side of the door, and when I tried to push it open, it didn't budge. The bar must be drawn across it, which confused me even more. Could they be sleeping? Why had they shut the world out?

I knocked even louder. "Dee?" To hell with being proper.

When I still got no reply, I turned on my heel, heading to my own rooms instead. A hidden network of passages in the palace connected my room to hers, and though that door might be barred too, I expected it wouldn't be. She always left it open for me.

A few minutes later, I pushed open the secret door into Dee's room, only to find the chamber completely empty. The bar had been drawn across the main door, as I suspected, but there was no sign of Dee or Elodie. The bed remained fully made and the windows open. It looked like they had just stepped out, but where would they have gone and why wouldn't they have used the door?

I almost missed the note on the bed until a gust of wind through one of the windows caught the edges, making it flap lightly in the breeze.

Striding over to the bed, I snatched it and scanned the page as quickly as possible.

Cass,

I'm afraid I've been taken hostage yet again - this time by a need to help my dear friend set her mind at rest.

Should you wish to find us, you could start at the inn where we made our escape from Arabella's men. There's a good chance we'll be there tonight. I believe your father will agree this is an exception to his rule, but if you really can't get away, perhaps you could send Sean instead.

All my love,

Dee

She had to be kidding. She couldn't really have left the castle on her own...?

I couldn't even finish that thought. Of course she could have. We were talking about Dee, my fearless, unpredictable princess with a huge heart. She would do anything to help those she cared for. She often spoke about Elodie's selflessness, not seeming to realize that she shared that same quality.

Well, if she could slip out of the castle undetected, so could I. Returning to my room, I packed my travelling bag, wrote a note of my own, and headed down to the stables. My favourite charger was missing and I had no doubt that Dee had taken it for herself. The stablehand quickly confirmed as much when I asked him about it.

"Did Princess Cordelia and her lady take some horses earlier?"

"Yes, Your Highness. They said they were going for a short ride. Matthew and William went with them but they're not back yet."

A short ride? The lie nearly made me snort. At least she had taken some of her guard, which eased my worry a little. Though I knew Dee could defend herself against a lot of things, I felt better knowing she had company. It also meant I wouldn't need to bring my own escort; if I could catch up with them tonight, we'd have plenty of backup.

After tying my bag to a different horse, I pulled out the message I'd composed and passed it to the man next to me. "Take that to the king, make sure it is placed in his hand only."

The man nodded at me seriously as he took the note and a thrill of excitement ran through me at the idea of getting away from the palace for a while, not to mention going on another journey with Dee. It seemed that life would never be boring with her around.

They probably had a head start of about three hours, I estimated, based on the amount of time I had spent with my father after Dee left us. I would be riding faster than them, but even so, I might not catch up with them until the inn. I knew exactly which inn her note referred to. Every moment of that last journey with her had firmly imprinted itself on my memory. I could retrace it step-for-step if I needed to.

The sun had nearly set by the time I arrived at the lodgings and tied up my horse. No one paid me any attention. Few people here would have ever seen Prince Cassian in person before, so on my own, without an entourage and travelling under an assumed name, no one had any reason to suspect I might be anything other than what I claimed to be: a man on his way to meet his wife.

The innkeeper, a man of my father's age, gave me a warm smile when I told him I had come to meet my wife who had arrived earlier. "The pretty blonde one? You're a lucky man."

He didn't have to tell me.

He pointed me to the door and I found William standing guard outside it. "Your Highness," he greeted me sheepishly. "We had no idea what Her Highness had planned until we'd left the castle."

Blaming him would be pointless. No one could stop Dee once she got an idea in her head. "She's inside?" I asked instead.

He nodded. "Lady Elodie is next door, and Matthew and I are beside her. I waited here for you to arrive. Her Highness seemed convinced you would."

Of course she did. How could I resist? "Thank you. You can turn in for now and tomorrow, we'll discuss our next moves."

He bowed to me and headed to his own room while I knocked on the door, setting my face into a frown. I didn't want her thinking she'd got away scot-free just yet.

The door opened just a crack and Dee's face appeared, her blue eyes offering a silent apology. "How angry are you with me?"

"Let me in and we can discuss it," I told her, trying my best to keep a stern expression on. She stepped back to allow me to pass, closing and barring the door behind me, and when she had finished, I turned to face her. "You really can't just run off like this, Dee. It's dangerous for anyone, but especially for you if anyone were to recognize you."

"I know." She did sound truly sorry. "I didn't mean to worry you, which is why I left the note. But you should have seen Lodee, Cass! Maybe we can't do anything to help Bran, but if she feels like we're trying, it will help to keep her mind off..."

I placed a finger against her lips to stop her explanations. My lips were twitching as I tried not to smile. "I understand why you did it, but you will need to be punished for it."

Her eyes widened in surprise before she swallowed bravely. "I will accept full responsibility. What is the punishment to be?"

I stepped closer to her, lowering my voice. "No one here knows who we are. As far as they know, we're just a newly married couple, and before the night is over, I want every person here to have heard you screaming my name."

If I thought her eyes were wide before, it didn't compare to how big they went when she realized exactly what I meant. "Cass!"

"Not that name," I told her, giving her a wink as her own gaze grew more heated. "Tonight, you can call me Sean."

~Cordelia~

The gleam in Cass' eyes made my knees weak. At first, when he appeared at the door, I believed his anger to be genuine. He'd never directed such a serious, disapproving look at me before. I'd seen him use it on other people, Eric in particular, but never on me.

But after what he just said, I understood now that it had only been for show. He was playing a part and inviting me to play with him, and though I didn't know exactly what kind of 'punishment' he had in mind, I had a feeling I wouldn't find it very unpleasant at all.

"What can I do to show you how sorry I am, Sean?" I asked, using the name he'd given himself when we first met and the name he told me he wanted me to call him now. For just a moment, I could see him again the first time I laid eyes on him, before I knew his true identity. I thought him handsome then, but knowing him as I did now, he appeared more attractive to me than ever.

"Turn around," he instructed, his voice thick with need as he pulled at the ties of his breeches. "And bend over."

He often behaved impulsively and playfully with me, so unlike the prince most people saw in the king's great hall, and I loved the idea that I could bring out this side of him. One night, as we lay in bed together, I asked him about the other women he'd bedded before, the mistresses he'd had. I knew they existed and it made me curious whether he felt the same way with them as he did with me. I'd never been with another man, so, although I suspected no other man could ever make me feel the way Cass did, I had no concrete experience to draw from.

Cass told me in no uncertain terms that it had never been the same with any other woman. "I desired them, yes, but only at that moment. If we were interrupted, I could simply walk away. I could never do that with you, Dee. What I feel for you, it's more than just desire. You're like air or water to me. I'd die without you."

Though the mischievous part of me wanted to call him out on that, to tease him that what he just said would be impossible, the truth was that I knew just what he meant. When we were alone together and uninhibited like we were now, my body ached for him so badly that it felt like I'd never be whole again without him.

Here in our little room at the inn, on his command, I leaned over onto the bed, that now-familiar aching already strong between my legs. A moment later, Cass lifted my skirts and ran his hand across my naked bottom.

"Did your father ever punish you when you were young, Dee?" he asked, his hand still stroking my backside. "Did he ever spank you here?"

The question took me by surprise, but my reaction to it surprised me even more. As soon as the idea crossed my mind of Cass smacking my bottom as punishment, a jolt of longing went through me and the ache inside me grew even stronger. Did married people really do this? *Should* I like the idea?

"He did," I admitted. "But only over my dress. I used to wear extra layers when I knew I'd done something bad so that it wouldn't hurt as much."

Cass groaned, the sound coming from low in his throat. "I should have known you were naughty even then, Dee."

My body reacted again, the space between my legs growing damper as he called me naughty. *Why* did I like that? I still had so much to learn.

"You've always had a mind of your own," he continued, still rubbing circles around my bottom. "Sometimes, it gets you in trouble."

His hand left my skin, and I had my mouth open to protest when suddenly he brought it down on me; not too hard, but not soft either. I jumped in surprise before pleasure flooded through me once more.

Yes, I definitely liked that. I wanted him to do it again.

"It's not entirely my fault," I told him, spreading my legs wider. "If you had just agreed to come with me in the first place, I wouldn't have had to run away."

His hand connected with my skin again, making me even wetter. "That doesn't sound like an apology."

"I'm just saying, we're equally to blame..."

He spanked me again, harder this time, before driving a finger deep inside me, groaning as he felt just how wet I was.

"Are you going to be good for me now, Dee?" His voice plucked something deep inside me, sounding almost as deep and needy as it had been the first night we were together, and the memory of that night sent another shiver of desire through me. "If you promise not to do it again, I'll give you your reward."

His thumb brushed against my most sensitive spot, giving me an indication of what that reward might be.

Still, I couldn't give in that easily. "And if I can't make that promise?"

His finger immediately left me, leaving me feeling even more empty than before. "Then I'll have to leave you here and go spend the night in Matthew and Williams' room instead."

He had to be bluffing? He wanted this as much as I did, I would swear, but in the end, I couldn't take that chance. If he left me now, I really might die of need. "I promise, Cass. I won't run away without you again."

"Sean," he reminded me, and I felt him pressing against my entrance again but not with his fingers this time.

"Sean. I'm sorry, and I promise not to do it again."

In one smooth, firm stroke, his cock filled me and I cried out before remembering that we weren't in the castle with its thick stone walls. The wooden walls dividing the rooms of the inn wouldn't muffle sounds very well at all, and I clamped my hand over my mouth.

"Don't hold it in," Cass ordered as he pulled out of me and thrust in deeply again. "I want to hear you screaming my name, remember?"

As he drove into me once more, I had no choice but to obey. "Sean!"

My hands gripped the blankets on the bed as Cass held my hips in place and buried himself in me, over and over again. All the aching for him, the need built up by my punishment and the pleasure of my reward, all pooled together inside me, growing deeper and deeper until I had no choice but to let go and drown in it, my pleasure completely overwhelming me and pulling me under as I moaned his name into the air.

His movements slowed behind me and I could feel his cock pumping deep inside me as my own body contracted around him. A soft chuckle filled the air behind me. "Damn it, Dee. I wanted that to last longer, but you feel too good."

"We can always try again later," I teased him, standing back up as he pulled out of me, his cock slick with the proof of my pleasure. "I'm sure I'll do something else that needs punishing before too long."

He smiled down at me, his expression full of affection, desire, and most of all, love. "I'm sure you will. I can't wait."

CHAPTER THREE

My stomach twisted nervously as I sat in the dining room with William and Matthew the next morning, waiting for Dee and the prince to come and join us. After last night, my nerves were a mess, making it impossible to eat, and when they finally appeared, I had to force myself to stay seated rather than jumping up and running over to her to make sure she was okay.

She looked fairly well, with no obvious signs of distress I could see. She even smiled at us all as she took a seat next to me. His Highness whispered something in her ear before going over to the kitchen to speak to the innkeeper.

Now that we were mostly alone, I leaned over to her myself, keeping my voice hushed. "Are you alright, Dee?"

Her face wrinkled in confusion as she looked back at me. "Why wouldn't I be?"

It made my heart ache to think she had to lie to me. We had never lied to each other before. Maybe she put on a brave face so we wouldn't add to my worries about Bran?

I got even closer to her so no one could possibly overhear. "I could hear you last night, Dee. His Highness beat you for your disobedience, didn't he?"

I expected her to blush or, perhaps, to cry. I certainly would have, but to my surprise, her eyes simply widened a second before crinkling in amusement as she laughed. "Oh, Lodee, it's okay, I promise. He did hit me, a little, but only for fun."

Fun? What could possibly be fun about that? "But it sounded like you were in pain. And why were you calling him Sean?"

Now, her cheeks did colour. "You really could hear everything?"

"Yes," I confirmed urgently as Prince Cassian began to walk back over to us, holding two steaming mugs for him and Dee. "It sounded awful."

She laughed softly once again before giving me a wink. "I'll tell you all about it later, but you really don't have to worry. Everything is fine."

That didn't clear anything up, but we couldn't continue the conversation as her husband sat down beside her, so I kept my mouth shut as they moved on to talking about other things instead.

The prince addressed Dee's guardsmen once he had gotten himself settled. "I'm not sure exactly what story Her Highness told you two, but she wants to travel to Lassaria to help her brother."

"Yes, we know, Your Highness," William admitted sheepishly. "She told us that once it became clear she had no intention of heading back to the castle."

The men had been surprised, to say the least, when Dee refused to turn around yesterday, but they could hardly abandon her. After a few weeks of guarding her at the castle, they were ready for a change of pace anyway, and by the time we arrived at the inn last night, they were almost as excited about the trip as Dee herself.

"Are you riding, Lady Elodie?" Cassian asked me curiously. "I didn't think you enjoyed it very much."

"I don't," I admitted. "But it will be faster if we're all on horseback, and I would like to get there as soon as possible. Matthew kindly took me on his horse."

I wouldn't say I enjoyed it either way, but I preferred riding with someone else who would control the horse. Hopefully, on the way back, I could ride with Bran. The thought of his strong arms around me filled me with such a sudden heat, I almost got worried I might be coming down with something.

"I told the king I would be gone for no more than two weeks," Cassian explained to us all. "It will take us three days to get to the Lassarian court if we ride most of the day, and then we need to try to track down Arthur and Eric, so time is against us. It's not going to be a pleasure trip. Does anyone want to go back to the Silatrian court now?"

He looked around the table at all of us but no one moved a muscle, and his face broke into a grin.

"Good. Me neither."

"I think it would be best to drop the 'Your Highness' and 'Lady' titles while we're travelling," Dee suggested. "We don't want to draw too much attention to ourselves."

"We could also do with some less showy clothes," Cassian mused, pulling out a small pouch of coins. "William, take this and see what you can find for me and the ladies. Pay people for the clothes off their backs if you have to. Matthew, secure us some provisions for the journey, we'll need to eat on the move."

Both men left to take care of their assignments and Cassian turned to me with a warm smile. "It will mean a great deal to Bran that you are going to such lengths to try and find him."

I had to set him straight, not wanting to take credit that belonged to someone else. "I had very little say in the decision to come."

That made him laugh as he shot an affectionate look at his wife. "I'm sure I can guess who made the final call, but you are still coming with us and braving your discomfort, all to find him. He will appreciate it."

To be honest, Bran's appreciation paled in comparison to the desire to see him safe, and to look Westley Eastam in the eye and tell him exactly what I thought of him and the things he had done to the people I cared about. Dee would probably laugh if I told her that, but I meant it. I had several days to come up with the right words and I planned to speak my mind to him once and for all before Dee's father put him on trial for all his crimes. I had been writing a few of the better ones down in my book in preparation.

"What's our plan when we get there?" Dee asked the prince as she munched on her breakfast, already behaving far less like a princess than she should. I would have to keep an eye on her over the next few days.

"I assume Arthur will be keeping your father updated on their whereabouts. We'll check at court first to find out where they are, and then we can try to meet up with them. Hopefully, they'll have some leads on where Eastam might be, and Bran along with him. What did you bring for weapons?"

"I've got my bow and arrows," Dee replied. "The men have their swords. What about you?"

"I've got my sword and a few additional knives. I can teach you how to use one if you like."

Dee's eyes lit up in excitement. "Can I learn how to throw it?"

Cassian chuckled. "Maybe eventually. Let's start simple, okay?"

Neither of them asked me if I wanted to learn to use one too. Among our small party, I alone had no weapon and was not even riding by myself. It would probably be easier for everyone involved if I *did* just go back to the Silatrian court and let them go on without me. However, the idea of sitting alone in Dee's room with the other ladies, waiting by the window for news to arrive while Dee and Cassian were out here *doing* something, convinced me otherwise.

For Bran's sake, I would do this. I would ride and I would fight, if I had to. I would step out of my comfort zone and force myself to be a little more like Dee, if it meant rescuing the man I loved.

~Zara~

A shiver ran through my body as I woke in the cold, stone house by the sea. The cold had become a near-permanent sensation for me. Ever since I left my home, no matter what I did, I couldn't entirely chase away the chill that seemed to have seeped into my bones.

The house where I woke up belonged to the man who had brought me to this particular kingdom: Westley Eastam, my current 'employer', for lack of a better word. Captor might be closer to the truth, though there were no chains binding me. Instead, he held the only thing I truly wanted in this world, and so long as he had it, I had to do his bidding just as surely as if he had a sword to my back.

I didn't care what his petty squabbles were about or who the men were he wanted me to lie to and steal from. I would rather not know. If I succeeded, Westley had promised to give me what I wanted, and nothing else mattered. I had learned long ago that everyone in this world only watched out for themselves, so if you wanted to survive, worrying about anyone else did you no good. Someone else ended up getting stabbed in the back, so it would be better to be the one doing the stabbing.

As always, I began my day in training, out on the rocky shore near the house. My speed and my skill with my weapons were my greatest asset. These things had been taught to me by my grandfather in the far-distant land where I'd been raised. Most people considered girls like me unworthy of learning such skills, but not my Jadi. He said there would come a time when I needed to defend myself and he wanted to be sure I would be ready.

He had never anticipated that I would need to do it here, in this cold land full of pale-skinned people, but he always said that life was full of surprises and unexpected turns that we must adapt to. That summed up my current ambition precisely: adapt and survive.

And find my way home again.

As I ran through my daily exercises, I could sense someone watching me even though the landscape around me seemed empty. Scanning the windows of the house, I found the source of my feeling: the tall, pale man with the red hair who I had found listening to Eastam and me the night before.

Again, I knew neither his name nor why Eastam held him. Those things were none of my business. If he hadn't wanted to be caught, he should have done a better job of hiding, or he should have escaped when he had the chance.

I couldn't afford to worry about anyone else. I could only look after myself, as I'd been doing for so long.

When I returned to the house, Eastam sat in the hall where we'd met the night before and he beckoned for me to come in and join him. "We'll be leaving later this morning. My man with Arthur has let me know where they're heading next, we can intercept them there."

At first, I couldn't see why Eastam needed my help at all. He had spies everywhere, people he paid out of his enormous wealth to do his bidding and betray those they were meant to serve. If he wanted Prince Arthur dead, there were a hundred different ways he could achieve it. But he soon explained to me that murder wasn't his goal. He only wanted the prince disgraced and humiliated, his shame known to the whole kingdom so they would be clamouring for his removal.

It made no sense to me why Eastam cared so much about being king in the first place. Why would he want to tie himself to the responsibilities that came with running a kingdom? Men like him were obsessed with power, not realizing that he already had the most important things in life: wealth and freedom. I would take those over being a queen any day.

After being dismissed, I returned to my room to prepare my few things for the journey and to change into something more suitable for a lady. My dark skin drew looks no matter what I did, so I chose to highlight it. Since it couldn't be hidden, why not use it to my advantage? The light blue dress I wore today served as a stark contrast to the darkness of my features. I barely noticed the stares anymore. People were repulsed by me on occasion, but equally often, they were fascinated, especially the men.

It didn't surprise me. Back home, it had been the same when lighter-skinned women would visit and I overheard the men of our household talking about them. They were always interested in something exotic and different. Here in Lassaria, and the kingdoms I had travelled to prior to my arrival here, men wanted to know if, besides the colour of my skin, there were any other differences beneath my clothes. If they offered me the right price, I would let them take a look. Beggars couldn't be choosers.

None had refused the offer of my bed yet except for Eastam himself. When we first met, I tried to offer him my body in return for what I wanted, but he simply laughed. "I'm not interested in sticking my prick somewhere hundreds have been before," he told me crudely. "There's only one thing I want from you, and when you've given it to me, you can have everything you want."

All I had was his word to go on, but I trusted it because he and I understood each other. If he double crossed me, he would die by my hand; he knew it as well as I did. That uneasy understanding kept us in this unlikely partnership which, finally, seemed to be nearing its end.

When the small travelling party had assembled, it surprised me to see we were bringing the tall red-haired prisoner with us. "Won't it make travelling more difficult if we need to watch him?"

"He's needed to set our bait," Eastam replied bluntly. "The other men will watch him. You stay focused on your task."

In other words: *mind your own business, Zara.* I could do that well enough.

I mounted my horse, riding astride it like the men, though Eastam gave me a look of disapproval as I did. Luckily, his opinion made no difference to me. Riding this way was more comfortable and better for control. I wore pale breeches beneath my dress so no one could accuse me of indecency. He had no cause for complaint.

Nearly eight hours later, we reached our destination, a small town just off the road that connected the king's castle to the main port. A popular place for travellers and merchants to stop for the night, it had a higher than usual number of inns for a town of its size.

"Arthur and Eric will be staying at that one," Eastam told me as we passed by one of the lodgings. "So that's where you're staying too. My men and I will be just up the road here. We'll get settled first and then one of them will take you to where you can meet Arthur, and confirm for you which one he is."

I could probably figure it out on my own. A prince would stand out, no matter what company he kept. I'd known princes before and they were all the same: arrogant, vain, convinced of their importance. But I accepted Eastam's suggestion and accompanied him and his men to their inn, ignoring all the subtle and not-so-subtle looks thrown in my direction, until Eastam dispatched his man to take me back to Prince Arthur's lodging.

Soon, we found ourselves at a table in the dining room and made ourselves as inconspicuous as possible, though my appearance made that difficult, as usual.

We had to wait nearly an hour until the prince's entourage arrived. As a group of men entered with a tall, dark-haired man at the centre, I figured that must be him. His eyes scanned the room arrogantly, like a hunter sizing up his prey, and when they fell on me, his eyebrows raised in surprise and interest.

It seemed this would not take long at all.

"That's Eric," the man with me told me in a whisper. "Eastam has other plans for him."

Damn it; wrong prince. Hopefully, Arthur would find me just as note-worthy.

Another group of the prince's men soon followed and this time, none of them matched my mental image of the prince. It took me by surprise, then, when my companion leaned closer to me. "That's him: the blonde one at the rear."

My lips parted in surprise as I realized who he meant. The blonde man dressed no differently from the other men and held himself no differently either. He seemed friendly and almost humble, not like any nobleman I'd ever come across, let alone a prince. And when his eyes met mine, as men's eyes always did, he simply looked away quickly as a hint of colour rose across his cheeks.

Well, that made things more of a challenge, but I had no intention of backing down. I didn't come this far to fail now. I simply needed a new plan.

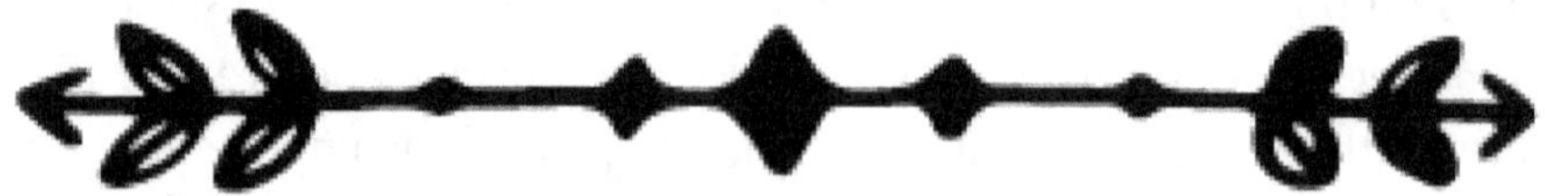

~Arthur~

After another frustrating day of searching for Westley Eastam with no results, I simply wanted my bed. As we tied up the horses outside the inn that one of my men had chosen, I had to listen to Eric reminiscing about the two women he'd been with the night before and speculating on what we might find in this town.

Between our lack of success and Eric's one-track mind, this journey had really begun to wear on me. When I walked into the dining room, a quick meal was my only goal. But when I caught sight of the woman in the corner, my hunger faded, replaced with a storm of nerves unlike anything I'd ever felt before.

I had only seen people who looked like her once before, a few years earlier when I took a diplomatic trip with my father. At the court of one of the bigger, more important kingdoms, we were introduced to a delegation from a kingdom far to the south whose skin glistened darkly. There were no women among their group, only men, and I had foolishly asked my father if women existed who looked like that. His look told me he found my question ridiculous. "Where would more of them come from without their own women?"

He made a valid point, I supposed, but I had still never seen one. And now, suddenly, one sat here in a random inn in my own kingdom. What could a woman like her be doing here in Lassaria?

Even discounting the exotic nature of her appearance, she was exquisitely beautiful, and when I realized our eyes met, a warm flush spread across my cheeks. I quickly averted my gaze and went to take a seat at the table next to Eric.

He clapped my shoulder as I sat down. "You've been holding out on me. You never mentioned Lassaria had any women like that."

"We don't," I answered, before shaking my head at my response. Obviously, that couldn't be true, since we both saw her sitting there. "I mean, I've never seen any before."

"She must be well-off," he mused, staring at her with no compunction about doing so. "That dress is expensive and to travel here from her home would have required a lot of time and money. Perhaps she's royalty wherever she comes from."

If that were true, why wouldn't she be at my father's court? His suggestion seemed unlikely, but I had no other explanation.

"I'm going to go find out," he said next, getting back to his feet and giving me a wink. "This would definitely be something I haven't tried before."

A bitter taste filled my mouth as I watched him walk over to the woman and her companion. He really had no shame. The man she sat beside could be her husband, and yet, Eric walked right over to try to work his charm as if no one could possibly refuse him.

It made no difference to me anyway, I tried to tell myself. My curiosity about her only had to do with how she ended up here, nothing more than that.

A few minutes later, Eric returned, his expression considerably less pleased than before.

"What did you find out?" I asked, unable to contain my curiosity.

"Not much. They said they are simply passing through Lassaria, but she wouldn't give me any further details than that, not even where she comes from. She's far too reserved and proper."

Reserved and proper definitely weren't qualities that held any appeal for Eric, so he turned his attention to the serving girl instead as we were all fed with stew and ale. I ate and chatted with my men but my eyes kept returning to the beautiful, mysterious woman. When she and her companion got up and left part way through our meal, a strange feeling of loss went through me, sadness at the idea that I might never see her again.

Perhaps all this travelling had started messing with my head. I had no reason to feel anything towards her at all.

Draining the last of my ale, I excused myself, figuring I would turn in early and get a fresh start in the morning. I made my way carefully to my room down the dark hallway, illuminated only by a few candles placed along the walls.

The man who had arranged our lodging had told me my room number and I found it easily enough. As I walked in, candles had already been lit, to my surprise, and, even more surprising, the woman from the dining room stood next to the bed.

Half-naked, in the middle of the room.

Her dress had been opened in the back and pulled off her shoulders, exposing her breasts as she stood facing the small dressing table. I had only a side view of her as I walked in, but even so, I hadn't expected to see anywhere near that much.

With a gasp, she pulled the fabric back over herself and looked at me in horror. "What are you doing in here?"

My face flushed hotter than ever as I stuttered out an apology. "I'm sorry, this is my... that is, I thought... I think this is my room."

"It is *my* room!" she exclaimed, her words tinted with an intriguing accent. "Leave at once or I will call for my guard."

"Of course." I took a step back, nearly running into the door that stood open behind me. "I'm sorry."

I managed to stumble back into the hallway and close the door behind me, my heart racing like a galloping horse in my chest.

I had seen a woman's breasts before, but not at such close quarters, and none like hers. Her skin looked smooth and dark and... enticing, I had to admit, and as my mind replayed the image over and over in my head, my body reacted in arousal.

Oh, God, I didn't need that right now.

Trying my best to think of other things, I returned to the dining room and asked for clarification on which room had been allocated to me. My men assured me that I did, in fact, have the right room, despite what had just happened. "There is someone else in there," I told the man who had made all the arrangements.

He gave me a funny look. "Then tell them to leave, Your Highness. No one can refuse you."

He made it sound so simple, but ordering people to do my will had never been my style. I wanted to lead by consensus, not command, and besides, the woman seemed to have no idea of my rank anyway or she wouldn't have spoken to me like that in the first place.

My heart still pounding, I returned to the room and knocked on the door this time. A moment later, the woman's stunning face appeared. She had dressed herself, this time in a stiff linen nightgown, but she still looked no happier to see me. "What do you want?"

That confirmed my suspicion about her ignorance of my position. No one would dare speak to a prince so imperiously.

"I'm very sorry, my lady, but you seem to be in my room. Where is your guard? We need to sort this out."

"He is next door," she said, pointing to the room to our right. "You can sort it out with him."

The door closed again in my face and I almost laughed in surprise. She reminded me of Dee with her blunt manner, and I had always loved my sister's spirit, as much as it drove my mother crazy.

Following her directions, I knocked on the next door and, after speaking to her man, we discovered that he had, in fact, put her in the wrong room. He apologized to me profusely as he went back to my room to tell the woman she had to move.

"I am already settled," she complained, looking over at me with a look that, while not quite an apology, had lost its anger. "Perhaps you can take my room instead."

That solution seemed fair to me, so I bid them both goodnight and went to the room she should have been in instead. Smaller and less luxurious than the one meant for me, it didn't bother me in the least. In fact, I preferred her having the more comfortable room. I had no need of it, and I rather liked the idea of her being better provided for.

Taking off my clothes and climbing into bed, I tried to focus on what the next day might bring, but as I drifted off to sleep, I couldn't get the unusual woman out of my head.

CHAPTER FOUR

~Bran~

As soon as we arrived at the inn, I began looking for a way to escape. Things seemed pretty hopeless when they locked me back up after my last attempt to break free, but here at the inn, my chances looked a lot better. Why Eastam had brought me along on this journey, I couldn't say; I could only count my blessings that he had.

They kept me restrained on the way here so that even if I did manage to get off the horse, I wouldn't be able to go far. Running made no sense anyway, not when they were leading me straight back to Arthur and Eric. By coming along quietly, I'd narrowed my obstacles down to the man assigned to watch me and the confines of the inn. I liked those odds much better than being locked within the stone walls of Eastam's manor house.

I still didn't know what to make of the mysterious woman who had thwarted my first escape attempt. From the window of my locked room, I watched her this morning, practicing some maneuvers with an unusual curved sword out by the sea. With intense concentration and impressive skill, she handled her weapon expertly, and I wouldn't fancy going up against her. Hopefully, if I did manage to get out of here, she wouldn't be waiting for me on the other side of the door.

Luckily for me, it seemed Eastam had other plans for her, from what I overheard. She would be trying to get close to Arthur, though her ultimate goal still eluded me.

I also knew now that Eastam had a spy among Arthur's men. That would be very important information to pass onto him if I could find a way out of here.

The man who had been given the job of watching me scowled at me from behind his thick beard, his equally thick arms crossed over his chest with a large scar down his left forearm. I could only guess it came from some old battle. From what I had seen, plenty of former soldiers worked for Eastam, and some former convicts too. It seemed he paid them all well, probably with the funds he had siphoned from the Silatrian treasury. The man in front of me certainly seemed motivated to keep me in one place.

I tried to lull him into a false sense of security by being a model prisoner, lying down on my bed and pretending to sleep. I figured nighttime would be my best chance to make a move since he had to sleep at some point too. But midnight came and went with him still sitting there, staring at me, unmoving, barely blinking. At last, a knock at the door broke the monotony, but it only signalled the arrival of another man to relieve the first one.

Finally, I figured I would need to take matters into my own hands and told the man I needed to use the privy. The inn had one large communal room in a shed behind the main building, which he took me to now.

After relieving myself under his watchful eye, I refastened my breeches and went to step back towards the door before pretending to trip over something on the floor. As the man went to steady me, I grabbed hold of him and, using all my strength, tossed him headfirst into one of the holes above the cesspit. He didn't fall all the way in, but it would take him a moment to right himself, a moment I would use to my advantage.

The sound of him gagging followed me out the door.

When we arrived in the town earlier that day, Eastam pointed out the inn where Arthur and Eric would be staying, so I knew exactly where to go. Despite the late hour, a few men with tankards of ale still stood outside the inn, and one of them recognized me as I walked up. "Bran? Where on earth did you come from?"

Alfred had been arranging all the travel plans for Arthur's group, which made him the perfect person to run into. He would know exactly where to find the prince. "Which room is Arthur in? I need to see him right away."

He gave me directions and I made my way to the room, knocking quietly on the door before letting myself in. Only a small sliver of moonlight streaming through the closed shutters provided any light at all.

"Prince Arthur?" I whispered, not wanting to startle him as I approached the bed.

The rustle of fabric from the bed preceded a flash of white in the moonlight, and suddenly, my knees hit the floor thanks to a well-placed blow to the back of my legs.

"You again!" The woman's voice above me sounded surprised, but not nearly as surprised as I felt.

"What have you done with the prince?" How could Eastam's woman be in the prince's room? Was I too late? Had she already harmed him?

"You are making a nuisance of yourself," she replied, not answering my question, and a thudding noise rang in my ears as something hit the back of my head. Darkness enveloped me as I hit the ground.

~Cassian~

We made good time to the Lassarian castle, partly because at the end of the first day, when I suggested that we rest for the night, Elodie insisted that we keep going as long as there was any daylight to be had.

"This is the last inn for some time, my lady," I pointed out. "If we keep going, we will need to make camp when night falls."

"That's fine," she assured me, to my surprise. I glanced over at Dee, who merely shrugged at me with a rather surprised look of her own. It seemed Elodie intended to get to Bran as soon as possible. We slept beneath the stars in a sheltered spot in the hills, and as day broke, we were back on the road.

I gave Dee one of the knives to hold as she rode, so she could get used to the feel and weight of it in her hand. Elodie surprised me once again by asking to hold one too.

I held it out to her rather nervously. "In some situations, it can be worse to be armed than not. If your enemy can get your weapon from you, they'll be even more dangerous. You need to be able to defend your weapon as well as yourself."

"I will learn," she told me firmly, even as her delicate arm seemed to tremble beneath its weight.

The second night, we did pause at a small country inn, and by the third afternoon, we arrived at Dee's former home. Somewhat ironically, I had never been to the castle before, since my trip to meet her there in the first place had been interrupted by Eastam's attempt on my life.

The king and queen greeted us with no small amount of surprise, and Dee wasted no time in getting to the point of our journey: "I need to know where Arthur is."

"Forgive us for not visiting with you properly, Your Majesties," I added, trying to smooth over the rough edges of Dee's impatience. "But it is important. Time is of the essence."

They gave us the latest information they had, which thankfully only dated back to yesterday. They were receiving regular updates from Arthur on his whereabouts and the most recent message had just arrived this morning. If we were fast enough, we might even catch up with Arthur and Eric tonight.

We promised Dee's parents we would come back again sometime when we were in less of a hurry, and then we returned to the road.

When we reached the town where Arthur had last stopped, we could see several inns along the main road. Luckily, the message to Dee's parents had included the name of the inn where Arthur should be, and the presence of men in Lassarian colours tending the horses in the inn's stables quickly confirmed we were in the right place.

Dee slid off her horse and made her way into the inn before the rest of us had even come to a full stop. By the time I helped Elodie dismount, gave William and Matthew instructions, and joined Dee inside, she had already tracked down her brother in the inn's central hall. The small building resembled many of its counterparts around the region with a wide entrance, a dining room and common room, and a series of bedrooms down a long corridor.

"Cassian," Arthur greeted me with a rather stunned look. "What are you all doing here?"

"I told you: we came to help," Dee told him, poking him in the arm. "How could you lose Bran?"

"I didn't do it intentionally," he protested before turning to me. "We are trying to find him."

"I'm sure you are, but in this case, a few extra bodies might help, especially when they're highly motivated. We're just glad we caught up with you."

"It's a lucky break," he agreed. "We were meant to move on today but one of my men took ill, so we spent an extra day here."

"Fill me in on what you've been doing so far."

Dee and Elodie went to get settled while Arthur and I went to his room. We were soon joined by Eric, who looked less than pleased to see me.

"Are you checking up on me?" was his opening greeting.

"You sent me the message about Bran," I reminded him. "Did you really think I wouldn't come?"

"I thought the king wouldn't allow it."

He had a point, but I kept my own disobedience to myself. "Well, in any case, I'm here now, but I don't have long. Let's make the time we do have count. Let's track this bastard down once and for all."

~**Cordelia**~

After Cass left us, Elodie and I went to get washed up in her room at the inn after our three days of travelling. She helped me out of my dress first, and when I helped her out of hers, I gasped at the bruises on the back of her thighs. "Lodee, what happened?"

Wincing, she reached down to try to cover them from my view. "I'm not used to riding for so long. The position got uncomfortable after a while."

"Why didn't you say something? We could have stopped or you could have changed position or..."

"I wanted to get here," she said simply, cutting me off. "And now we've arrived. Don't worry about me, Dee."

She could say that all she wanted, but of course she had me worried. In her concern about Bran, she had forgotten to take care of herself. "Bran will kill me if he finds you all battered and bruised like this."

Her cheeks flushed a bright red as she looked up at me with wide eyes. "Bran isn't going to see my legs!"

"That depends on how quickly you get married," I teased her, laughing as she turned even redder. "Oh, Lodee, your husband seeing you naked is nothing to be embarrassed about."

"I just can't imagine having any man looking at me like that," she admitted, dipping her cloth into the basin of water that had been left for us and beginning to wash the dirt of the road off of me.

"You want children, don't you?" I reminded her. "He'll need to lift your skirts for that to happen."

She groaned in embarrassment. "I know that, Dee, but he doesn't need to look at me. It can be done in the dark, can't it?"

"It can, but then you miss half the fun. Don't forget, you get to look at him too."

I couldn't have imagined her face turning any redder but somehow, it happened anyway. "I don't want to look at him!"

I suspected her view on that would change once she actually got to that point, but I could see I wouldn't be able to convince her otherwise right now, so I simply moved on to my next question. "Does Bran have much experience with women?"

This time, she nearly dropped the washcloth in surprise. "It's not any of my business. I haven't asked him but I imagine he has some. Most men do, don't they?"

It certainly seemed that way. Truthfully, I appreciated that Cass had known what to do, and I couldn't help thinking that it would be good for Lodee if Bran had enough confidence in his own abilities to make up for her hesitance.

"I suppose they do. Society and biology grant them more freedom in the matter."

"Do you think he has been with other women on this trip?" Her face tightened unhappily, and I could have kicked myself for putting the thought in her head.

"Of course not. I'm sure no other woman has crossed his mind since he met you. He loves you, Lodee, and he's an honourable man. He's not like Eric."

A shudder ran through us both at the thought of Cass' younger brother. Hopefully, he wasn't corrupting Arthur while they were spending time together. Although my younger brother probably had his share of experience too, he never flaunted it. He had never kept an official mistress, like Cass had, and he certainly didn't go around bedding random women as Eric did. Whatever his bedroom activities were, he kept them discreet.

Maybe he would rub off on Eric instead of the other way around, though that seemed a lot to hope for.

When Elodie and I were both clean and dressed in some fresh clothes, we took our dirty things to the inn's launder woman to have them cleaned before making our way to Arthur's room where, as I expected, he, Eric and Cass were still in discussion, looking over some maps they had laid out on the bed between them.

"This room is quite small," I pointed out to my brother as Elodie and I squeezed our way in. The one Elodie and I had just been in must have been twice the size.

"Yes, there was a misunderstanding about the room," Arthur explained, which didn't really explain anything at all. "But it's fine. We won't be here much longer anyway."

I looped my arm through Cass' as I found a spot on the bed next to him. "So, where do we think Westley is?"

"It's easier to say where he isn't," Eric replied in frustration. "Which is pretty much everywhere."

Arthur nodded in grim agreement. "It feels like we've been chasing our own tails. People will send us a message saying they've seen him and by the time we get there, we're told he's back the way we came."

"Are people feeding you false information?" Cass asked.

"Maybe, or maybe he's being warned that we're on the way?"

"That's also possible," my husband mused. "How much do you trust the men with you?"

"They're all men I've known for years. I don't know what they'd have to gain from working with Eastam."

"Maybe you can answer that, Eric," Cass suggested, and the younger prince gave his brother a dirty look.

"He is very persuasive," was Eric's clipped reply. "He has a way of making you think that he's the only person in the world who can give you what you want, even though it generally isn't true and he has no intention of giving it to you in the first place."

"Let's keep a close eye on your men then," Cass suggested to Arthur. "If he's gotten to one of them, it could explain why you haven't had any luck yet. In the meantime, where are you planning to go next?"

Just as they bent over the map again, someone knocked at the door. I couldn't see how anyone else could possibly fit in this room, but luckily, the man at the door simply had a note to deliver.

"A man just dropped off for His Highness, Prince Cassian."

We all exchanged looks of surprise. Who would have sent Cass a message here and how would they have known where to find him?

"It must be from my parents," I offered. They were the ones who had told us where to find Arthur.

Cass took the envelope from the man and pulled out one of his small knives to break the seal. When he opened the note, his eyes widened in genuine surprise. "It's not your parents. It's from Eastam."

"What?"

All of us immediately crowded around to try to read it, but in a rare moment of forwardness, Elodie snatched the paper from Cass' hands.

"Read it out loud," I urged her and she did in a trembling voice.

Cassian,

I see you have come to join the search for me. I'd be honoured, but I suspect it is your man that you want more than me. I will be happy to return him to you in exchange for a face-to-face meeting to discuss a partnership for our mutual benefit. I will send you the coordinates in three days' time. You must come alone. If you don't follow all my instructions, your friend will meet an unfortunate end.

And since you are probably wondering how you can trust that I haven't harmed him already, you can look out the window now to judge for yourself.

Eastam

Elodie's startled eyes looked up from the paper and we all immediately rushed to the small window of the room, throwing the shutters open.

Sure enough, in the street outside, sitting astride a strong black horse, was none other than Eastam himself. Next to him, on another horse, sat a man I didn't recognize, but I certainly knew the man he had tied up behind him.

"Bran!" Elodie's voice rang out in shock and desperation, and Bran's eyes went wide as he caught sight of her.

"Elodie?"

He sounded completely bewildered to see her there, and I could hardly blame him for that. We had no opportunity for any explanations or further questions as, with a tip of his hat to us, Westley kicked his horse into a gallop, the other man close behind him.

Cass and Arthur both swore as they almost fell over each other, trying to get out of the small room and to their own horses. Eric followed behind them but Elodie and I stayed put. No matter how much I wished otherwise, I knew their chances of catching him were miniscule. By the time they got out to the stables and got their own horses saddled, Eastam would have nearly a five-minute head start and he could have gone in any direction.

They set off anyway but it didn't surprise me at all when they returned an hour later, dejected as they joined us in the dining room.

"He's just playing with us now," Arthur exclaimed in frustration. "What does he want?"

"I don't know." Cass' grim expression eased slightly as he sat down next to me, giving me a kiss on the cheek, but it returned when he addressed the rest of the group. "At least we know how to find him in three days' time now."

"You're not actually going to go and meet with him?" It had to be a trap.

"We'll come up with a plan, Dee," he promised me before looking over at Elodie with a sympathetic smile. "We'll get Bran back, I promise. We know he's safe now, which is something."

Safe for now, I added in my head, though I didn't say that in front of my friend. I had no idea what Westley's intentions were, but knowing him, I had a feeling things were going to get worse before they got better.

CHAPTER FIVE

With my eyes closed, the room around me faded away and I could almost pretend to be back in my home. The gentle splash of the fountain in the courtyard sounded in my ears as the warm breeze moved against my skin, the quiet only occasionally broken by the hum of the servants as they moved around the riad or the song of the bright coloured birds my father kept in cages in his office.

My chest tightened as it always did at the thought of my father, but I forced myself to breathe deeply, expanding it back out again. The point of this meditation was to relax and distract myself from my anxiety, not focus on it.

Focusing on the beating of my heart, I waited until it slowed again and, once my mind had cleared, I began to review the current state of my assignment.

His initial reaction to me made it clear that I would need to approach Arthur differently from anyone else I had seduced before.

My plan had been to have him notice me in the dining room. Most men I had targeted before would approach me after our eye contact, and I would flirt with them just enough to pique their interest. Afterwards, I intended to arrange to be in his room and, as most men did when told they were wrong, he would argue with me, our passions gradually inflaming until, helpless to resist the temptation, he would fall into my bed.

If my target were Eric, I could almost guarantee it would have played out just that way, but Arthur kept his distance in the dining room. He cast the occasional stealthy look in my direction, but made no move to speak to me. I hadn't counted on him being shy in public.

I could handle that, though. I would just need to be a little bolder in response.

Hence, my half-naked state when he walked into the room meant for him. Men responded well to visual stimuli, I'd found, so the sight of part of me should get him thinking about the rest. When I ordered him out of the room, I fully expected him to refuse, to move towards me instead and pull my dress the rest of the way off.

None of that happened. Instead, he backed away, apologized, and disappeared. Men rarely surprised me anymore, but this Lassarian prince had managed to do it. I had just changed into my nightdress, trying to decide what my next move should be, when he knocked at the door again.

Convinced I had him now, I played my imperious part again, waiting for him to take control and put me in my place, but once again, he backed down, taking my room with hardly a whimper of protest and leaving me in a state of confusion. What sort of a man was this prince? What kind of man let a woman he just met direct him, putting her wishes above his own?

The only man I had known who would do such a thing was my father. In this foreign land, they didn't seem to exist at all. Or I hadn't thought they did, until now.

Sleep refused to come as I tried to decide what my next move should be. I didn't have a lot of time to play with. Westley wanted me to have completed my task in just over three days from now, to coincide with some other scheme of his, and initially, I hadn't thought that would be a problem. Now, I couldn't be so sure.

As a result of my restlessness, I was still awake when I heard the quiet knock on my door in the still darkness of the night, and when the door opened, I figured it must be Arthur. Perhaps I had gotten through to him more than I realized. Maybe I had been wrong about him. Maybe he would make a move on me after all.

However, the man who entered whispered Arthur's name and I realized it couldn't be the prince. It must be someone looking for him instead, and when the moonlight caught his face and I recognized the man from Westley Eastam's house, I could barely believe it.

How did he get away again? Eastam's men were obviously idiots, and that had been way too close. If he told Arthur about the conversation he overheard between me and Eastam, I could be arrested, or worse, and then I would never get what I wanted.

So, although I respected the man's perseverance, I had no choice but to turn him back over to Eastam again, with the advice to get rid of him before he caused any further problems.

"He won't get away again," Westley promised me darkly. "But I still need him alive, at least for a little while longer."

It seemed too great a risk to me. "I hope you will not regret it."

He gave me a condescending sneer. "You stick to your business. Let me worry about mine."

"I will, as long as your business does not put me in danger. If I catch him again, I will kill him myself."

Eastam sent me back to my inn with a reminder of his deadline for me.

And now, I had spent all day in the room, waiting for a signal from either of my two men on the outside, the one serving as my guard or the one working for Arthur. Both were under instructions to let me know when and where I could find Arthur alone, but frustratingly, he had been occupied the entire day. Night would be falling soon and my time grew ever shorter.

At last, a knock sounded at the door, and I opened it to reveal my travelling companion with a tray of food for me. He brought it inside before passing on his news: "They are all in the dining room now, but after they eat, they intend to visit the other inns in town to try and find any information they can about Eastam's current whereabouts."

Westley must have made his move if they knew he had been here. "Will Prince Arthur be alone?"

"They are splitting up. He may have one other man with him, but I can distract him."

Since I had no other opportunity, I would have to make the most of it. After eating some of the meal I'd been brought, I checked my hair and dress in the mirror before setting out into the streets of the town with my chaperone.

The small town bustled with travellers and tradespeople along the main road, everyone making the most of the pleasant evening. Stalls had been set up to sell items that people on the road might need, or food for those who couldn't afford the prices at the inns. As always, people stopped to stare as I went by, but I ignored them as I always did. Sometimes, I wondered if they realized that if they came to my home, *they* would be the odd ones out. I doubted they would appreciate the stares and whispers any more than I did.

The man with me had been informed which direction Arthur had headed, so we went that way now, walking slowly so as not to miss him. Sure enough, before long, he exited from another building and turned towards us, frustration written across his face as he spoke to the man next to him.

He hadn't noticed me yet, but I knew just how to get his attention this time, now that I knew more about what kind of man he was.

"Oh!" My loud gasp pierced the air, making several people on the street look over at me, including Arthur and his friend. I stumbled to make it more convincing before falling to the ground.

Several people moved towards me but Arthur reached me first, squatting down and steadying me with his surprisingly strong arms. "My lady, are you alright?"

The concern in his voice sounded genuine and I brought tears to my eyes as I looked up at him. "I'm fine, I simply tripped. Please forgive me for disturbing you."

"Nonsense," he assured me, helping me back to my feet. This close up, he smelled of horses and leather, like a man of action. The comparison to my father weakened. "You haven't disturbed me at all. Can you walk?"

I took a tentative step before letting my knee buckle. "Oh, I don't think so."

"I can get a cart for you, my lady," my companion suggested. "It will help to bring you back to the inn."

"Good," Arthur agreed, naturally taking charge of the situation. "Garrett, you can go and help."

The man with him nodded and the two of them set off, leaving me and Arthur alone, precisely as I'd intended. "There is a bench just inside," he told me, pointing to the inn he had just come from, only a couple of buildings from where we are now. "Can you make it that far?"

"I will try." I offered him a tentative smile as his arm wrapped tightly around my waist for support. Limping, I took a couple of steps before declaring defeat. "No, I'm sorry, it hurts too much."

"Would you allow me to carry you?"

His manners really were impeccable. Not many men would bother to ask, not with a woman like me.

"If you're sure I'm not too heavy for you, sir."

"Hardly," he replied with a smile, lifting me up as easily as if I were a child. I couldn't help but be impressed.

Striding purposefully down the street, he took me to the inn and set me down gently on the bench inside before offering a small boy idling nearby a coin to go wait in the street and tell us when the cart arrived.

"We weren't introduced properly last night," Arthur said once we were truly alone. He accompanied his words with a sheepish grin, no doubt recalling the state in which he found me. "My name is Arthur."

"Zara." Normally, I wouldn't tell men my real name, but in this case, the risk seemed minimal. If all went well, in just over three days I would be leaving this place forever anyway.

"Zara." He repeated it in wonder, turning the word over curiously in his mouth. "It's beautiful, but unusual. Where are you from?"

"I don't actually know the name of the place," I admitted truthfully. "It is far from here."

He laughed gently. "I gathered that. Are you staying in Lassaria for long?"

"It depends. I am here to find something; when I find it, I will be leaving."

His eyes travelled across my face, examining it as though he found it uniquely interesting. "Well, in that case, for the sake of all Lassaria, I hope it takes you some time to find it. We are richer for having you here."

I had heard many lines from many men before, but something in the way he said it set off a little flutter in my stomach anyway. Almost as if I actually believed he meant it.

That would be foolish, though. Everyone was playing a game, and that was all our interaction could be too.

A game that I had to win.

~Arthur~

Sitting next to Zara on the small bench in the inn, I couldn't help thinking that some kind of strange trick of fate had brought us together. Someone like her being in our small kingdom in the first place was unusual enough, and even if we had only met in the dining room last night, that would have been memorable.

But then we had the mix-up with our rooms, and now I came across her in the street right at the moment she needed help. It felt like someone sending me a message that this woman and I were meant to be connected somehow.

Her rather brusque manner from the night before had disappeared. She must have only interacted with me that way because I startled her when I walked into the room and caught her unaware, and I couldn't really blame her for that. I would have been annoyed in her shoes, and I respected how she had stood up for herself.

But now, her expression appeared warm and almost shy as she looked up at me. "Do you speak for all of Lassaria?" she asked, her tone light and teasing.

I had just told her that the whole kingdom was better for her presence in it, and I supposed it did sound rather presumptuous to her since she had no idea that this kingdom did actually belong to me.

And in that split second, I decided not to tell her my exact title. She said her stay here would be temporary, until she found the thing she sought, and though the thought of her leaving didn't please me, it also gave me an idea. Dee had told me all about how she had pretended to be a lady-in-waiting when she met her husband Cassian, who had pretended to be one of the prince's men. It sounded foolish, but it had helped them to get to know each other as real people rather than simply as their titles.

I wouldn't have to keep up the pretense for long. Perhaps this would even be the last time I saw her, though I hoped that wouldn't be the case. But maybe, in whatever time we did have, Zara could get to know me as simply Arthur and not the crown prince of Lassaria.

Therefore, I kept my reply purposefully vague. "I know my country-men. If they have any taste at all, they will agree with me."

Something dark flashed in her deep eyes. "Most are not so gallant as you, my lord."

My heart sank at her words as I tried to imagine what gave her cause to say so. "Have you encountered any problems on your travels? Please let me know if anyone has mistreated you and I will..."

I trailed off, not sure how to finish that sentence without revealing the amount of influence I had, and Zara laughed. "You will what? Change the hearts of men who fear what is different?"

"Maybe," I agreed sheepishly. "I can try, at least."

"I almost believe you would." Though warmth radiated from her smile, that hint of darkness remained in her eyes, something that spoke of a pain deeper than she let on. She had known loss; I had seen the look often enough to recognize it.

"If it's not too bold of me to ask, Zara, what is it that you're looking for? I know Lassaria very well. Perhaps I can help you find it."

She examined my face carefully, a half-smile pulling at her lips. "You do not even know me, my lord."

"A condition I am attempting to remedy," I pointed out.

That made her smile fuller. "You are far more bold tonight than you were yesterday in my room."

She was teasing me now, I felt fairly certain, so I responded in kind. "You are far less intimidating with your clothes on."

She gave a genuine laugh, her eyes sparkling, and my breath caught in my throat as I looked upon her. I had never seen anyone so beautiful. "In that case, the next time we meet, I will be covered from head to toe so you may be at ease."

I had my mouth open to reply, to tell her that the last thing I wanted would be for her to cover up any of her beautiful features, but before I could get any words out, the young boy I had paid came running back in. "The cart is here, my lord."

I bit back a groan of disappointment. I would have very much liked to keep talking to her.

Zara also seemed reluctant to go, but she took a deep breath and gave me one more smile. "Thank you for your help, my lord. I won't forget your kindness."

"Please, call me Arthur." I didn't like her calling me 'my lord', partly because I had a different title, but mostly because I wanted her to use my name instead. "Are you sure there's no way I can help you in your search?"

I still didn't know what she needed to find or why, and I had my own search to continue, but I still wanted to help if I could.

"I don't think so, Arthur." She said my name shyly, but even so, it sounded wonderful in her beautiful accent. "We are leaving in the morning to go to a small town on the coast. I believe it's called Fingate?"

My lips parted in surprise at the remarkable coincidence. "I am heading there myself tomorrow. I have some business to attend to during the day, but I will be there in the evening."

It had just been decided over dinner. Alfred would be making all the arrangements for us now, sending messengers ahead to ensure we had a place to stay for the night. What were the odds that we would be going to the same place? It seemed almost impossibly unlikely.

Her face lit up at my words for just a second before she looked down, hiding her reaction. "Well, perhaps I will see you there, then."

'Perhaps' sounded far too unsettled. "Would you have dinner with me? There is only one small inn there and I don't know what the food will be like, but if you would like to..."

"I would love to." She cut me off before I could make any more apologies and she got to her feet, wobbling slightly on her injured leg. "Travel safely, Arthur, and I will see you tomorrow."

I insisted on helping her out to the cart and once she had safely settled upon it, she gave me a sweet wave as the man who had been with her earlier pulled her away.

Only once she had disappeared from my sight did I realize she hadn't actually answered my question about what she was looking for. I had asked several times, but she somehow managed to answer me without answering each time. Still, I knew that I would see her again, and hopefully tomorrow, I would have the chance to find out much more about her and what brought her here.

~Elodie~

After dinner, most of our party went out to search the town for any sign of Westley Eastam or his men. Prince Arthur went out and so did Prince Cassian and Dee along with him.

I volunteered to go, but Dee told me to stay put. "You're still recovering from our long ride," she reminded me. "You should get some rest."

I didn't want to rest, not when Bran might still be nearby, but Dee had already left the room before I could protest.

William also stayed behind to act as my guard and he gave me a kind smile. "Would you like to go back to your room now, my lady?"

"No." Maybe I couldn't go out searching the town, but it didn't mean I had to sit around and do nothing. "I'd like to go to the stables and practice with my knife."

William's eyebrows raised in surprise but he made no argument, simply bowing to me and following behind me as I went to my room to retrieve the small knife that Cassian had given me and leave my book behind so it did not get damaged. The stables were empty when we got there, other than the horses, so I went into an empty stall where I had some space. William stayed outside the stables where he could keep an eye on the inn and make sure no one caused any trouble.

Cassian had already shown me and Dee a few basic moves when we stopped to make camp during the ride so I repeated those now, trying to make the movements sharp and fast, like he said. The knife already felt less heavy in my hand than it did just a few days ago.

When I finished my small repertoire of exercises, I looked around for something I could actually try stabbing. Waving my knife around was one thing, but if I actually had to stick it into something, or some*one*, I wanted to be prepared for it. Unfortunately, the only thing in the stall, besides me, was a large pile of hay in the corner. Hardly ideal, it would have to do for now.

Getting down on my knees on the ground, I raised the knife with both hands and brought it down into the pile of hay.

"Ow!"

Terror filled me as the pile of hay yelped and began to move. What in the world? It felt like one of my most horrifying stories come to life. I had once told Dee a tale of a blanket that came to life and smothered the person lying beneath it, and I couldn't sleep for a week afterwards.

A moment later, I realized that the hay hadn't actually spoken, but rather, a man who had been lying beneath it, a man who glared at me as he pulled my knife out of his arm.

"Why were you trying to kill me?!"

His justifiably angry tone did nothing to calm my racing heart. "I'm sorry, Your Highness, I did not see you there."

Prince Eric gestured down at his wound. "Really? The hole in my arm would suggest you did."

As he looked back up at me again, his brow furrowed in confusion.

"Wait, you aren't the woman I slept with last night."

I shook my head vigorously, my eyes wide. "Definitely not."

"Well, now I really don't know why you want to kill me." He tossed the knife back over to me, but I completely missed it. Thankfully, it simply hit the floor and not me, so I quickly bent down to pick it up. When I stood back up again, Eric's eyes were still on me. "So, who are you, then?"

I supposed I shouldn't be surprised he didn't recognize me. He must have so many different women in his memory, it would be hard to keep them all straight. "I'm Lady Elodie Auclair, Princess Cordelia's lady-in-waiting."

It took a minute for him to put that together, but I saw the moment it clicked. "Ah. Right. And why are you out here stabbing haystacks?"

"I'm practicing," I explained.

He raised an eyebrow at me. "You anticipate a lot of haystack stabbing in your future?"

"The haystack... never mind." Obviously, he wanted to fluster me, and I wasn't going to let him. I tried to turn the questioning back on him instead. "Why are you hiding in a haystack anyway? Shouldn't you be out searching the town with the others?"

Eric's face darkened as he rubbed at the wound on his arm again. The knife really hadn't gone very deep considering I had used nearly all my strength. I really did need to practice more.

"They won't even notice I'm not there," he scowled. "No one pays any attention to me when Cass is around."

His sullen self-pity made him look like a little boy rather than the lecherous man I knew him to be, and I had enough practice dealing with Dee's brothers growing up to know how to deal with pouting little boys. They needed a firm hand, so I took a deep breath and did my best to channel Dee's mother and the way she used to speak to her sons.

"Maybe they would pay more attention to you if you behaved like a proper prince more of the time."

He obviously hadn't expected that. A bewildered expression crossed his face as he looked over at me. "What did you say?"

I crossed my arms as I had seen the Queen do, taking care not to cut myself with the knife in my hand. "You are the one who conspired with Eastam in the first place, putting your own brother in danger, and now you're upset because people like him more than they like you? What reason have you given them to like you?"

"I have been working as hard as any man here to track him down," he protested. "Now Cass turns up and everyone acts as though he's our saviour. 'It will all be fine now that Cassian is here'."

He put on a fake high-pitched voice for the last sentence and I struggled to keep from rolling my eyes at his childishness.

"Prince Cassian has earned his reputation through hard work and decency," I pointed out, uncrossing my arms. "If you did the same, perhaps people would treat you more equally."

I hadn't even realized I'd pointed the knife at him as I made my point, but Eric eyed it warily. "Put that thing down before you hurt someone. Probably yourself."

"I'm not going to hurt..." I protested, but before I could even finish the sentence, Eric had the knife out of my hand and at my throat.

"You were saying?" His eyes glinted dangerously at me for just a moment as my breath caught in my throat. Should I call for help? Before I could make up my mind, his expression cleared and he took a step back, offering the knife back to me handle-first. "You need a lot more practice, my lady."

Apparently, I did, and as I looked at the easy way he handled the weapon, I began to get an idea. I needed training and Eric needed to improve his reputation and stay out of trouble. Maybe we could help each other out.

"Would you teach me how to use it properly?"

He hadn't been expecting that at all and his face broke into a grin. He resembled Cassian more when he smiled, and I found myself thinking he should do it more often. "I don't know if I'll live long enough to achieve that."

I pursed my lips at him. "Very funny. I would appreciate any training you could give me, and in return, I can teach you how to behave more like a prince."

He gave a very ungentlemanly snort. "What do you know about being a prince?"

"

"I grew up with three of them in the Lassarian castle. I know the rules of etiquette inside and out, and I know what people like Princess Cordelia and Prince Arthur value in a man. I could help you behave in a way that would impress them."

My offer intrigued him, I could tell, but he still hesitated. "We don't have a lot of time, my lady. This meeting with Eastam is in three days."

"You're right," I agreed before giving him my most confident smile. "Which is why we need to start right now."

CHAPTER SIX

We only went a couple of miles out of town before Westley led us onto some private farmland. Just out of sight of the main road, we were all ushered into an outbuilding containing only a few chairs and a few thin blankets piled on one side of the dirt floor. With the door shut firmly behind us, his men freed me from the ropes that bound me to the man beside me and my limbs screamed in protest as I stretched them out, every part of me aching. Getting tied up was getting very old, very fast.

Westley had stepped up my security, not taking any chances after my escape the night before. I couldn't see any opportunities to get away now, even though my motivation had increased exponentially. When I heard Elodie's sweet voice calling to me across the dusty road, I couldn't believe it. I thought my mind must be playing tricks on me. How could she be here? Our location might be a mystery to me, but I knew we were nowhere near the Silatrian castle where she should be, safe and secure next to Princess Cordelia.

However, as my eyes fell on her in the window of the inn, I quickly saw that she hadn't travelled alone: Cordelia and Cass were also there. How on earth had Westley enticed them to come? Obviously, he knew exactly where they were, but how he'd managed to pull it off, I had no idea.

And now, stuck with him and several of his men in this building, escaping seemed hopeless. One of the men sat on a chair directly in front of the only door, and even if I could get away, we had travelled miles from the town and I couldn't be sure of the direction. I might be able to evade capture if I got free, but that wouldn't do me any good if I couldn't get the information I needed to convey to Arthur and Eric, and now to Cass too.

It especially didn't help me get back to Elodie.

So, as much as it pained me, it made more sense to stay here with Eastam and his men and wait for us to get close to the others again. Obviously, Eastam had some kind of scheme in motion, so maybe if I could find out more about what he intended, I could figure out how to stop it.

"Are we staying here overnight?" I asked him. He sat across the small room from me, talking quietly with one of his men, but he looked over when I spoke.

"Is the accommodation not good enough for you?" he asked with a smirk. "I'm sure I could find a latrine to put your head down if you wanted."

The man next to him scowled, which helped me identify him as the man I'd left in the privy last night. He looked ready to kill me, but Westley seemed to find it funny.

"You shouldn't have let him get the drop on you," Westley scolded the man before turning back to me. "You're very determined, I'll give you that much. I could use a man like you on my staff. Are you sure you won't reconsider my offer?"

I couldn't ask for a better opening. If I wanted to get the details of exactly what he had planned, pretending to be on his side seemed the most likely way to achieve it.

"You said I could have anything I wanted?" I asked, trying to still sound suspicious rather than eager. He wouldn't buy a complete change of heart.

He looked surprised that I even went that far, but he answered me readily enough. "That's right. What is it you want, Bran?"

This time, the surprise belonged to me. He'd never called me by my name before. Did he hear Elodie shout it? "How do you know my name?"

"My informant found it for me. There's nothing I can't find out if I want to, nothing I can't procure. Whatever it is you want, I will give it to you if you pledge your loyalty to me."

If I didn't know exactly what a scoundrel he was, I could see why the offer would be enticing. Had he made the same bargain with all the men with us? How many promises did he have to fulfil if he ever achieved his goal? It seemed it would be hard to keep track of and almost impossible to do.

I decided to stick as close to the truth as I could, hoping it would make everything else I said more believable too. "I want the woman we saw at the inn today, the one who called out to me."

An amused expression settled on his face. "It seems you already have her heart. I'm not sure you need my help for that."

A flush of pleasure ran through me at the thought, but I would need to give him another reason why I needed his help. "Prince Cassian doesn't want us to marry. He's seen his brother be distracted by women and he wants the men closest to him to be devoted to their duty without that kind of distraction."

That couldn't be more of a lie, and I could only hope Westley didn't know Cass enough to know that he would never interfere in my life that way. In fact, the prince had only ever expressed delight about me and Elodie, but I kept my face as neutral as possible as Westley looked me over, trying to judge the truth of my words.

"Feelings can complicate things," he finally said. "I understand Cassian's point of view. Some men turn into blithering idiots as soon as a woman catches their eye. There's nothing worse than a man who thinks only with his prick."

Apparently, Westley had never been in love, but that came as no surprise. Someone as selfish and manipulative as him probably wouldn't be capable of it, and I couldn't imagine the woman who would find him attractive.

"So, you won't help me," I guessed, trying to goad him.

"I didn't say that," he quickly amended, just as I expected. "I have no problem with the men beneath me dipping their wick wherever they like, so long as it's not on my time."

Keeping the disgust from my expression proved a real struggle. A man who could speak about any woman that way, and especially a woman like Elodie, deserved no respect, but I had to pretend to give it to him anyway if I wanted to pull off this subterfuge.

"I can make sure you and your lady are married," he continued. "I'll even set you up with a house of your own with money for your expenses, the perfect family life. All you have to do is help me."

Now, we were getting to the heart of things. "Help you to do what, exactly?"

"I want to be king," he told me bluntly, which again, came as no surprise. "It is my birthright as the eldest son of the current king."

Eldest *bastard* son, I couldn't help adding in my head. Right or wrong, those were the laws of the land. Bastards held no legal right to any title or property from their fathers.

"I had it all worked out," he continued with a scowl. "With the support of Silatria behind me, the king would have to concede, but as long as Cassian is the Silatrian heir, that support is not available."

At least he could see that clearly: Cass would never support him.

"But your precious prince is another of these men who let their actions be swayed by a woman. From what I hear, he's completely under the thumb of my ridiculous half-sister, and knowing that, I'll make him an offer he can't refuse."

My heart beat faster as I tried to guess what he meant. "What kind of offer?"

"His throne or his wife's life."

I should have guessed. "You plan to take Cordelia."

Westley inclined his head, a smirk on his lips. "I knew he wouldn't come without her. The meeting with me is merely a distraction. Everyone will be expecting something to happen when we meet, but instead, my men will take the opportunity to grab Cordelia. When he realizes she's gone, he'll be more willing to negotiate with me."

I had to hand it to him: for someone who had so little of it himself, he seemed to understand human emotion very well. "It sounds like you have it all figured out. What do you need me for?"

"Cordelia trusts you, yes?"

I nodded. After all we had been through together, I certainly hoped so.

"You will lure her away. She'll go with you willingly enough and the others won't realize anything has happened until it's far too late."

I had a pretty good picture of what he had in mind now, so I tried to broaden my scope and gather as much other information as I could. "And Arthur? What are you doing with him? What does the dark-skinned woman want with him?"

Westley's face immediately closed off. "You don't need to worry about that. I only need you to help with Cordelia. The rest of it is my concern."

It might not be all the information I wanted, but I knew a lot more than I had before. Now, I just had to figure out how to get that information to the others before anything could go wrong.

~Cassian~

Dee and I got back to the inn before Arthur, which we hoped meant he had more luck than we did. We'd visited two other inns and a couple of drinking houses along the main road and everyone claimed not to have seen anyone of Eastam's description. It didn't seem possible. He must have stayed or eaten somewhere while waiting for us to arrive. Arthur had compared his movements to a ghost earlier, and it had started to feel eerily true.

Because he *had* been waiting for us, as unlikely as it seemed. Did he simply guess that I would come because he had Bran? Did he know about Bran's connection to Elodie, and Elodie's connection to Dee?

He seemed remarkably well informed about everything, including our movements. We had barely been at the inn an hour before he delivered his message. Someone had to have been watching us, and combined with what Arthur told us earlier about how Westley kept managing to avoid them, I grew more certain by the minute that Arthur had a spy in his midst.

We could try to ferret out the spy, or perhaps we could take a page from Westley's own book and use it to our advantage. I wanted to speak to Arthur about it now, as soon as he returned from his own rounds in the town, so I left a message with his men telling him to come to my room as soon as he arrived.

When he showed up, his flushed face and shortness of breath immediately caught my attention.

"Are you okay?" Dee asked him before I had a chance to.

"Did you find him?" I added. Perhaps he had been running after Eastam?

"No, there was no sign of him," Arthur relayed, looking as frustrated by that fact as I felt. He gave his sister a nod of confirmation. "And I'm fine. I assume your search came up empty too?"

I shook my head. "He's as slippery as ever. Where's Eric?"

Arthur looked around the room in confusion. "What do you mean? Didn't he go with you?"

"I thought he went with you." Why couldn't my brother just go where he should and do what he'd been asked to do? Although my father had hoped this time with Arthur might make him more responsible, it didn't seem to be working. "Never mind, it doesn't matter. I want to talk to you about the plan for tomorrow. Let's have a seat."

Without a lot of room in the small bedroom, Dee and I both sat on the bed while Arthur took the chair.

"Are you sure you're okay?" Dee asked her brother as we got settled. "You seem... different, somehow."

Arthur's face turned red again but this time, it seemed to be with embarrassment.

"Actually, Dee, I hoped to talk to you about something after we're finished here."

He glanced over at me and I got the message: whatever he wanted to talk to his sister about, he didn't want me to hear it, and I didn't mind. I actually quite liked that they could confide in each other. "That's fine. Once we're finished, I'll see if I can go track my brother down."

I would probably find him in some random woman's bed, if I knew him at all.

"So, about tomorrow...?" Arthur asked, obviously eager to move on.

"Right. So, we suspect you've got a spy with you." Arthur nodded in confirmation. "I have an idea how we could try to figure out who it is. We're going to this town on the coast tomorrow evening?"

Arthur nodded again, his lips curving into a small smile. "Fingate."

"Right," I repeated. "I suggest that when we get there, we tell everyone that I've made contact with someone who's going to give me information on Eastam. Meanwhile, you secretly tell each of your men a different location where I'll be having the meeting with the informant. We each stake out one of the locations, and wherever Eastam or his men show up, we'll know that the person given that location is our mole."

Arthur nodded, following along with me entirely. "That's a great idea. Do we have enough men to stake out each place?"

"We've got me, you, Eric, William and Matthew."

Dee cleared her throat beside me. "And me. And Lodee."

"I'm not sending either you or Elodie out alone where Eastam's men might find you." No matter how persuasive she might be in general, I had no intention of budging on this point.

"Then Lodee and I will go together," she countered. "It's one more place we can cover."

Arthur's lips twitched as he watched us argue. I had to guess he'd been on the receiving end of Dee's logic a few times himself and he knew as well as I did how futile trying to convince her to consider her own safety first could be.

"We've got six then," I conceded, turning back to Arthur. "How many men have you got? How many different locations will we need to monitor?"

"Six, but..." He grimaced as he trailed off. "I don't think I can take part. I already have plans for dinner tomorrow."

Dee spoke up before I could ask any follow up questions. "Then we choose your most loyal man, the one least likely to betray you, and give him the unguarded location. If nothing turns up at any of the other sites, we can find a way to lay another trap for him."

I still had to wonder what dinner plans could be more important than uncovering our mole, but I gave in to Dee, as was fast becoming our usual dynamic. "Alright. I'll go see if I can find Eric now and fill him in. I'll be back soon."

As I left the room, their heads were already close together in conversation. I envied their relationship, the easy, comfortable way they were together. I would like to have that kind of relationship with my own brother, but unless something drastic changed with him, I couldn't see how it would ever happen.

~Cordelia~

As soon as Cass had gone out of earshot, I pressed Arthur for information. I had covered for him with Cass, but my curiosity had certainly been piqued. "Dinner plans? With who? Why?"

He blushed again, which I had barely ever seen my brother do before. In our personal lives at the castle as well as in all his public interactions, he was usually self-assured and confident. What could have flummoxed him so much?

"I'm meeting a woman for dinner," he confessed. "And I could use some advice."

A woman? I knew absolutely nothing about Arthur's love life. We had never talked about it, partly because as a princess, I had never had any kind of romances. I simply had to wait until a husband was chosen for me, but as a married woman, my experience had increased greatly. Perhaps that explained what brought him to me for advice now.

"Is this someone you've been seeing for a while?" I asked, trying to gauge the situation. "Are you officially courting her?"

I tried to guess who it might be among the noblewomen in my father's court. None of them jumped out at me as someone I could see Arthur with.

"No, we've only just met," my brother told me, taking me by surprise once again. It seemed he might be a secret romantic, believing in love at first sight. I wouldn't have guessed. "I've only really spoken to her for a few minutes, but she's really unique. Unlike anyone I've ever met."

I knew that feeling well enough. It described how I felt when I got to know Cass, back when he still posed as Sean.

As if he read my mind, Arthur got to his question for me. "The thing is, I didn't tell her that I'm the prince. She's not Lassarian and she doesn't know the difference. I thought maybe it would help her to get to know me for me, like what happened with you and Cassian, but now I'm worried that I'm simply being dishonest."

My heart melted as I listened to him. He obviously felt quite strongly about this woman already and sincerely cared about making the right impression on her, and once again, I could completely sympathize. I had agonized over keeping the truth from 'Sean' too.

"Do you think she would treat you differently if she knew you were a prince?"

A soft smile crossed his lips as he thought back to some memory I couldn't guess at. "I don't think she would. She doesn't seem the type to be concerned about title or position."

A tug of worry pulled at me as I registered the clear interest on his face. I loved that he had found someone who would make him happy, but we had to be realistic. "If she's not Lassarian, what kind of future could there be for you?"

My father had always been clear about this: I would marry a foreign prince and my younger brothers would marry from the Lassarian nobility. Arthur *might* be permitted to marry a foreign princess if it served the kingdom's interests, but otherwise, he would also be expected to choose a local noblewoman. Arthur's marriage would not be arranged as mine had been, but he had a limited list of candidates to choose from. He could not simply choose any woman he liked.

"I don't think there is one," he agreed, looking saddened by the idea. "She is only here temporarily, but I feel like we have a connection. Am I just setting myself up for disappointment, Dee?"

How could I answer that? I had pretended to be someone else and convinced 'Sean' to pretend to be my fiancé, all the while thinking I had to marry Eric. I was hardly a shining example of how to avoid potential heartache. Luckily, everything had worked out for me, but it seemed unlikely that Arthur's mystery woman would turn out to be a foreign princess in disguise. Lightning didn't generally strike twice.

So, in the end, I told him only what I had told myself in those moments of madness where I let myself fall for Sean even though I believed we could never be together. "It's better to have the memory of true happiness than to never experience it at all. As long as you understand it has to end, why deny yourself a few moments of joy?"

Arthur nodded, his jaw setting in determination. "That's what I thought. Thank you, Dee."

He stood to go but I called out after him. "Wait, do I get to meet her?"

"We'll see," he replied vaguely. "I don't want you scaring her off before I can make a good impression."

"Scaring her off?" I repeated, highly offended by the implication. "I don't know what you mean. I am a perfectly charming, friendly, model princess..."

"Goodnight, Dee." My brother left the room, grinning and shaking his head at me.

CHAPTER SEVEN

The ride to the coast the next day seemed to go on forever. Westley had left orders for me to ride 'properly', like a lady, in case we happened to run into Arthur and his men on the road. Personally, I couldn't see it making a difference, at least not enough of one to make it worth the trouble. If someone came across us, I could always think of an excuse. Talking myself out of situations was one of my strengths, but it didn't work as well by proxy. Knowing that, Westley simply left his orders and disappeared, and if I disobeyed, the man with me would waste no time in running to Westley to report me. Getting on Eastam's bad side would be best avoided now that I could practically taste my reward.

On a positive note, the slower pace we had to move at thanks to my unsteadiness on the horse gave me plenty of time to think over everything that had happened with Arthur so far and how I should approach the dinner tonight.

He had really surprised me the previous night during our brief conversation in the entranceway of the inn. Unlike the flustered, almost submissive man I'd encountered in my room, the Arthur who helped me on the street and spoke to me afterwards couldn't have been more charming or confident. He attributed it to me being fully clothed, and perhaps that did explain it. Maybe the sight of me half-naked had made him uncomfortable rather than turning him on. I could think of no other reason for the change in him.

And my nakedness hadn't made him uncomfortable because of any lack of attraction on his side, I felt certain. He didn't look at me with the disgust I saw in some men's faces, and he had invited me for dinner tonight, all of which suggested an interest in me. It simply seemed he actually wanted to speak to me and get to know me as a person rather than simply sleep with me.

Maybe he truly was a gentleman. That would be a surprise.

And it made what I had to do more difficult, but I couldn't let any personal feelings I had on the subject get in the way. I had come so far and gotten so close, and I couldn't let anything distract me now. Not even a handsome prince with the kindest eyes I had ever seen.

He seemed like something out of a dream or one of the tales my tutors used to tell me when I was a child. Maybe if we had met in another time and another place, if our roles weren't already so clearly defined, we could write a completely different story. Unfortunately, the ending of this one had already been predetermined, written in the orders Westley Eastam had given me and the promised reward he held over my head, bending me to his will.

Appealing to the gallant side of Arthur had worked far better last night than the more direct approach in his room the night before. Now, I needed to find a way to combine the two, a way to appeal to his more noble instincts but also to get him into my bed. It wouldn't be easy, but I never backed down from a challenge, especially with so much at stake.

Finally, we reached the bustling port town of Fingate, having encountered no one of importance on the road and therefore making the whole sidesaddle exercise completely pointless. Westley had already arranged for me to have a room at the same inn as Arthur again, but it appeared we had arrived first. As I looked around the grounds of the inn, I could see no sign of the prince or his travelling party.

"I'm going for a walk," I told my own travelling companion. I hadn't bothered to learn his name.

"You're not going anywhere on your own," he grunted back at me.

I couldn't stop myself from rolling my eyes. "Where am I going to go? I'm indebted to Eastam as much as you are. If I wanted to run away, I would have done it by now. You can go have a nap or a drink, but I don't need a babysitter."

Perhaps I sounded convincing, or maybe his laziness got the better of him, but either way, my argument seemed to work and he walked away from me, leaving me on my own.

Making my way out of the inn yard, I followed the smell of salt water down to the sea as people on the streets stopped and stared at me, as always. One child began to cry, but I had heard it all before. Sometimes, children asked their parents if I had been burned. Sometimes, parents told their children I must have been punished by God and that the blackness of my sins had been etched into my skin. Nothing they could say could surprise me anymore.

The town had a small harbour where fishing boats were going in and out, unloading their catches before returning for one more run in the late afternoon sun before night fell. Market stalls sat around the harbour, allowing people to buy the fish straight off the ships. The whole area heaved with people, too many people for my liking, so I quickly turned away and followed a trail up the small cliffside next to the harbour instead, where I could see the harbour and the sea but where no one would bother me.

The smell of the fish and the sea reminded me of another town and another harbour, far from here, though the two locations were really nothing alike. While the grey, choppy sea in front of me looked cold and uninviting, the waters in my memory were deep blue and calm. If I closed my eyes, I could almost see it: a warm sunny day, the harbour bustling with people, all of whom looked like me. The large ship ahead of us looked like a mountain to me, so tall and so big, and I bounced with excitement as I tugged on my father's arm, trying to hurry him as he bid farewell to my mother and sisters.

"I wish you wouldn't take her," my mother said, not for the first time. "Zara is too young for such a big journey."

"I travelled regularly by her age," my father pointed out with the special smile he always had just for my mother. "And she is just as smart and brave as I ever was. It will be a month at most and then we will return, and the things she sees will feed her imagination for a year afterwards. It will be worth it, *habib*."

She gave in, as she always did when he smiled at her that way, but her hands trembled as she held my face and kissed my forehead. "Take care of your father for me, Zara. Come home to us safely, the both of you."

That must have been almost ten years ago now, and I hadn't seen her, my sisters, or our home since then.

"Zara?"

The sound of my name made me spin around, holding my arms out in front of me in a defensive position. I had got so caught up in my memories that I had forgotten to be aware of my surroundings. I never made such a mistake anymore.

"I'm sorry, I didn't mean to startle you." Arthur raised his hands to show me he had no weapon, or perhaps simply to calm me, as he might do with a frightened animal. He looked nearly as surprised by my reaction as his presence made me feel.

With my heart still racing, I tried to control the quiver in my voice as I lowered my arms. "What are you doing here?"

I should be following him, not the other way around. Why had he snuck up on me?

He shrugged as he offered me a sheepish explanation. "We just arrived in town and were visiting the harbour when I saw you climbing up here on your own. I wanted to make sure you were alright."

He really had no motive other than ensuring my safety? I tried my best to calm my racing heart, pulling my mind firmly out of its thoughts of the past as I offered Arthur a smile. "We keep running into each other, my lord."

"We certainly do." He smiled back before turning to look over the sea. "It's a lovely view, isn't it? You would hardly know that just beneath the water lay rocks which have wrecked hundreds of ships over the years. It's one of the most treacherous places to sail, especially for the inexperienced."

"It is sometimes hard to tell what is beneath the surface," I mused, gazing out at the water myself. "Things are often not quite what they seem."

"I sometimes wonder about the men who choose to go out there, day after day," he continued, his eyes still fixed in the distance. "The risk they take. When their boat goes under, do they still think it worth the chance? Or do they wish they had simply stayed on land instead?"

The question reminded me so much of the things my father and I used to speak about that I had to struggle to hide the tears that came to my eyes. No one had spoken to me in such a way for so long, as if I had opinions and ideas worth considering. I had almost forgotten how it felt.

"Staying on land might be safer, my lord, but then you would never know what you had missed. Personally, I think I would rather have the experience than live with the regret of never trying."

I hadn't even been aware of us moving closer to each other, but when he turned his head to look at me, suddenly, our faces were only inches apart. His eyes were a soft shade of blue and this close up, they had almost a mesmerizing effect. He held my gaze for a moment and then his eyes dropped to my lips and, to my surprise, my heart began to beat faster again, but not from fear this time.

I had kissed dozens of men before and it had never affected my heart rate before. But the idea of Arthur kissing me, the mere anticipation of it, filled my whole body with a lightness I had never felt.

However, in the end, my anticipation proved fruitless. He didn't kiss me at all. Instead, he turned away again, clearing his throat. "Well, when I finished at the harbour, I intended to go to the inn to get settled and find you. It looks like I've already accomplished the second part, so will you do me the honour of letting me escort you back?"

He held out his arm like the perfect gentleman he really might be, and together, we walked back down the path and through the town, back towards the inn and the dinner which awaited us there.

~Arthur~

It had been another day of disappointment in our search for Eastam, but for once, the failure didn't get me down. The thought of what awaited me when we reached our destination kept my spirits high even as we visited a farmhouse we'd received a tip about. Someone thought they saw Eastam heading there last night, but when we arrived, we found he'd vacated it less than an hour earlier.

"I'm sorry, Your Highness," the farmer apologized to me, bowing his head. "I didn't know you were looking for him or I would have kept him here for you. They just turned up at my door with a sack of coins, which a man can always use, you understand? They asked for nothing, they just stayed out in the back house and kept to themselves."

I couldn't blame this man. Ideally, we could let the whole kingdom know that Eastam shouldn't be trusted, but getting the word out would be next to impossible, not to mention he'd probably just go by a different name in that case. I tried to look on the bright side: we had only missed him by an hour. We were getting closer.

"Did he have a man with him: very tall, with light reddish hair and a kind smile?" Lady Elodie asked the question as Dee and I exchanged smiles. I wouldn't have described Bran quite that way, but the farmer seemed to know who she meant.

"Yes, my lady, I saw him. I wasn't sticking my nose in, you understand, but I did notice he seemed to be tied up when they arrived yesterday but not when they left this morning. Today he seemed willing to go with them all on his own."

We couldn't read too much into that, but it intrigued me nonetheless. Why wouldn't Eastam have restrained Bran today, and if he hadn't, why didn't Bran run? Hopefully, Eastam hadn't found a way to turn him against us. He seemed to be very good at getting people to do what he wanted, and I suspected it would break both Cassian and Elodie's hearts if Bran turned out to be one of the ones Eastam could manipulate.

I suspected I would never be able to completely respect anyone who had fallen for his lies.

We made a few more stops along the way but we got no further breaks. Eastam seemed to have vanished into thin air again and Cassian's frustration showed as we arrived at Fingate.

"Welcome to my life," I told him sarcastically. "This has been what the past month has been like."

He shook his head. "I don't know how you've managed. I'd have lost my patience a long time ago, but hopefully, if we can pin down our mole, we won't have too many more days like this. Have you given all your men the locations?"

As we'd discussed, I'd found time to speak with each of my men today, giving them each a different location where Cassian planned to meet with a mystery informant later. We hoped our mole would pass that information to Eastam and when he or, more likely, one of his men turned up at the location, we would have the identity of our spy.

"I've spoken to all of them. And you all know the plan, right?"

No one was to engage with Eastam's men. We simply wanted to know where they turned up so we could identify the mole; Eastam himself could wait. No sense in anyone taking unnecessary risks.

"It's all clear," Cassian assured me. "We'll get settled in at the inn and then we'll go stake out our assigned spots. And you have your... dinner plans?"

He couldn't hide his curiosity about exactly what had me occupied this evening, which meant that Dee had kept our conversation secret. I appreciated that, and I kept my answer brief: "Yes. I'll come and find you when I'm finished."

He accepted my brushoff, and once we had the horses tied up in the inn stables, the others all went inside while I spoke to the innkeeper to make arrangements for dinner.

"Have you seen a woman arrive?" I asked as casually as I could after everything had been agreed on. "Young and very pretty, travelling alone with an escort?"

"You mean the dark one?" he replied bluntly. "Kind of hard to miss her."

He must mean Zara, but I didn't particularly appreciate his tone. "Do you know which room she's in?"

He pointed it out to me but as I began to head towards the door, he called me back. "She's not there though, I saw her heading out a short time ago."

Disappointment shot through me, but I did my best to push it down. Having some time to kill could be a good thing. I could use a short walk myself to clear my head and try to get in the right frame of mind for a pleasant dinner. I would prefer to keep my mind clear of Eastam or anything connected with him during the short time Zara and I had together.

As I made my way down to the harbour, I caught sight of her, a flash of pale white fabric catching my attention as she climbed the narrow path that led to the top of her cliff. She didn't seem to have anyone with her for protection, which seemed dangerous to me, so I followed her just to ensure her safety and *not* because I couldn't wait any longer to speak with her.

Or so I told myself.

Now, we were walking back to the inn, her arm in mine. She had seemed comfortable with it as we made our way down the hill, but when we reached the town, she looked around almost nervously. "Are you sure you want to be seen with me, my lord? I mean, looking so intimately acquainted? People are staring."

Were they? I hadn't noticed a thing, I'd been so focused on her, but as I glanced around now, I could see she spoke the truth. Dozens of eyes were turned our way, some shamelessly gawking while others pretended not to be looking even as they were.

"Perhaps they have never seen such a beautiful woman with a man like me," I suggested, hoping to make her laugh.

A quick smile did flash across her face, but it disappeared almost as fast as it came. "It is normal for me, my lord. People always stare, but you do not have to endure it if you don't want to."

"I thought I asked you to call me Arthur," I reminded her. "And I am used to people staring at me too, usually for far worse reasons than having a lovely lady on my arm."

I squeezed her arm with my free hand to let her know I had no intention of letting go. It saddened me to know she had come to accept this as normal. Some people were simply looking out of curiosity, which I could understand. I had done the same thing when I first saw her, confronted with someone so unique and unexpected. But the people who continued to stare or the ones whose lips curled in disapproval were the ones who bothered me and, I assumed, her as well.

"It will be the same in the inn dining room," she warned me. "You can change your mind about dinner if you like."

I had no intention of backing out, but I already had a solution for her worries. "Actually, if it's alright with you, I have arranged for us to eat in my room. It will be more private there, with fewer interruptions. Your guard is welcome to join us if you feel it would be inappropriate for us to be alone."

I held my breath, hoping she would decline that offer, and to my relief, she did. "That's not necessary, my lo... Arthur." She corrected herself at the last moment. "I trust that you are a man of honour."

"I certainly try to be."

We therefore headed straight back to my room when we returned to the inn and there were some cold meats and bread already laid out for us. The main meal would be brought later.

"This is very generous of you." Her eyes widened with surprise as she looked over the table. "I did not expect anything other than the daily stew."

"It may be one of your last nights in Lassaria," I pointed out, though my chest tightened as I said the words. I didn't want them to be true. "I'd like you to leave with a good impression of us."

She turned her captivating eyes on me. "You have a habit of speaking for the entire country, Arthur. Are you aware of it?"

The question both made me laugh and impressed me. She missed nothing. "I do, don't I? There is actually a good reason for that, and I would like to tell you about it. Perhaps after a drink?"

She accepted my invitation to sit down and I poured us both a drink from the jug that had been left for us. When we had both quenched our thirst, I took a deep breath and prepared to make my confession.

"There is something I have not told you, Zara. I haven't hidden it, exactly, but I have not been straightforward about it either, and if we are to be friends, I would like to start off with a clean slate."

She blinked a couple of times as she absorbed all of my declaration. "Is that what you want, Arthur? For us to be 'friends'?"

She put an emphasis on the last word which made it sound far more intimate than the type of friends I usually had.

I wanted to respond to that, but first, I still needed to get my confession off my chest. "What I would like is for you to know exactly who I am. My name is Arthur, as I told you, but my full name is Arthur Riseley."

I expected some kind of reaction to that, but she continued to look at me blankly, and I realized that, as a visitor here, my family name would mean nothing to her either. I would have to explain further.

"My father is the King of Lassaria."

That brought a reaction, at last. Her lips parted in surprise as her dark eyes looked into mine. "But that would make you a prince."

"It does," I agreed. "The crown prince, actually."

"You are the crown prince of Lassaria?" Perhaps I should have anticipated the doubt in her voice. Any man could claim to be the crown prince, especially a man dining alone with a beautiful woman, hoping to make a good impression.

"I am," I confirmed, and to prove it, I turned over the ring on my finger so she could see the crest engraved into it. "This is my royal seal."

She leaned closer, studying it for a moment before looking back up at me in genuine confusion. "Why are you telling me this?"

"Because you said you were looking for something," I reminded her. "And I want to help. Now that you know who I am, you can see that I have resources at my disposal, resources I could use to assist you. So please, Zara, tell me: what is it you're looking for?"

~Elodie~

"I'm glad to see you survived, Lodee," Dee teased me as we both got changed out of our travelling clothes in my room at the inn by the road in Fingate.

"Survived?" I repeated, not sure what she meant. "We didn't ride that far today. The journey from Silatria was far worse."

"Not the ride itself, but the company," she explained as I undid the laces of her rough riding dress, covered in the dust of the road. "You were riding with Eric nearly the whole time. I wanted to come and rescue you but Cass wanted to talk strategy. I hope the prince wasn't too inappropriate with you."

On that point, I could set her mind at ease. "Actually, he behaved as a perfect gentleman."

Dee scoffed as she stepped out of the dress. "We're talking about the same guy, right? The one who tried to have my husband killed so he could marry me instead?"

When she phrased it like that, it did sound pretty bad. "That's not exactly what happened, and you know it. Besides, I think there is actually more to him than we realized."

Dee's gaze softened as she looked back at me. "You could see the good in anyone, Lodee. Next you'll be telling me Westley Eastam deserves another chance."

My eyes narrowed at the thought of him holding Bran against his will. "Never. That man is beyond redemption."

My passionate declaration made Dee laugh. "Well, at least we agree on that point. Now, let's hurry, we need to get to our hiding spot."

Dee had told me about this plan when we were getting ready this morning, how we were all going to split up to try to figure out which of Arthur's men might be working with Westley. Part of me couldn't believe that Cassian had actually agreed to let Dee and I go on our own, but then, knowing for myself exactly how persuasive Dee could be, the other part of me understood it completely.

I secured my small knife in its scabbard to my skirt so the layers hid it from view but it still remained accessible if I should need it, while my book got tucked more firmly beneath my dress. Eric had already taught me a few basic maneuvers with the knife last night and he had agreed to teach me more tonight, once we had all returned from our stake-outs.

The place Dee and I were assigned to watch was a small fisherman's house near the harbour. Arthur's man, Alfred, had been told this location would be the site of Cassian's clandestine meeting, and Cassian thought it would be safest for us because there would be people around, so if we ran into trouble, we could always call for help. The other locations were more remote.

After checking in with the others to go over the plan one more time, Dee and I set off together through the town. Even though we were wearing our plainest clothes in an attempt to blend in, we still attracted some attention. Dee always stood out in a crowd, no matter what. She simply had that quality about her, while I much preferred to be in the background.

Finally, the crowd began to thin as we approached the harbour until the only people around were us and a few fishermen going about their business. They were too busy to pay any attention to us, so by the time we found the house we wanted, no one noticed us at all. Cassian had chosen well. There were people close enough that if we screamed, someone would hear us, but not close enough to be paying any attention to what we were doing. Dee took a quick look around just to confirm that we were, in fact, not being watched, and once she'd confirmed it, we both ducked into a small alley between two wooden buildings where we had a clear view of the front door of the house in question.

"Now, we wait," Dee whispered to me as I tried to ignore the smell of rotting fish that seemed to surround us.

Arthur had told each of his men that Cassian would be meeting his informant when the evening church bells chimed. We had arrived roughly early enough to avoid being seen, and we had been instructed to wait half an hour. If no one showed up by then, we could assume that Alfred had not passed the information on to anyone.

Speaking to each other could give our location away, so we waited in silence as my hand went to the handle of my knife, trying to review the moves Eric had taught me in my head. I couldn't tell for sure how much time had passed, but eventually, we heard the crunch of boots on the rocky road and Dee and I both pressed ourselves further into the shadows, trying to ensure we stayed out of sight while still keeping an eye on the house across from us.

The steps grew louder until two men appeared in our line of vision and I couldn't stop myself from gasping out loud.

One of them was Bran.

CHAPTER EIGHT

No sooner had we arrived at another farmhouse for the evening, a short distance from a coastal town I didn't recognize, than a messenger came riding up with a note for Eastam. Westley scanned it quickly, his eyes narrowing in thought before he looked around at all of us.

"Change of plan," he announced. "Bran and Tom, you're going into town to check on something for me."

As he explained the information that he'd just been given - that Cass would be meeting with someone who had promised him details of Westley's movements - and that he wanted me to go along to try to intercept whoever that person might be, I did my best not to show my excitement. This couldn't be any better. If I could get to Cass, I could tell him everything I knew and hopefully bring this whole ridiculous adventure to an end. Overpowering my companion shouldn't be difficult, especially with Cass' help.

I couldn't believe Westley would trust me this much after only one day with no escape attempts. Perhaps he wasn't the brilliant tactician we had made him out to be.

That proved wishful thinking. As Tom and I made our way into town, it quickly became apparent we weren't alone. We were being followed by at least two other of Eastam's men, and realization sank in: he didn't trust me at all. This must be some kind of test to see if I really had switched sides. If I made a wrong move, they probably had orders to put an end to me right there and then.

Still, I clung onto some hope. Maybe there would still be a way to get a signal to Cass, some method to give him the most vital information, if not all of it. I would have to wait and see how things played out.

We left our horses at the harbour so as not to attract attention, which turned out to be a good move as the street around us grew quieter. Besides the calling of the gulls and the rhythmic splashing of the waves against the rocky shore, our own footsteps were the only sound as we headed to the house matching the description we'd been given. The men tailing us had disappeared from my view, but I was under no illusion that they were truly gone. They must be concealing themselves. We were still being watched; I could feel it.

Just as we approached the front door of the house, a noise came from behind us, a sharp, almost high-pitched intake of breath. Tom paid no attention to it but every nerve in my body instantly roared to life. I knew that sound, or to be more precise, I knew the person who made it. Sure enough, when I turned to look, I could just make out Elodie and Cordelia, hidden between two buildings on the other side of the street.

What on earth were they doing here? Were they waiting for Cass? As my eyes connected with Elodie's across the distance between us, it took every ounce of strength I had not to run to her. My pounding heart urged me to, but I had to remember our situation. I had to consider the man beside me and possibly the others watching us too, and drawing their attention to the two women could be disastrous. Luckily, Tom didn't seem to have heard Elodie's gasp; he remained focused on our immediate task.

"I'll go in," he grunted at me. "You stay out here in case he tries to escape."

Without waiting for my agreement, he burst through the door of the small house while I scanned the surrounding area. With a little effort, I could see the two men who had followed us, and there were two more besides them, further away but still watching me too closely for it to be a coincidence. I couldn't say which side they were on, but it made my choice even clearer, as much as I disliked it.

If I tried to approach the women, I would put them in danger. If I tried to run, I would *still* put them in danger, since the men would look for me and might discover them instead. The only way to keep them safe would be to continue to play along.

Tom exited the house in what felt like only seconds. "It's empty!" he scowled. "Either someone set us up or tipped him off."

He began to look over in the direction where Elodie and Cordelia were standing, so I quickly shifted my position to block his view. "We had better get back then," I suggested. "Eastam won't want us to waste time."

He grunted in response and set back off down the street. With one last, fleeting glance at Elodie, trying to tell her with my eyes what I couldn't explain in words - how my actions were meant to protect her and nothing had changed for me - I turned and headed back to the harbour and back towards Eastam's hideaway.

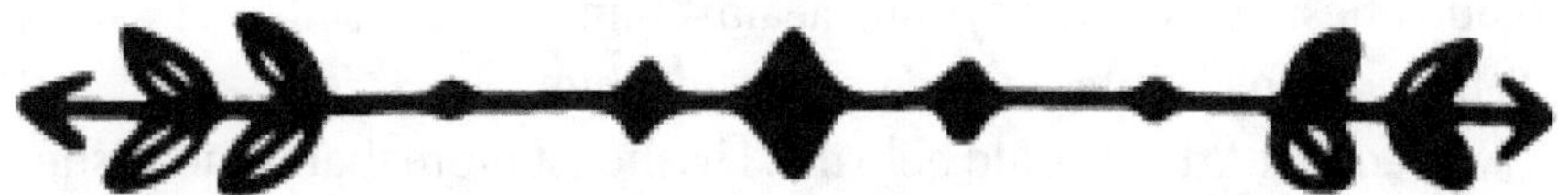

~**Zara**~

Of all the confusing things Arthur had done since the first time I laid eyes on him, this confused me the most.

I already knew he was the prince. Westley had told me all about him, but I didn't know why Arthur would tell me so now. What did he have to gain from it? In other circumstances, I might have thought he wanted to get me into bed with him, but he'd already had opportunities to do that and hadn't taken advantage of them.

And then, without me even asking, he showed me his seal, the very thing I had been tasked with getting from him. Westley hadn't known where he would keep it but he guessed it would be on his person, most likely in a small pouch designed to be hidden. His informant among Arthur's men said that he always had it with him since he used it regularly no matter where they were, but he had never actually seen him take it from its hiding place. I had been planning to go through his clothes once they were on the floor of my room and he had gone to sleep.

Now, he practically handed it to me on a silver platter. I had noticed the ring on his finger before, but I hadn't made the connection. The seal rested against his hand, cleverly concealed to fool any unscrupulous person like Westley who might want to take it from him, and yet he had shown it to me without a moment's hesitation.

Like he trusted me.

Like he thought I was someone worthy of his trust.

And then he said he wanted to use the power of his position to help me, though he still had no idea what I wanted or what I had come here to find.

Could he honestly be this good, this decent? It seemed impossible, and the thought that it might be true made my heart ache. How could he ever defeat someone like Westley, someone with no morals who wouldn't hesitate to use anything against him?

Who wouldn't hesitate to use *me* against him.

I wished that Arthur could help me. I wished it more than I had wished for anything for a very long time. Things would be so much simpler if he could, but I knew otherwise.

The information I needed lived inside Westley Eastam's head. No amount of wealth or power could pry it free if he didn't want to give it up, so I had to do what he asked of me. He demanded my compliance as payment for the information I so desperately needed to know.

Obviously, I couldn't tell Arthur any of that, but perhaps I could still tell him the truth about what had brought me here. I needed to tell him *something*, and the truth would be easier to remember than a lie.

Besides, it might be nice to talk to someone who took a genuine interest in what I had to say, even if nothing more could ever come of it.

"It is not a short story," I warned him, leaning back in my chair and taking another drink from my cup. The cool liquid set my dry lips and helped to drown out the guilt in my stomach. "And I'm afraid there are pieces missing. I was quite young and the places and times are not all clear in my mind."

His eyes sparkled with curiosity, not at all put off by my disclaimer. "Well, now I am even more eager to hear it."

He encouraged me to take some of the food from the platters in front of us as I tried to decide where to begin. I had never told anyone the whole story before, only sharing bits and pieces when absolutely necessary.

"I grew up far from here," I started, hesitantly. "As you can probably guess."

I gestured down at my body, at my skin, and Arthur's gaze followed my point, his eyes tracing every line. By the time he looked back up at me, his cheeks had gone slightly pink.

He really was rather adorable.

"My father occupied an important position in our kingdom. He worked in the king's palace and he frequently took trips to meet with other important men and make deals with them, deals to help our kingdom grow stronger and wealthier."

Arthur nodded, listening to me intently as he put some of the bread in his mouth. I couldn't help watching his strong jawline as he chewed, noticing the way the muscles in his neck tightened. As well as being kind and generous, he was also a very handsome man, I would have to be blind not to notice that.

I forced myself to focus back on our conversation. "He would tell me the most incredible stories of these journeys and the people he met on them. I remember the first time he told me about people with skin as pale as paper. I thought he must be teasing me."

That made Arthur smile, his eyes crinkling warmly.

"As I got older, I began to beg him to take me with him. Each time he would tell me that I wasn't quite old enough and maybe the next time. He said it so many times I began to think he would never agree, but at last the day came and he told me I could accompany him on his next trip."

"How old were you?" Arthur asked.

"I'm not completely certain," I admitted. "Perhaps 12 or 13? My mother thought we should wait for a few more years, but my father assured her we were visiting friendly territory on a safe route. He couldn't think of a less dangerous destination, and so we set sail. We made a stop at an island nation along the way and the people there fascinated me. They did indeed have lighter skin than mine, though not as light as my father had described. When I pointed that out to him, he simply laughed and told me we had not reached our final destination yet."

A knock on the door interrupted my tale and Arthur called for the person to enter. My mouth remained closed as one of the kitchen servants brought even more food for us, a plate of warm vegetables and cooked meats. The prince had really gone to some effort for tonight and I found it rather sweet.

When we were alone again, I resumed my tale. "Eventually, we reached a large city full of people with even paler skin than those I had seen before. Not as pale as yours, but still the lightest I had ever seen. Their clothes were different and they spoke a strange language. All of it fascinated me, and as we visited the homes of the men my father had come to speak to, I got to see the way they lived, the way they ate, the games their children played. The experience exceeded every daydream I'd ever had about it, and I couldn't wait to get home and share everything I had seen with my friends and family. On the day before we were meant to return, the king of this place finally granted my father an audience."

"Do you know which kingdom you visited?" Arthur asked before shaking his head at himself. "I'm sorry, I didn't mean to interrupt."

I took no offense at the interruption since it came from sincere curiosity.

"That's alright, but no, I don't know where we were. I remember the castle very well. If I were ever to go back there, I would know it immediately, but beyond that, I can't say. In any case, the king had a son a few years older than me, perhaps as old as eighteen. He stared at me the whole time our fathers were talking, which I found very rude, and when the business had concluded, he told his father that he wanted to keep me."

"*Keep* you?" Arthur repeated the words in shock, almost as startled as I had been when the interpreter had shared them with us. "In what way?"

"He didn't specify, but I imagine as a pet of some kind. An oddity that he could show off. The king asked my father what price he wanted for me but my father told him I was not for sale. Although he kept his temper, I could see the way his hands trembled in anger and the way the muscles in his face twitched. I had never seen my father so upset."

Arthur's eyes were troubled as he waited for me to continue, seeming to anticipate that we had reached the difficult part of my story, and he had it exactly right.

"The men were waiting for us when we went to return to our ship the next day for the journey home. I don't know if they were sent by the king himself or if they were merely men who had overheard the exchange and wanted to curry favour with their king. Whatever the motive, they arrested my father on entirely false charges of having stolen something from the royal court. I never left his side the whole time we were there, so I know he couldn't have stolen anything. Even if he could have, he would not. My father was an honest man, always."

"What did they do to him?" Sympathy filled Arthur's quiet question.

"They sentenced him to forced labour and sold him to a man taking people to work in the kingdom of Lassaria."

Arthur's eyes widened in surprise. "Lassaria? They brought your father *here?*"

"That's what they told me," I clarified. "I had no other information to go on."

"And what happened to you?" He asked the question as if he were afraid of the answer.

"The king took me in, out of the 'goodness of his heart', and gave me to his son, just like he wanted in the first place."

Arthur swallowed painfully hard. "And what did he want with you?"

He anticipated the worst, but I simply shrugged. "I don't know. I didn't stay around to find out. As soon as I saw an opening, I escaped and found my way aboard a ship getting ready to depart. The destination made no difference to me as long as it took me closer to Lassaria. I vowed to find my father and bring him home with me, or die trying."

The story didn't end there, but I had been talking for a long time already. The food had disappeared, though I had barely noticed either of us eating as we spoke, and the evening shadows outside the window grew longer by the minute. Not wanting to draw this out any further, I tried to sum everything up as quickly as I could.

"It took me a long time to get here, many years. I learned several new languages and I met many people who offered to help me only to find they had their own interests at heart. But I have survived and I am here, and now, after all this time, I will find my father. I have to. It is the only thing I am still living for."

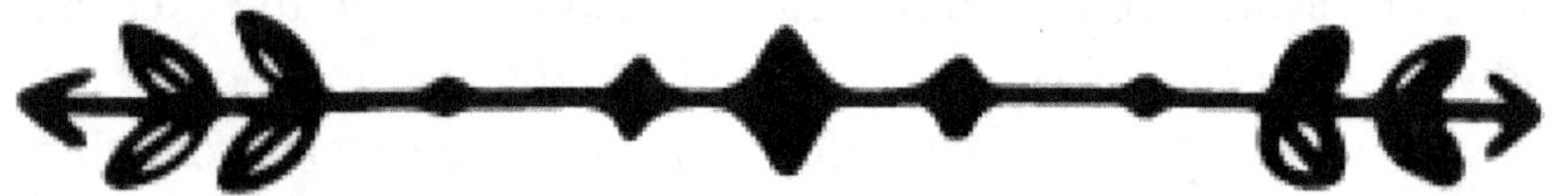

~Cordelia~

When Bran and the other man walked away from us, I could finally let out the breath I'd been holding ever since Elodie gasped. Time seemed to stop as I clapped my hand over her mouth to stop her from calling out to him like she had in the inn. Bran had definitely heard her, I felt certain. He looked right over at us, and even with the shadows concealing us, he couldn't have missed us. If he gave us away, we would be trapped. We could only wait to be discovered.

Bran, however, remained stoic. He acted like he hadn't seen us at all and then, despite the fact that he didn't appear to be restrained in any way, he left with the man he arrived with, casting one last glance in our direction before he departed.

The whole encounter confused me, but not nearly as much as Elodie.

When a couple of minutes had passed and I could be certain they were out of earshot, I released Elodie from my grasp and she immediately looked up at me with hurt, worried eyes. "What just happened, Dee? Why didn't he come to us? I know he wanted to."

It certainly looked that way to me too, which must mean he had a reason not to. "He had the other man with him," I reminded her. "Maybe he couldn't speak to us without getting us in trouble?"

I noticed the way he looked around while his companion searched the building. He seemed tense, suggesting there might be more going on than what we could see.

"He avoided us to protect us," Elodie said slowly, turning the idea over in her head to check if it made sense before she nodded firmly at me. "That must be it."

"I really think it is," I assured her. "We'll tell Cass what we saw. He'll know what to do."

After peering around the corner to check the coast was clear, Elodie and I set out back towards the inn. Just as we reached the door, Eric arrived from the opposite direction, also returning from his lookout point.

"What a waste of time," he scowled. "Watching an empty street for half an hour."

To my surprise, Elodie cleared her throat at him. "I'm sure you got some satisfaction from knowing you were doing your part, whether you got the glory or not."

Where on earth had that come from? I expected Eric to brush her off or, worse, make fun of her, and I prepared myself to jump to her defense. But to my even greater surprise, he did no such thing. He dropped his scowl instead and straightened his shoulders. "You're right, my lady. I'm simply frustrated that I don't have any information to share. Did you have any better luck?"

Had someone put something in the drinking water? Nobody had behaved how I expected them to tonight: first Bran, then Elodie, and now Eric too.

"Actually, we did," she shared. "We're certain we saw Eastam's men."

"Really?" His eyes lit up in genuine appreciation. "This might be the break we need. It's about time."

I could agree with that. "I certainly hope so. I'm just going to find Cass and tell him..."

I trailed off as Cass himself walked up behind us. "Tell me what? Good news, I hope. I didn't have any luck."

"We did. Come on, Elodie and I can tell you all about it in our room."

Surprising me once again, Elodie hung back. "Actually, I will stay here with Prince Eric, Dee. You can tell His Highness what we saw."

Cass gave me a look full of curiosity, but I had no idea what to tell him so I simply shrugged. "Alright. In that case, Lodee, I'll see you in the morning."

We all said goodnight and Cass and I went alone to our room. He had already arranged for some food to be brought in so we sat down to eat while I told him exactly what had happened.

"I'm sure Bran saw me and Lodee, but he pretended he hadn't."

"There's a chance there were others with them, out of your sight," Cass guessed. "Maybe more than he could overpower."

I exhaled in relief. "That's what I thought. He can't have turned against us. Right?"

I couldn't help adding the last question. Although I had assured Elodie it wouldn't be possible, I couldn't completely quiet my worry. Eastam had a habit of pulling off the impossible.

Luckily, Cass had no such doubts. "There's no way. I know Bran, and he must have some kind of plan. There's nothing Eastam could offer him that would convince him to betray us. Unless, I suppose, he threatened Elodie's life, but Elodie's safe with us, so we don't need to worry about that."

My mouth dropped open in horror. "It hadn't crossed my mind until you just suggested it!"

Cass chuckled at my reaction. "Honestly, Dee, I feel better after what you've just told me. It means Bran's got Westley to trust him, at least somewhat. He's working his side the same as we're working ours. I'd bet my life on it."

That wager was solid, but not as strong as it could be. "Would you bet mine?"

His eyes narrowed at me playfully and possessively. "I wouldn't bet your life for anything in this world, Dee. Now, let me go find Arthur and take care of our mole, and then I'll come back and show you just how precious you are to me."

I liked the sound of that, but I didn't want him disturbing Arthur in case his dinner with his mysterious woman hadn't ended yet. "I believe Arthur's still busy, but why don't you get Eric to help you?"

Cass exhaled with obvious reluctance. "I suppose I could, if I have to. Now turn around."

Though he gave me no hint about his intentions, I trusted him completely so I did as he said. As quickly as he could, Cass untied the laces of my dress.

"Now, you can get out of your clothes and wait for me in that bed," he suggested, gesturing to the small bed in the corner with a devilish smile. "I'll be back as soon as I can."

CHAPTER NINE

~Cassian~

The look of anticipation in Dee's eyes when I told her I'd be back to join her in bed had me hurrying down the hall in a fairly un-princely manner. Propriety be damned; I wanted to get back to my wife as soon as possible, but first, I needed to deal with this mole.

Eric's room sat empty, however, nor did I see him in the dining room. Where had he got to now?

Before I could find out, William and Matthew walked in the front door of the inn and came over to me as soon as they caught sight of me. "We didn't see anyone at our assigned location," William told me in frustration.

"Don't worry, we've found out who the traitor is. You're just in time, I need some backup while I apprehend him." I could worry about Eric later.

They quickly fell in behind me as we returned to the inn's dining room where I had spotted some of Arthur's men and, sure enough, they all sat there drinking their ale to pass the time.

I thought I could identify the guilty party, but it wouldn't hurt to double check. "Alfred?" I asked, my tone authoritative but not too stern so as not to give myself away just yet.

The others all turned to look at the man at the end of the table. "Yes?" he asked, looking at me curiously. I had never spoken to him before.

"Could I speak with you for a minute?" Again, I didn't want to alarm him. It would be best if we could do this quietly.

"Certainly, Your Highness." He placed his cup down on the table in front of him and got to his feet while I turned around for him to follow me. Unfortunately, as soon as I broke eye contact, he bolted, darting away towards the other door.

"Damn it," I swore under my breath before shouting out the order: "Stop him!"

The room erupted in chaos as William and Matthew took off after him and the other men, some more sober than others, tried to help as well. Another body following behind wouldn't help and chances were that if he wanted to run far, he'd need a horse, so I headed to the stables instead, using the more direct route.

Less than a minute after I got there, footsteps approached across the courtyard, coming in quick, and I concealed myself behind one of the pillars at the front of the stable. As soon as Alfred ran past me, heading for the horses, I grabbed hold of him from behind, bringing him to his knees.

"I guess you know what I wanted to talk to you about," I grunted at him as he struggled to get free.

William and Matthew weren't far behind and between the three of us, we soon had him subdued. "Tie him up and keep him in your room tonight," I instructed. "Arthur and I will question him in the morning. If he gets free, I'm holding you personally responsible."

"Yes, Your Highness." They both bowed their heads, giving the situation the seriousness it deserved. They were good men and I whispered a silent thanks to my mischievous wife for bringing them along in the first place.

With the mole taken care of, I dusted myself off and headed back towards my room, my anticipation, among other things, growing by the second at the thought of the naked woman on the other side of the door. Only two doors away, I passed Lady Elodie's room and heard the low sound of a man's laugh coming from inside.

My earlier words to Dee came rushing back to me. Had Eastam found a way to get to her? Dee would never forgive me if I didn't check, so not wasting a second, I threw the door open, ready to defend her from whatever danger she might be facing.

Sure enough, I walked in to find a man threatening her, his back to me. She had her small knife out in self-defense, and I immediately regretted giving it to her in the first place. He would have it from her in a second.

Both of them turned to look at me as the door slammed open, their faces frozen in surprise, but my shock had to be greater than both of theirs.

"Eric? What the hell are you doing?"

Could he still be working with Eastam? Maybe we had more than one mole. I really hoped he had learned his lesson, but it seemed I had been too optimistic.

"It's not what it looks like..." he tried to tell me, but I'd heard that before.

"I can't believe you. Were you working with Alfred this whole time?" Years of frustration with his selfish behaviour bubbled over into the angry accusation as my nostrils flared.

Confusion and hurt flashed across his face. "What? Of course not. We were just..."

He honestly thought he could talk his way out of this? "I should have known you couldn't be trusted. You've never been able to think of anyone but yourself."

"Your Highness?" Lady Elodie's voice took me by surprise with its firmness. "Prince Eric meant me no harm. I understand it may have looked that way, but we were simply practicing with my knife. He has been helping me learn how to use it."

She held up the small weapon in her hand and I looked between it and Eric cautiously. "Is that true?"

"That's what I was trying to tell you," he grumbled. "But you always assume the worst of me."

For good reason. "You did almost have me killed," I pointed out. "But in this case, if I have misjudged you, I apologize."

As I left them alone, heading back to Dee at last, another thought crossed my mind: Eric might not be trying to physically harm her, but I still didn't trust him alone with any woman, especially the sweet, innocent one my best friend had fallen for.

I would have to keep an eye on this unlikely pairing, but not right now. At this moment, Dee waited in my bed, and nothing in the world mattered more to me than that.

~Arthur~

When Zara began her story, I never could have guessed how it would end. My heart ached for her and my stomach felt like lead as I tried to imagine what she had gone through, on her own for all those years, travelling through strange lands far from her home and everything familiar and comfortable to her.

How did she get money or food? How did she manage to survive? The details might be painful, and yet, I wanted to know it all. She seemed not to want to talk about it anymore, and perhaps that meant she had done some things she wasn't proud of, but I could hardly blame her for that.

The fact that she hadn't given up and still sought her father all these years later seemed truly heroic to me. She was obviously a woman of true loyalty, capable of deep, selfless love. I couldn't imagine any of the women in the Lassarian court undertaking such an endeavour... except, perhaps, for my stubborn sister.

Dee would like Zara, I felt certain, and that only made me more convinced that she was someone worth liking.

More than anything, I wanted to be able to help her in her quest, but I had to admit I didn't know where to begin. I had never seen anyone with her skin colour in Lassaria before. Surely, if her father had been in the kingdom for years, word should have got to us somehow. We were a small kingdom and gossip travelled fast.

On the other hand, the Eastams had managed to keep the news of Dee's twin sister a secret from us, so perhaps there were more secrets out there than I cared to admit.

It also disturbed me to hear of one of our subjects buying indentured labour in the way Zara had described. That practice had gone out of favour in our kingdom even before my father's time. We had servants, yes, but they were free to leave and make their living elsewhere if they chose to. No one 'owned' anyone else, not anymore.

So, if someone in the kingdom held Zara's father against his will, I wanted to know about it, not only to help Zara but also to ensure that there weren't others like him. It should be clear that Lassarian society would not tolerate treating people that way.

"Thank you for telling me," I managed to say, trying to find the words to convey everything her tale had stirred up in me. "If he is here in Lassaria, I will help you find him. You have my word on that."

A soft smile graced her full, pretty lips. "I do believe you mean that, Your Highness, but the thing is: I've been told he's not in Lassaria at all. They took him somewhere else instead. I am just waiting to find out where and then I will be leaving to go there myself."

My heart sank at her words, both in disappointment for her and for myself. "You came all this way only to find he had never been here after all?"

She nodded as she swallowed. "Apparently, the man who bought him was Lassarian but he did not bring him here because he thought he would draw too much attention. He sent him to one of his properties abroad instead."

"Who is the man?" I asked in both curiosity and anger. "Do you know his name?"

She hesitated for just a moment before answering me. "No. I am only dealing with someone who knows him."

For the first time, I felt that she had not been entirely honest with me, but the reason for the lie escaped me. "Who are you dealing with? Perhaps I can speak to them myself to get the information for you faster."

Although she smiled, she cast her eyes downward, not meeting my gaze. "I don't think you can help me with this, Your Highness, but I appreciate the offer all the same. Now, I have taken up enough of your time this evening, I'm sure you have more important things to do than to talk to me all night."

As she got to her feet, I did too. "I asked you to call me Arthur," I reminded her once again. "That still applies even though I'm the prince."

Her eyes searched my face as though she didn't quite believe me. "There are not many princes like you, Arthur."

That seemed an odd statement for her to make. "Do you know a lot of princes, then?"

"I have known enough." Her eyes took on that far-away quality again, as if she had returned to her memories. "Princes and would-be princes alike, and I can honestly say that you are unlike any of them."

"I hope that is a good thing?"

This time, when she smiled, her eyes focused on mine. "It's a very good thing. Thank you for dinner, Arthur."

She put her hand out and I took it, kissing the back of it. As her hand slipped from mine, her fingers seemed to catch on my ring. If it were looser, it might have fallen off, but it had been purposefully designed to be snug. I didn't want to ever lose it, since it could cause a lot of damage in the wrong hands. It remained firmly in place as her hand dropped back to her side.

"May I walk you to your room?"

My suggestion made her laugh. "It is only down the hall, but if you would like to, I would be honoured."

Offering her my arm, I led her down the far-too-short hallway until we reached her own door. I lingered there a moment longer, reluctant to let her go. "What are your plans for tomorrow?"

"I am hoping to meet with the man who has information for me. I will be staying here until we can meet. Are you moving on tomorrow?"

I needed to catch up with Cass and Eric and see if they had found the spy before I knew exactly what our plans were, but I couldn't stop myself from making her an offer anyway. "If we are, it won't be before breakfast. Would you like to join me back in my room in the morning so we can dine together again?"

"I would like that." She let herself into her room before turning back to me. "Thank you for listening to me tonight, Arthur. I enjoyed speaking with you."

"As did I." I bid her goodnight as the door closed behind her, but I stood there a moment longer, looking at the door and thinking things over before heading back to my own room. I may not have the answers she wanted, but she had given me enough information to start looking for them, so once I returned to my room, I sat down and wrote a number of letters, to my father and to others in the court who might have information that would be helpful.

For the fee I offered, I had several volunteers to ride through the night to deliver my messages. They should be at the castle in the early morning and return to me by tomorrow evening. Hopefully, if all went well with my own duties for the day, Zara and I could dine together again and I would have some answers for her then.

It seemed that fate had brought us together for a reason and somehow, I would find a way to help her.

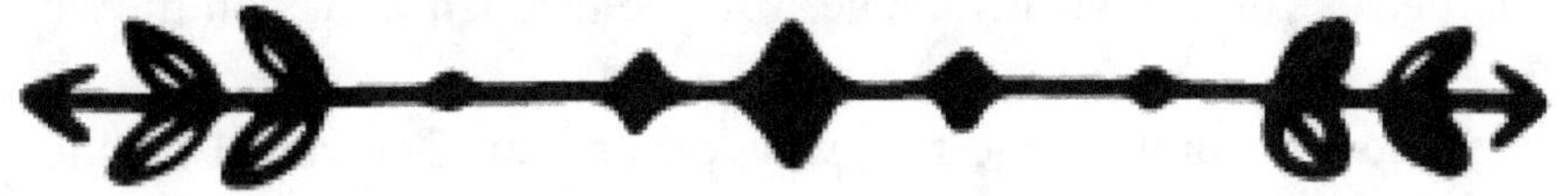

~Elodie~

Eric's face settled into its usual scowl after Cassian left us.

"This is pointless," he pouted, gesturing back towards the door. "He'll never see me as any other than a screw-up."

"It's been one day," I countered. "His perception isn't going to change overnight. You have to make a consistent effort and then he'll see it. He's a fair man, he will give you a chance if you deserve it."

I already knew that from the things Dee had told me and what I'd seen myself in the Silatrian court, not to mention the way he had just apologized to Eric for his mistaken assumption. Somewhere inside, Cassian wanted to be able to trust his brother; Eric just needed to give him a reason to do it.

"You really think so?" Eric's pout morphed into an almost boyish look of hope.

The relief on his face made me smile. "I'm sure of it. Now, let's resume the exercise, please."

We took up our positions from before we were interrupted, Eric advancing on me while I held the knife out, still in its scabbard so that I wouldn't accidentally stab him. He had insisted on that stipulation after I slightly nicked him the night before.

As he'd instructed me, I kept my eyes locked on his face, waiting to see the signs that would tell me which way he intended to move, and then I went in the opposite direction, getting to his side and laying the knife flat against him.

"Not bad." He sounded genuinely impressed. "Let's do it again."

We ran through several more scenarios, with Eric getting the upper hand about half the time and me the other half. I still had a long way to go, but the tally had improved a lot on the previous evening and Eric told me so when we stopped for the night.

"You have good instincts, Lady Elodie. You can read people well, which gives you a huge advantage. You see through what's on the surface."

No one ever praised me that way, other than Dee, and I blushed beneath the weight of his words. "I think you are just a good teacher, Your Highness."

"Don't sell yourself short." His eyes scanned my face curiously. "I suppose you do that because you have been so long in the princess' shadow."

"Dee does not try to hide me," I protested, not quite sure what he meant by that.

"Not on purpose, perhaps, but I think if you spent a bit more time in the sun, you'd be surprised what you could do."

With those confusing words and an even more confusing wink, he let himself out of my room, closing the door behind him. After drawing the beam across to bar the door, I began to get ready for bed but I couldn't stop thinking over what Eric had just said. Perhaps he had stumbled upon a small truth. I did let Dee speak for the both of us while we were in public and deferred to her wishes most of the time, but custom demanded it. She was my superior, after all, as well as my friend. Someone like Eric, someone born into the second-highest position in his kingdom, couldn't really understand spending time with someone who outranked him so significantly.

Not in the same way Bran could. Bran occupied the same position I did so he understood it completely. He would never tell me to change anything about myself, which was just one of the reasons I loved him. I wanted someone who accepted and understood me, someone dependable and trustworthy.

And someone who walked away from me tonight rather than running to me because he evaluated the situation logically and placed my safety above everything else.

What would Eric have done in his position, I couldn't help wondering? Probably something far more impulsive and far more dangerous. The kind of thing I would have scolded him for afterwards and told him to be more cautious about.

It would have been reckless and irrational for Bran to do anything other than what he'd done. I knew that. So why did I wish he had done it anyway?

~**Bran**~

Eastam's jaw set angrily when we returned to the farmhouse and told him there had been no one at the meeting place.

"Your man must have got his information wrong," I suggested, though I suspected I knew the truth. It occurred to me on the way back that

Cass and Arthur must have pegged Alfred as a mole and fed him false information, trying to draw Eastam out. I could think of no other reason why Cordelia and Elodie would have been anywhere near the place.

Although, in that case, why on earth would he have sent them on their own? Unless they knew a mole existed, but not his identity? Perhaps there had been traps set up for us all over town? Cass would certainly do something that clever. It must have just been bad luck that the ladies were assigned to the location given to the real mole. Nothing else made sense to me.

Eastam quickly came to the same conclusion, to my frustration. "He must have been compromised. They must know about him."

I had to suppress a groan. It would have been better if he didn't figure that out, if he had tried to establish contact again, but at the very least, he had still lost his man on the inside. We would have to count that as a win for now.

"Do you want us to try to turn one of the other ones?" the man who had gone with me asked.

Westley considered that for a moment but shook his head. "No, I think it's time to pull out our secret weapon. I want to meet with Eric tomorrow."

Eric? Surely Eastam didn't still have Eric in his pocket? Just the thought made my blood boil. After the second chance the king and Cass had given him, could he really still be messing around with this madman?

"Bran, you can come with me," Eastam added.

That surprised me, but I quickly nodded. I definitely wanted to know more about Eric's involvement, and I might be able to try to get a message to Cass, even indirectly. The closer I stayed to Eastam, the better.

"My lord, I thought you were meeting with the woman tomorrow?" one of the other men reminded him.

Westley raised his eyebrows, looking unimpressed. "I'm sure I can fit them both in. We'll speak to Zara first, then Eric."

With that, he dismissed us all to get some rest. Sleep didn't come easily though, not when I could still picture the confused look in Elodie's eyes as I walked away from her. Hopefully, it wouldn't be too long before I got a chance to explain myself to her and to find out exactly what had been going on while I'd been away.

CHAPTER TEN

Darkness still lay over the room when I woke up to Dee's hand trailing across my body. We were both still naked since there hadn't seemed to be much point in getting dressed after our evening together, not when the room and our own body heat were enough to keep us comfortable. The feel of her warm, soft body next to mine gave me a pleasure that only seemed to increase the more often I experienced it. Though we had been married for more than a month already, waking up next to her still managed to surprise me each time with how much I enjoyed it. I couldn't imagine ever getting tired of it.

"What are you thinking about?" Dee's soft voice murmured in the stillness of our room. "Even in your sleep, you were tense."

Was I? Vague images filtered through my memory, pictures of Westley, Bran and Eric. In the dream, Westley played the villain, that much I knew, but everyone else's motives seemed murky. I didn't know who to trust, and I had to figure it out urgently, as Dee's safety depended on it somehow.

Shaking my head, I tried to put the dream behind me. We had real problems to worry about, so I wouldn't waste energy and emotion on something my subconscious had dreamed up. "I guess I was thinking about how fickle people can be. You think you have someone's loyalty, but in the end, they're only looking out for themselves."

"Do you mean Eric?" As usual, Dee didn't miss a thing.

"He's one example," I admitted. "But it's not just him. Ever since I started working with my father more closely, I see the men who come and speak to him, saying all the right things, and then as soon as his back is turned, they're making their own schemes, directly contradicting what they've just said. Investigating all the people who betrayed us to help Eastam has only made things worse. In most cases, the reward he gave them couldn't even be called significant. They just liked feeling important, and he must have given that to them. How can I run a kingdom full of people whose loyalty might change at any time? How do I rule those who could betray me?"

"Loyalty isn't a permanent thing," Dee pointed out, propping herself up on her elbow so she could look down at me in the pale moonlight that seeped in through the holes in the shutters. "It must be continually fed to be renewed, through trust and respect."

"I know that." With a soft touch, I reached up to cup her face. Dee had my trust, my respect and my eternal loyalty, and she had earned it just as she described. "I just wish there could be an easier way to determine who's on whose side. How can you tell whether someone is really trying to change or if they're just saying what they think you want to hear?"

Now I *was* speaking about Eric specifically, and Dee understood that instinctively. "I think you have to give him the benefit of the doubt. He's made mistakes but it doesn't mean he's beyond redemption. Maybe if you show him that you trust him, it will encourage him to try harder."

That had been what my father had been trying to do with this assignment for him, but perhaps me showing up in the middle of it had made him feel that he'd lost that opportunity. Maybe I needed to show him I hadn't come here to take over but to work together with him.

"Thank you for talking about this with me, Dee. I really don't have anyone else to talk to, especially with Bran gone. Even Arthur can't completely relate. His brothers have never tried to have him killed."

That made Dee laugh, as I knew it would. "No, my younger brothers are far too practical for that. Neither of them wants to be king, they'd much rather have the titles and lands without all the extra responsibility."

There were days that sounded pretty good to me too, especially when I imagined getting to spend my days alone with Dee, just like we were now.

And since we had this time, I saw no reason to let it go to waste. My hand curled around the back of her head as I pulled her mouth down towards mine, all thoughts of traitors fading into the back of my mind. Her body melded to me instantly and she giggled into the kiss as she felt my firm cock against her.

"You just woke up," she pointed out, whispering against my lips. "How can you already be turned on?"

"I have the most beautiful princess in the world naked in my bed. How can I not be?"

Using both hands, I brought Dee's body fully on top of me and then, in a quick move learned from years of combat training, I flipped us over so that she lay on her back with me covering her. I loved being with her in any position, but this might just be my favourite, when she surrendered herself to my control completely.

"Cass," she moaned as my cock began to grind against her, teasing at the junction between her legs.

"We know I'm ready," I reminded her with a sly grin. "Are you?"

Her legs spread around my hips and my cock slid lower, slipping through the wetness already gathered there.

"Damn it, Dee." How did she always feel so good? How did I want her more every time I had her?

We were both so ready that we needed no further preparation. I pushed into her, coating myself in her sweet dampness before withdrawing and pushing in deeper. The sigh that came from Dee's lips had to be the most perfect sound I'd ever heard, my very favourite sound in the world. It said she'd rather be here than anywhere else in the world, beneath me with me buried inside her.

"You know," she said as she caught her breath. "If you did this with all the ladies in Silatria, you'd never have to worry about keeping anyone's loyalty ever again. They'd be yours forever."

A laugh burst out of me. I had never met a woman who thought like Dee and I never knew what would come out of her mouth next.

"Their husbands might have an issue with it," I pointed out as I thrust into her again, every nerve on edge, every sensation heightened as she took me in. "To get them on my side too, I'd have to let them have you, and that's never happening. You are mine and only mine, princess."

"You sound pretty sure of that," she teased, her legs tightening around me as she raised her hips to meet me.

"If there's anything in this world I'm certain of, it's that."

Before she could say anything else, I covered her mouth with mine, my tongue thrusting into her mouth at the same time my cock sank deep into her. Her hands gripped my back, pulling me even closer until every single part of us seemed connected, body and soul. Her pleasure was mine and mine hers. We were truly one.

As our movements grew more frantic, my cock tightening as it pressed against her most sensitive spot until we reached our peaks together, I realized I had answered my own question. I wanted to know how I could rule those whose loyalty I couldn't be sure of, how I could live as king in a world of uncertainty, but the answer had always been right in front of me.

With Dee by my side, I could do anything at all.

~Cordelia~

As soon as we were up and dressed, Cass and I went to see Arthur to talk about what to do with Alfred. Besides that, I also wanted to know how my brother's dinner with his mysterious woman had gone, but I hesitated to bring it up in front of Cass. Arthur seemed to want to keep the whole thing quiet.

Once we had knocked, Arthur opened the door with a warm smile on his face, which quickly faded as he got a full look at us. "Oh. Good morning."

"Good morning to you too," I replied sarcastically, teasing him for his lack of enthusiasm as I walked past him into his room. "Were you expecting someone else?"

My brother glanced out into the hall. "No, of course not. What's going on?"

Cass got right down to business. "We got the mole, and I have some ideas about what we should do with him."

"Right. We should take care of that right away." Arthur sounded slightly disappointed about that, for some reason, but he quickly shook it off. "I just need to send a message to someone, hold on."

He disappeared for a moment, speaking to one of the men standing guard out in the hall, before returning to us.

"Where's Eric?"

Arthur made a good point. Eric *should* be involved if Cass wanted to give him a chance to prove himself. I raised my eyebrows at my husband to remind him of that, and he gave a sigh. "I'll go get him."

As soon as he'd left the room, I pulled Arthur over to the table and sat him down across from me. "So, tell me about your dinner last night? Did you end up telling your dinner companion who you are?"

"I did," he confirmed.

"And?" I prompted when he didn't immediately continue. "How did she react? Was she surprised? Upset? Thrilled? What happened?"

My enthusiasm made him smile. "Surprised, I think. We actually ended up speaking about her far more than me."

"You told her you're the crown prince and it didn't dominate the conversation?" That seemed almost impossible to me. When I found out about Cass' true identity, we had talked of nothing else.

"She has her own concerns," he said vaguely, looking towards the open door. "I might actually want your help with something, Dee, but it will have to wait until we have more time to discuss it."

His cryptic words piqued my curiosity even further, but before I could ask for any further details, Cass and Eric arrived, closing the door behind them as they came in and over to us.

"Now that we've got our mole, we need to figure out what to do with him," Cass began, addressing us all.

"What do you mean?" Eric asked. "We lock him up and punish him, that's what we do."

"That is one option," Cass agreed, making an effort not to shoot down his brother's suggestion out of hand. "Or, we try to use him to flush Eastam out. That's what Westley would do in our position, I'm certain of it."

"How would we do that?" The suggestion intrigued me, but I didn't really understand how it would play out. "He might already be compromised. Bran and the other man from last night know that Alfred gave them false information yesterday, so they might suspect we're already onto him."

The look Cass gave me contained both respect and affection. "You're right, it's entirely possible. It's also possible that even if Alfred agrees to work with us, he might double cross us again."

Those all sounded like reasons not to do it, then. I had to be missing something. "What are you suggesting?"

"I'm suggesting that we send him in with someone else, someone who can keep an eye on him but also convince Eastam that Alfred can still be trusted."

"Who could do that?" I still couldn't see the big picture of his plan.

Cass' eyes moved to Eric, and Arthur and I both turned our heads to follow his gaze, while Eric looked back at us all with wide eyes.

"Me? You want me to work with Alfred?"

Cass nodded. "Eastam already thinks he can manipulate you." He diplomatically left out the fact that Westley not only thought he could but had rather successfully manipulated Eric not all that long ago. "He'll find it far more believable that you are willing to work with him again than if we send in someone fresh."

"And you trust me with this?" Eric sounded so uncertain of that fact that I had to hide my smile behind my hand.

"It's an incredibly important responsibility," Cass replied, not directly answering the question. "You'll need to try to meet with Eastam himself. He's nearby, I'd wager my life on it. I can almost feel him breathing down our necks."

"And then what?" Eric asked, still sounding surprised at the turn this conversation had taken.

"Then you tell us as much as you can about what he's planning, and you tell us if Alfred is sticking to what we agreed."

Eric nodded slowly. "And if Eastam wants me to do something for him?"

"Then you agree and tell us what it is he wants you to do."

Cass made it sound fairly simple, but I suspected it wouldn't be quite that easy. Eastam hadn't gotten as far as he had by being sloppy. He would have his guard up, I felt certain, so both Eric and Alfred would have to be very convincing.

Once Eric had agreed, we all went to speak to Alfred, who had spent the night tied up in one of the neighbouring rooms. His eyes were full of fear as the three princes approached him.

"I'm sorry, Your Highness," he addressed Arthur, bowing his head and not even trying to claim innocence. "I didn't mean to betray you. In a way, I'm glad you caught me so that I don't have to do it anymore."

"If you were so eager to be caught, why did you try to run?" Cass asked, his voice taking on that hard, unforgiving edge it had when he carried out his official role. It also reminded me of the way he'd spoken to me the night he 'punished' me and a thrill of excitement ran through me.

Concentrate, Dee.

"I was afraid of what you'd do to me," Alfred answered with apparent honesty. It seemed like a reasonable reason to run.

"Why did you do it?" Arthur asked, his voice filled with genuine curiosity and hurt. "Why did you work with him? I've always treated you well, haven't I?"

"You have, Your Highness. It's just that my family's farm is failing and Eastam promised me he would give them new land from his own family's territory. He knew all about what we needed, and he said I only had to keep him informed about where you were going to make sure you didn't catch up with him."

"But that's not all you ended up doing, is it?" Eric guessed, and Alfred hung his head once more.

"No. He began asking me to do more, to tell him about things I saw or overheard. At first, I said no, but then he threatened to expose me for what I'd already done and I'd be sure to lose my position. The only way to keep him quiet was to do as he said. I just kept getting in deeper and deeper and before I knew it, I couldn't see my way out of the hole anymore. So, although it sounds crazy, it's really true: I'm glad you caught me and pulled me out, even if it means being punished."

Cass exhaled in frustration. "I don't understand the power this man has over everyone!"

"He's very charming when he wants to be," Eric muttered. "He makes you feel you can do anything."

Those kinds of skills could be so useful if used in a constructive way. What a shame that Eastam chose to be selfish and manipulative with them.

Cass and Arthur explained to Alfred that they wanted him to try to get to Eastam and to take Eric along with him. Alfred looked more and more unsure as the plan unfolded. "I want to think that I'm strong enough to resist him, but after everything I've done, I don't know if I can say that for sure."

"I'll help you," Eric promised. "We can keep each other honest."

When all the details were sorted out, Alfred and Eric got ready to go make contact but Cass stopped Eric before they could leave. "Wear my doublet instead."

Confusion flickered across Eric's face, but he did as his older brother said, trading clothes with him while I watched curiously, trying to figure out what trick Cass had up his sleeve. When Eric had gone, I had to admit defeat. "What was the point of that?" I asked my husband.

He gave me a wry smile. "The pattern on the doublet is a message to Bran. If he's there, he'll see it and hopefully he can try to get a message to me in reply."

These men and their secret messages. I shook my head with both disbelief and admiration. "Do you think Eric will pass this test?" I appreciated that Cass had given him a chance, but I knew he'd be judging the results carefully.

"I hope so," he answered with a sigh. "If he doesn't, then I don't know what chance there is left for us at all."

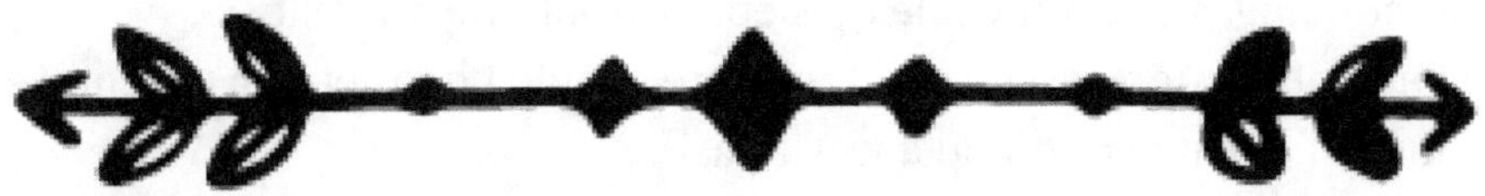

~Zara~

When I woke the next morning, I expected to feel regret over my conversation with Arthur and just how much I had shared with him, but to my surprise, it didn't come. Instead, when I thought back to his reactions, an odd feeling of warmth ran through me. While almost every other man I had told this story to before, in any shape of form, tried to find a way to twist it to put me in their debt, Arthur wanted none of that. He simply listened and sympathized with me, offering his support in whatever fashion I wanted it.

Why did he have to be so kind? It made what I had to do so much harder, but I still couldn't see that I had any choice in the matter. Perhaps if my father had been brought to Lassaria, the crown prince could help me to find him, but the information I'd been able to find told me that he had been taken somewhere else by no less a person than Westley Eastam's father.

Westley swore he knew my father's location, and he would not only tell me where to find him, he would release him from his bondage, so long as I did what he asked. He tasked me with delivering Arthur's seal to him and then to be on standby for the rest of his plan, though I didn't know exactly what that entailed. He swore that as soon as he had succeeded in disgracing Arthur, he would give me what I wanted.

After all these years during which I had sacrificed so much, I couldn't fall apart now over a man who, for all his kindness, had nothing to offer me of any true value to me.

As I got dressed for my breakfast with Arthur, I reviewed my options in my head once more. The ring was secure on his hand, unfortunately. I had tested it last night as we said goodbye, just to see how easily it would come off, and the answer seemed to be not very easily at all. There would be no way to get it off him while he was awake without him noticing, and even while he slept, it would be difficult.

The only option I could see, therefore, would be to get him to remove it himself. I just had to find a way to ask.

Since I had no ladies to help me fasten my dress, I had come up with my own method of securing them, and I had just finished doing so when a knock sounded at the door, making my heart leap in anticipation. I hadn't expected Arthur to actually come and collect me, just as he had walked me to my door last night. His chivalry continually surprised me.

But when I opened the door, Arthur's handsome face was nowhere in sight. Instead, my travelling companion, Eastam's man, stood there.

"He wants to see you," he grunted at me, and I didn't need to ask which 'he' we were talking about. We only referred to one man that way, one whose name we never said aloud.

"I already have plans," I countered. "They're important for the job he wants me to do."

"You'll have to reschedule."

I had my mouth open to argue when another man walked up, one I had seen with Arthur in the dining room the first night we met. "My lady?"

"Yes?"

"I have a message from His Highness. He sends his regrets, but he is unable to keep your appointment this morning."

The pang of disappointment that rushed through me surprised me with its strength. Why did I care so much whether I got to dine with Arthur or not? It must simply be because I knew I had so few opportunities left to achieve my task.

The man hadn't quite finished yet, though. "However, he has asked if you are free to dine with him this evening?"

So, he still wanted to see me. He must have just had something come up, much like I had. "That will be fine. Please send him my thanks and wish him a good day." The man bowed in acknowledgement and returned back down the hall while I turned back to the man in front of me with a sigh. "It appears I'm free after all."

He didn't bother to reply, leading me out to the stables instead and helping me up onto one of the horses since I had to ride sidesaddle once again. We rode a short distance out of the town to a nearby farmhouse where several men stood around the yard, practicing their knife skills or simply talking. To my surprise, the tall, red-haired man who had been held prisoner by Eastam stood among them, the one I had stopped from escaping twice before. Now, he appeared to be unrestrained, but made no move to get away.

Had Westley turned him somehow? He could be awfully convincing. The red-haired man and I both gave each other curious looks before my companion led me inside to where Eastam awaited me. We were soon left entirely on our own.

"Do you have it?" he asked before I had even fully settled in the seat across from him.

"Not yet." I kept my answer short and to the point. I had no intention of telling him I knew the location of the seal. If he knew about the ring, he could task one of his other men to get it and then I wouldn't receive my reward. I had seen the way he played his men against each other, offering them incentives to out-perform each other. The knowledge I had gained was the most valuable thing I had at the moment, and I would therefore tell him as little as possible.

"Time is running short," he reminded me, his eyes narrowing as he looked me over. "What's the problem? Is he not interested in your particular 'assets'?"

My jaw clenched at the implication but I forced myself not to react to his provocation.

"He is very interested, my lord. He's simply a gentleman who wouldn't presume to take advantage of a lady. I don't imagine you could understand."

Westley snorted. "I certainly don't understand any man who would consider you a lady."

"Did you summon me here simply to insult me, my lord?" I had no patience for his attempts at wit.

"No. I wanted an update, but I also suspect that my man with the prince's party has been compromised. See what you can find out and report back to me through your companion."

"This is not part of our deal." No matter what he might think, he couldn't order me around as he pleased like all of his other minions. I had agreed to do a specific task for a specific reward and that formed the full extent of our relationship.

"My plan might not succeed without it, and if I don't succeed, you don't either."

My nostrils flared in indignation but I couldn't really argue with that. His success reflected on mine, far more directly than I would like it to.

"Fine. Is there anything else, *my lord*?"

My emphasis on his title dripped with sarcasm, but he pretended not to hear it.

"Yes, one more thing. I'm about to meet with one of the Silatrian princes. I want you to keep an eye on him too, to see if he's going to double cross me."

"How many eyes am I meant to have?" I blurted the words out without thinking them through, but honestly! He asked too much.

"As many as you need to, *my lady*." My title sounded equally sarcastic in his mouth. "It all comes down to this. If I fail, we all fail."

I understood that. I had been telling myself the same thing all morning. And yet, looking at his smug, arrogant face, I couldn't help wishing that he not only failed, but failed spectacularly. The thought of Arthur locking Westley away in a prison cell somewhere brought me far more satisfaction than it should.

But then I would never find out what I needed to know. And so, I kept my opinions to myself, bowed my head to him as politely as I could, and left to make my way back towards the town.

Time *was* running short, as he'd said. I needed to figure out how to make the most of it.

CHAPTER ELEVEN

~Bran~

Only a few minutes after she entered the house, the dark-skinned woman walked back out again, looking even less impressed than she had when she'd gone in. The man she had arrived with spoke to her quietly, but not so quietly that I couldn't hear him.

"I need to speak to him for a minute. Wait here for me."

He went inside to Eastam while the woman looked around in frustration, obviously not wanting to be here at all. With her lips pressed tightly together, she headed back towards the tied-up horses they had arrived on, and I made my way over too, doing my best to appear as though I just happened to wander by rather than seeking her out.

"You know Eastam is using you, right?" I murmured, keeping my face turned away from Eastam's other men who were all keeping guard outside the house as he'd instructed. "He'll get what he wants from you and leave you empty-handed."

Her dark eyes scrutinized me carefully over the top of the horse as she pretended to search in the saddlebag for something. She obviously knew how to play this game.

"You must be working with him too or you would have tried to run again," she pointed out. "There is nothing stopping you now."

"Now that you're otherwise occupied, you mean?"

I raised my eyebrows at her and her lips twitched in either amusement or pride, or perhaps both.

Since I couldn't tell her my real intentions, not when she could turn around and share them with Eastam himself were she so inclined, I settled on something between the truth and a lie.

"I am working with him, but for my own reasons. He thinks it's for the reward but I don't care about that. Him achieving his goal helps me achieve mine, it's as simple as that, but I would never trust that he's going to do what he's promised to."

Her jaw tightened as she looked away from me and I could tell that she had reservations too, which didn't surprise me. She seemed far too capable and clever not to.

"Normally, I do not trust anyone," she admitted, those dark, deep eyes of hers returning to me, her mouth barely moving. "But in this case, I have no choice. He is the only one who can help me."

An unexpected pang of sympathy hit my chest. "In that case, you are in a very sorry state indeed."

"Do you know Prince Arthur?" she asked me suddenly, in what appeared to be a random change of subject. "Is he trustworthy?"

I answered as truthfully as I could. "I don't know him well, but by all accounts, yes, he's a fine prince and a decent man. I know his sister better, she is married to the prince I serve. She is of a strong character herself and she speaks well of her brother, which makes me think highly of him."

The woman nodded slowly as she processed all that. "And if Arthur were to capture Eastam, could he make him talk?"

She asked some hard questions. Eastam was unlike any prisoner I'd ever dealt with, which made it hard to be certain. "He could punish him, certainly. Strip him of his titles and land easily, but make him talk? I'm not sure."

She nodded again, more sadly this time. "That is what I thought."

The door to the house opened and her travelling companion came out, forcing me to move away before we were spotted together. After mounting their horses, they rode off together and I went back into the house to see Westley. "Eric is coming next?"

Eastam nodded, his eyes fixed on a small knife in his hand that he used to carve a hole in the table. He did it out of habit, I'd noticed. The twisting motion seemed to help him think.

"The man who just left will bring him back here. It should be within the next half hour. Wait outside until they arrive."

Having been summarily dismissed, I returned outdoors and waited impatiently for the next arrival. Every second spent here, away from Elodie, felt like one too many. At last, three horses approached, and my eyes narrowed as I got a look at the men riding them. Along with the man who had just been here and Eric, which I had expected, they were accompanied by the man I had spoken to the night I tried to break free and find Arthur, the one who sent me to the woman's room instead. He must be the spy who had been working for Eastam, but in that case, why would he be here? Cass should have apprehended him last night after Cordelia and Elodie saw us in town.

Confused, I followed them into the house and sat down next to Westley while the three other men sat across from us on rickety stools. Eric refused to meet my eye, pretending he couldn't see me, and disgust raced through me. How could he betray Cass like this yet again? He had been incredibly lucky the king had given him a second chance after nearly getting Cass killed in the first place. There would be no further chances once Cass found out about this.

Eric spoke first, addressing himself to Eastam. "It's been a while, Westley."

"It has," Eastam agreed. The words seemed innocuous enough but their tones made it clear on both sides that the men disliked and distrusted each other. That should make for an interesting conversation. "I am giving you one last chance to make up for your earlier failure."

Eric's neck turned bright red. "*My* failure? You were only supposed to change the marriage contract! You're the one who tried to kill my brother instead and screwed the whole thing up."

Once again, his thoughts were only for himself and the indignities he had suffered. His selfishness beggared belief.

"Let's just say that neither of us got what we wanted," Westley growled. "However, we have a chance to rectify that now. You can still get your throne and I can have mine." Eric opened his mouth to say something but Westley held up his hand to stop him. "And your brother doesn't have to die, since that seems to be a sticking point for you."

It took every ounce of self-restraint I had not to punch Eastam right in his smug face. Or Eric, for that matter. Maybe both of them, if I could time it right.

"How can I have the throne if Cass is still alive?" Eric asked, sounding justifiably confused.

Eastam sighed, raising his eyes to the ceiling in a show of exasperation. "If he abdicates."

Abdicates? I had never heard him mention that plan before, and it didn't entirely make sense. Only the king could abdicate, and Cass was still just a prince.

Eric pointed out the same thing. "My father is still on the throne."

"Not for long." Those were the only words Westley spoke, but they were enough. Eric's eyes widened in the same way that mine did. Once again, he went to speak, but Westley cut him off. "That is not your concern. All I need for you to do right now is prove your loyalty to me."

Eric's eyes narrowed once again, regarding Westley with a healthy amount of suspicion. "How?"

"By killing him." Eastam pointed at the man next to Eric, Arthur's man, whose face immediately turned ghostly white.

"W-what?" the man stuttered. "My lord, that isn't funny."

"No, it's not," Eastam agreed, his voice cold as ice. "It's not funny that you sent me false information last night which could have exposed my men. It's not funny that you're probably only here because you struck a deal with your prince after he caught you out. And it's not funny that now I have to doubt whether His Highness here is in on it with you. This way, I'll know if one of you is clean, because I know for sure you both aren't."

Eric swallowed hard, his hand moving to the sword handle at his side, and the other man's eyes grew even wider.

"Your Highness, you can't! Tell him the truth, tell him..."

Whatever he wanted to say, none of us would ever find out. Eric's sword pierced his stomach skillfully as the man's face froze in shock and disbelief. Eric ran him through once more for good measure before kicking his stool over with his foot, letting the man crash to the floor as he bled out onto the dirt floor.

"Satisfied?" the prince snarled at Westley as he shoved his bloodied weapon back into its scabbard.

A hint of a smile crossed Westley's lips. "For now. At least we can talk about what you're going to do for me. Bran, you can leave us now."

What? I didn't want to go anywhere, not right when we were getting to what I wanted to know most of all. "My lord?"

"You heard me. Wait outside."

Damn it. Why had he brought me here to witness Eric's betrayal, only to send me away now? I had no idea what new game he had in mind, and enlightenment didn't appear to be on the horizon anytime soon.

Eric continued to avoid my gaze as I walked past him and I couldn't help tossing one last disparaging look over my shoulder at him as I went. In that last glance back, I saw it: the message from Cass on the back of Eric's doublet, looking like mere scratches to anyone else, but to me, they spelled out an invitation, clear as day.

Dusk. The ale house.

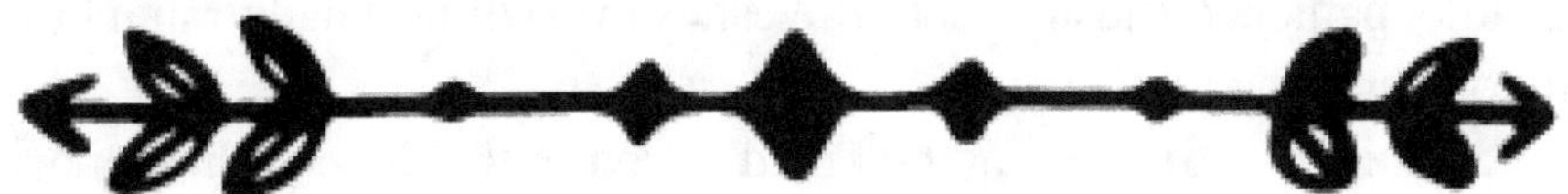

~Arthur~

While we waited for Eric and Alfred to return, Dee went to visit with Elodie, and Cassian and I passed the time talking about life as a crown prince. I had never really had the opportunity to simply sit and speak with someone else in my position about all the pressures and responsibilities that came with the job, and I found it quite illuminating. Things I thought were unique to me turned out not to be; he had experienced many of them too.

We also had similar philosophies on several things, especially around the welfare of our subjects. I could see several areas where we might be able to work together on things, given our close geography and now familial ties, and Cassian seemed to agree.

Despite all the time I had wasted on this search for Eastam, I found myself grateful for two things to come from the chase: the chance to get to know my brother-in-law better, and the fact that it had brought me into contact with Zara.

I had one ear trained on the door as I anxiously awaited any reply to the messages I had sent to the castle last night, but Eric returned first, on his own.

"Where's Alfred?" I asked as Eric entered my room, a deep scowl on his face.

"Dead," was his blunt reply.

Cassian and I looked at each other in surprise. Obviously, something hadn't gone to plan. "What happened?"

"Eastam knew he'd been turned. He told me to kill him to prove my own loyalty."

"And you killed him, just like that?" I couldn't speak for the laws of Silatria, but here in Lassaria, we considered that murder.

"I didn't want to," he growled. "I tried to think of a way out of it, but the idiot panicked and almost told Westley everything. I had to shut him up to keep my cover."

That might be true, or had he killed Alfred so that he couldn't report back to us that Eric was actually playing the other side?

I glanced over at Cassian again to try to gauge his read on the situation but his expression proved impossible to decipher. "Did Bran give you anything?" he asked instead. "Any kind of message for me?"

Eric's brow furrowed in confusion. "No. Why would he give me a message?"

"Tell me what happened between you," Cassian replied, not answering the question.

Eric explained how Bran had been in the room at the beginning and sent out after Alfred's death. After listening to his brother carefully, Cassian got to his feet. "Show me the horse you used."

Eric looked over at me as if to ask if I had any idea why this mattered, but I could only shrug my shoulders. Together, we went out to the stables where Eric pointed out the horse and saddle he had just used, and Cassian walked over to take a closer look, examining everything in minute detail.

"What is he looking for?" I asked Eric, who shook his head.

"I hoped you had an idea."

None the wiser, we both watched as Cassian looked over the saddle, running his fingers along it, until at last, his face broke into a satisfied smile. "He got it," he told us, though I still had no idea what he meant. "Let's go back inside."

Still offering no explanation, Cassian led us back to my room where we all sat down again.

"Tell us what Westley asked of you," Cassian prompted his brother.

Eric leaned back, crossing his ankle across his knee. "His instructions were vague, as usual. He wants me to create a distraction when Cass goes to meet with him, something to keep Arthur and the other men busy."

"For what purpose?" I asked.

Eric shrugged. "He didn't say, which is how he works. Everyone only knows their piece of the puzzle. He's the only one with the whole picture."

I tried my best to put myself in Westley's shoes and imagine what he might be trying to achieve. "So, he wants us distracted so that we can't help Cassian if he gets in trouble, perhaps?"

"Maybe." Cassian sounded unconvinced. "Or he wants to do something entirely different while none of us are around to stop him."

"Like what?" Eric asked, and neither of us had an answer for that. Getting inside the head of a man like Eastam would be nearly impossible, which explained why we hadn't been able to stop him yet.

"I'll think about it," Cassian announced, getting to his feet again. "I'm going to have dinner with Dee and then I'll be heading to the ale house in town. Would you like to join me?"

I felt bad about putting him off, but once again, I had other plans. "I'm afraid I'm busy again tonight."

The same curiosity as before flashed in his eyes, but he asked no further question, turning to his brother instead. "Eric?"

Eric looked up at him in surprise. "You were inviting me too?"

"Why not?" Cassian's tone might be mild, but we all knew why not. By making the offer, Cass held out an olive branch to his brother, who quickly accepted it.

"Okay, sure. Maybe we could bring the ladies with us." Cassian's eyebrows raised, and Eric rushed to clarify. "Princess Cordelia and Lady Elodie, I mean."

Cass nodded slowly. "Yes, perhaps we should. I'll come and find you after dinner."

With that arranged, they both said goodbye and left me on my own. I'd already made plans for food to be brought to my room again for me and Zara, but I had really been hoping to get news back from the castle before dinner, and the likelihood of that decreased with each passing minute.

Just as I'd thought it might be hopeless, someone knocked on my door and I quickly went to open it, hoping to find the messenger there. Instead, Zara herself stood there, looking fresh and lovely in a pale, yellow dress.

"Am I early?" she asked, glancing back over her shoulder. "You look like you were expecting someone else."

"I thought you might be from the kitchen," I lied, not wanting to get her hopes up about the messenger until I had some news to share. "The food isn't here yet, but you are more than welcome. Please, come in."

She entered my small room, and I thought again how fortunate I was to have met her on this journey. If we had met at the castle, I would have been busy with other duties and much more tied by convention. Here, away from the court, I could entertain her in my room without anyone interfering, and we could get to know each other much better.

It almost felt as if this had been meant to be.

"What do you think of Lassarian food in general?" I asked as a starting point for the conversation and a way of finding out more about her as we both took a seat. "Is it very different from the cuisine where you grew up?"

That earned me a smile as she reached back into her memory. I loved the warm look in her eyes whenever she thought about her home. "It is quite different, yes, but I am used to it now. I sometimes wonder when I go home if I will be able to handle all the different flavours again or will my tongue have grown dead from the blandness of the food here?"

Her blunt assessment of my homeland's culinary offerings made me laugh. "It can be rather repetitive, I admit."

"Repetitive?" She repeated the word in a teasing tone. "No, of course not. Some days I can have meat and vegetables and other days I can have vegetables and meat."

She looked younger when she smiled, like she did now. I liked the way it looked on her. "What else is different?" I asked curiously. "How do people entertain themselves after dinner?"

"We talk, as you do," she said, still teasing me, until her expression grew more reflective. "And we dance sometimes."

"Dance?" I repeated curiously. Men and women at the Lassarian court danced in elaborate, choreographed, pattern dances, but I suspected she meant something different.

"It is a more intimate thing than your dancing," she explained, confirming my suspicions. "We hold hands, for one thing."

"Would you show me?" The boldness of my question surprised me, but I asked it anyway since I wanted to keep that smile on her face. "I am not a great dancer, but I'm willing to try."

My enthusiasm seemed to please her. "If you would like to, I would be happy to show you what I remember. It has been a long time though."

"We'll figure it out together then," I offered, getting to my feet. "How do we start?"

Zara came to stand in front of me, her face tilted up so she could meet my eyes. Her lips parted, making me more aware of my own lips too. They seemed suddenly dry and I quickly ran my tongue along them to moisten them while I waited for her instructions.

She held up her hands, palms facing me. "First, we join palms like this."

Gently, I placed my hands against hers. The contrast was significant, both in the size and our colouring, and yet, they seemed somehow to go together.

"Next, we link our fingers." Her fingers spread and I copied her motion. As her fingers slipped between mine, entwining, a rush of desire ran through me. Though we were hardly touching, I had never been even this intimate with a woman before. My heart beat faster and my breeches grew tighter, making me blush. Hopefully, she wouldn't notice.

Zara, however, frowned as she looked at our intertwined fingers. "I'm sorry, Your Highness, but your ring is quite hard. Would you mind taking it off while we do this?"

It hadn't even crossed my mind that it would hurt her delicate hands. Even so, I hesitated to take it off. It never left my hand.

She picked up on my reluctance and her hands withdrew from mine, pulling all her warmth away too. "It is okay if you would rather not," she assured me, taking a step back. "We don't need to do this. It is probably not proper for a prince like you anyway, not with a woman like me."

I didn't want her to think that my hesitation had anything to do with her position, or whatever else she meant by that, so I quickly pulled the ring off and placed it on the table beside us, still in my sight but off my hand.

My hands bare now, I held them back up to her, palms out as she had done to me. "Please, Zara. You've got my full attention. I would like you to show me the rest."

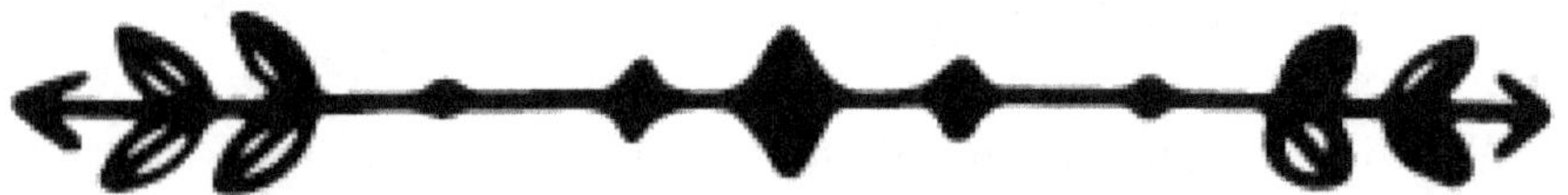

~Zara~

I couldn't believe it had been that easy. I only had to ask Arthur to take off his ring and he did it. As he placed it on the table next to us and turned back to me, his handsome face full of warmth and eagerness, a strong, painful rush of guilt ran through me.

I wished I didn't have to do this. I wished I could find another way to get the information I so desperately needed, but ten long years of bitter experience had taught me that wishing was not enough. Wishes only came true when backed up by action, and I knew exactly what action this situation required.

I had to get that ring.

But first, Arthur expected a dance, and I owed him that much. It was the very least I could do.

My hands slid back into place, my palms touching his as his strong fingers threaded through mine once more. Though he seemed to think of me as some kind of expert, I had only done this dance with my sisters before. Before I left home, I had been too young to dance with men, but we practiced all the time, preparing for the day when we would be presented at the court and paraded in front of all the eligible young men, looking for a suitable husband.

My mother harboured a secret hope that I would catch the eye of one of the princes, but my father disagreed. I had overheard them speaking about it one night when they thought I had gone to bed.

"She will have to learn to hold her tongue," my mother mused. "No man wants a girl who talks back as much as she does."

"She should not settle for any man who does not want to listen," my father replied mildly. "I listen to you, don't I?"

My mother pretended to be outraged, but I could hear the laughter in her voice. The room fell silent so I quietly snuck back to my own room. At the time, I thought they had simply gone to sleep, but now I knew better what that silence meant.

The same silence filled Arthur's room right now, the silence of tension and attraction and connection.

I led him through the steps methodically and without words, making my movements slow enough that he could copy me without getting lost. His movements were awkward, as he'd warned me. His height made him less than graceful, but his gentleness made up for it. He smiled every time he made a wrong turn, never getting upset or losing his patience.

When we had been through it a number of times, I took a step back. "Now, we can try it at full speed."

His eyes immediately widened in dismay. "It goes faster?"

I simply smiled and nodded, and he took a deep breath as he faced me.

"Very well, Zara. I'm in your hands."

I began to hum a tune, an old melody I barely remembered, and it almost seemed like the room around us faded. In my mind, I could see myself back in the courtyard of our riad, the warm summer night's air around me as a handsome man approached and asked me to dance.

A smile spread across my face as I pictured the shocked faces of my family when they took in his pale skin and blue eyes, so exotic and different, but in my imagination, he paid no attention to any of them. He had eyes only for me, just as I couldn't look away from him.

Our hands connected as our feet went through the steps. Lost in the moment, he let me lead him, hardly putting a foot wrong as we moved in the rhythm of the dance. His smile filled me with warmth and I could see a new heat in his eyes too, a heat that seemed to increase every time our bodies brushed against each other.

When it ended, we stood face to face, both of us breathing a little heavier, our eyes locked on each other as the room around us took shape once more. The heavy, humid, perfumed air disappeared as I took a deep breath. "You have the makings of a fine dancer, Arthur," I praised him sincerely. "You just need more practice."

"It is much easier with such a skilled teacher," he replied, his eyes never leaving mine. "I think there is a great deal you could teach me."

His eyes dropped to my lips and my heart seemed to skip within my chest. I had never *wanted* a man to kiss me before. I had let them, when I needed something from them that they would only give me in exchange for the pleasure they could take from me, but I had never sought it out myself, just for its own sake.

Yet, I couldn't lie to myself: I did want him to kiss me. I wanted to know what it would feel like with a man like him.

And to my great relief, he did not let me down. Gently, as always, he brought his lips down to mine and my eyes closed as our mouths pressed softly together.

This was not like any kiss I had ever known before. Most men kissed me almost painfully hard, as a way of staking their claim to me. It focused on possession, or domination, all about the way they were feeling.

Arthur's kiss had none of that in it. It felt tentative but sincere, like an invitation. He wouldn't go on if I gave him any sign I wanted to stop. The choice was mine as much as his.

And truthfully, I didn't want it to stop. The bubbly feeling in my stomach, the shot of pure longing that went through me, these were all new feelings for me, and I had to admit I liked them.

I liked *him*.

And for that reason, I couldn't allow this to go any further. Sleeping with him to get the seal was one thing. I had been prepared to do that, to let him have his pleasure in exchange for what I wanted, but we had moved far beyond that. He had no desire to use me, but I still intended to use him. I was the villain here, I could see that, and it would only hurt him if I led him on any more than I had already.

I didn't want him to be hurt when he realized I had gone.

I didn't want to hurt him at all.

With that in mind, I pulled back from his kiss, though it felt like leaving a part of myself behind, and his face immediately registered concern. "I'm sorry, Zara. I didn't mean to..."

I placed my finger against his lips to stop his apology. He had nothing to apologize for. Those words belonged to me. "It is not that, Your Highness. It's just that dinner is here."

I had heard the footsteps a moment earlier, and now the knock sounded on the door. Arthur laughed in surprise and relief. "Of course. Allow me."

As he stepped away towards the door, I saw my chance. With his back turned, I had the perfect opportunity to snatch the ring from the table and put it in the little pouch attached to the rope around my waist.

So, I did.

The ring almost seemed to scald my hand as I picked it up, the weight of my guilt seeming to weigh me down, but I did my best to push those feelings aside. I *had* to do this. I had to. After all this time, I had to find my father.

"Zara?" Arthur said my name just as I pulled the string of my pouch closed again.

I turned back to him and saw to my surprise that the knock at the door had not been our dinner, but a man in riding clothes. Arthur had a piece of paper in his hand and his eyes were filled with an emotion I couldn't identify.

Unfortunately, I couldn't stick around to find out what this all meant. I needed to get out of there quickly before Arthur realized the ring had gone, before he realized what I'd done. I couldn't bear to see the look on his face when he realized it. It would break my heart.

"I'm afraid I'm not feeling well all of a sudden," I lied, putting a hand to my stomach. "Please, excuse me."

I tried to move towards the door, past the two men, but Arthur put his hand on my arm to stop me. "Wait, Zara, this is important. It's a message from my father, the King."

I didn't see what that had to do with me. "Perhaps you can tell me about it another time."

I tried to move again, but he held me firm, and my heart beat even faster. Did he suspect what I'd done? Why was he behaving this way? He had never been forceful with me before.

"Zara, it's about your father."

Something in the way he said it made my heart sink, and I didn't understand what he meant in the first place. What would the king know about my father?

Arthur dismissed the man at the door and pulled me further inside, closing the door behind us. I swallowed hard as my means of escape seemed to vanish. "I don't understand," I told him truthfully.

Arthur explained to me how he had written to the court last night after our conversation, asking if anyone knew anything about my father or his location. Disbelief filled me as I listened to him. He had really done that for me? For no reason other than to help me?

Why did he have to be so good? The ring seemed to be burning a hole through my pouch, searing my skin, proclaiming my guilt.

"What does the message say?" I asked. I couldn't imagine he had received any further information than I had been able to gather over the years.

"I'm acquainted with the man who brought him here. His name is Eastam and his son has been a thorn in my side for a very long time." I already knew that, but Arthur had not finished yet. "However, Eastam did not send your father to one of his properties abroad, as you said. My own father bought out his sentence instead."

I had never heard that detail before and it did not fit with what I knew.

"That can't be true," I countered softly. "I have heard from good authority that Westley Eastam's father sent him out of the country."

"That's exactly right," Arthur confirmed, seeming to contradict what he had just said. "This is where it gets complicated. Eastam's mother's husband bought your father, but his birth father sent him away."

It took me a moment to piece that all together in my head, but eventually, I figured it out. "The king is Westley Eastam's father?"

Arthur nodded. "Westley is my half-brother, unfortunately."

That, I certainly had not known, but suddenly a lot of things made more sense, things I had seen and overheard with Eastam. He wanted the throne because he thought he had a legitimate claim to it, not simply from some delusion of grandeur.

As interesting as that might be, it paled in comparison to the rest of what Arthur had said. "So, your father sent my father away? Where? Do you know where he is?"

If Arthur had that information, then maybe I really didn't need Westley after all. For the first time in a very long time, real hope rose within me.

Arthur nodded again, but more sadly this time. "My father does not approve of holding men in such a way, and he suspected there might be more to the situation than he knew. Wanting to set things right, he granted your father clemency and released him. He paid for his return journey himself."

I heard the words, but I couldn't quite make sense of them. Return journey? To where?

"Are you saying...?" I tried to form the question, but the words refused to come. It seemed impossible.

Arthur filled in the blanks for me, his eyes full of sympathy. "All this time you have been looking for him, he has never been here. He has been at your home all along."

CHAPTER TWELVE

~Elodie~

Dee and I were talking in my room when Cassian and Eric knocked on the door and let themselves in. "I'm having dinner brought here for us and then we're all going out," Cassian explained.

"Out?" Dee's eyes lit up at the idea of an adventure. She had been going crazy staying indoors all day while we waited for news. "Out where?"

"A drinking house," her husband replied, and my mouth fell open in disbelief.

"We can't go to a place like that," I protested. "No respectable princess would ever associate with common, drunken men in a place like that."

Dee pursed her lips, trying not to smile. "Oh, Lodee, there are plenty of drunken men in the castle anytime there's a feast, but I've never been to a public house before. How exciting!"

It sounded far more dangerous than exciting to me, and as if he could read my thoughts in my face, Eric gave me a smile. "Cass and I will be with you the whole time. No one will dare to come near you, and if they do, we'll make them regret it."

I believed he meant it, but Cassian's next words were what truly made up my mind. "I'm hoping to meet Bran there."

Instantly, the hairs on the back of my neck stood up. "Bran will be there? How do you know?"

He explained to us about the messages that Eric had unwittingly relayed, one to Bran to inform him of the location of the meeting and the reply from Bran saying that he had received it and would do his best to be there.

"Surely he won't come alone," Dee pointed out. "How will you manage to speak to him without anyone noticing?"

Cassian gave a shrug. "I'm still working that part out, but for a start, we'll have to disguise ourselves as much as possible."

That excited Dee even more. "Will you wear a fake mustache?"

"Only if you do too," he teased her back, and they both smiled at each other in that special way that told me they'd completely forgotten anyone else's presence in the room.

When I glanced over at Eric, he had a confused look on his face as he watched them, and as Dee went with Cassian to pick out our disguises, Eric and I stayed in my room to wait for the food to be delivered from the inn's kitchen.

"They really seem to like each other," he said, gesturing to the door through which the prince and princess had just exited. "And not just in the bedroom."

How could he doubt it? "Of course they do. They're in love."

"Love?" he repeated with a huff. "I don't know what that means. I doubted it even really existed, but seeing the way they are together, maybe there is something to it. I've certainly never felt it. Perhaps some people just aren't meant to."

From all I'd heard of him before this trip, it didn't surprise me to hear him say that, but from the time I had spent with him in the last few days, I thought he might be selling himself short.

"There are some men who fall in love with every woman they meet," I explained, thinking of Dee's middle brother, Edward. He had a new crush nearly every day, it seemed like, and he considered each new woman the most perfect, beautiful creature he'd ever seen... until the next one. "But their love is not worth as much as the man who thinks he shall never feel it, and then feels it all the more strongly when he finally does."

Eric looked over at me with a curious, thoughtful expression. "You think everyone is capable of it?"

"Yes indeed, Your Highness. There is someone for each of us. When you meet her, you will know it. She will make you feel things you have never felt before and think things you have never thought."

His lips tightened as he turned that response over in his head. "And this is how you feel about Bran?"

The question took me by surprise. He had never asked me anything about my relationship with Bran before and I really didn't think he had any interest in it. But now that he had asked, I did my best to answer him honestly.

"Yes, that is how Bran makes me feel. From the first time I met him, I felt safe with him and comfortable to speak with him. I don't feel that way around very many people."

"You don't feel comfortable speaking to me?" he asked, sounding almost hurt.

Once again, I hadn't expected that question, but I answered him truthfully once more. "Not when we first met, but the more time we have spent together, the more comfortable it has become."

"So does love have to come on all at once, do you think, or can it grow over time?"

That was a good question and I paused to give it some proper thought. "I think it can grow, yes. Sometimes, we make judgements of a person based on limited information, and when we truly get to know them, we find that we were mistaken. In some ways, that may be a more lasting kind of love than the kind based on an immediate attraction, because it is rooted in who the person is rather than simply how they appear."

That answer seemed to please him enough that the hurt on his face began to clear, so I carried on with my reply.

"And in some cases, like Princess Cassian and Princess Cordelia, they are lucky enough to have both: an instant draw to each other that has only deepened as they got to know each other further."

We had no further chance to discuss it as the food arrived, and Cassian and Dee returned soon after. When our stomachs were full, Dee sent the men away while she and I got changed into the clothes she had brought for us.

I stared at her in shock as she held mine up for me. "I can't wear that! I will look like a man."

"That's the point, Lodee," she told me with a laugh. "We'll draw too much attention as women. If we wear these, keep our hair beneath our hats and keep our heads down, no one will notice us."

It seemed crazy to me, but if Cassian had agreed, I supposed I couldn't really argue. Dee and I helped each other dress, though she ended up being more helpful than me. Since she had helped Cassian dress and undress before, she knew where all the pieces of men's clothing went. I couldn't find a place to secure my book beneath the looser clothing so I would have to leave it behind.

When we looked at the finished product in the mirror, I could hardly believe my eyes. At first glance, we truly looked like any men one might pass in the street. Or perhaps boys, to be more truthful.

"Are you ready?" Cassian's voice sounded at the door along with a knock and Dee rushed to it, pulling it open and showing off her efforts to him. His eyes wandered over her as his teeth caught his bottom lip. "There is no reason on earth you should look good like this, but somehow, you do."

"Not quite as good as you did in my dress," she reminded him with a laugh. "Come on, let's go before you get any ideas."

We all walked side by side through the darkening streets towards the ale house. It felt strange to be out in public this way and not holding onto one of the men or to Dee, but I supposed men didn't do that when they went out together. I tried to keep my head down, as Dee had said, and not catch anyone's eye.

Most of the tables were already occupied as we walked into the small building that smelled of both strong ale and urine while raucous laughter and conversation filled the air. Doing my best not to gag, I followed the others to an empty table near the back wall. Eric almost went to pull out my chair for me before he remembered not to, but it surprised me to see even that much of a chivalrous gesture from him.

"I don't see Bran," I whispered to Dee as I scanned the room from our vantage point and she shook her head.

"No, nor do I, but perhaps he's still on the way."

Cassian went to get us all some drinks and I peered around curiously once more. I had never been around men before when they weren't aware of any women present. In some ways, it felt different: I noticed a lot more cursing and scratching themselves, for example. But in other ways, they seemed much the same as they were around us, and I had to admit, I found it fascinating.

Cassian had just sat back down when the door opened, and my head immediately turned towards it, watching as another small group entered, but my heart sank when I didn't see Bran's familiar red head among them. I had just looked away again when Dee grabbed hold of my hand beneath the table. "There he is!"

With my pulse kicking up a notch, my eyes quickly returned to the door where Bran had entered just behind the other group, him and two other men I had never seen before. They went and found their own table while we tried not to be too obvious about watching him and, after a few moments, Bran stood up to get a drink of his own.

"That's my cue," Cassian muttered to us all and, leaving Eric with me and Dee, he wandered casually over to where Bran stood.

My breath in my throat, I kept my eyes on the men Bran had entered with, who were watching him closely. Were they going to recognize Cassian? Would we all get caught? What would they do to Bran if we did?

And what would his reaction be if he looked over here and saw me like this right now?

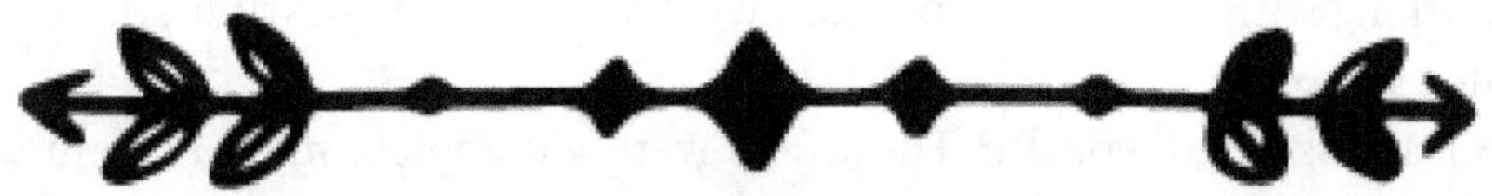

~Cassian~

By the time I got up from the table, Bran had already made his way over to the small serving hatch that led to the ale house's kitchen, where drinks were being dispensed by the establishment's owner. Careful to keep my eyes forward, I sidled up next to him and spoke to him under my breath.

"It's good to see you."

A quick smile crossed his face, though he immediately pulled it back down. "I almost didn't recognize you. Sean, is it?"

I had to fight not to smile too. It felt damn good to hear his voice after more than a month, but unfortunately, we had no time to catch up. We only had a small window of opportunity before his companions would begin to get suspicious.

"What can you tell me?"

As usual between us, he needed no further explanation. He knew exactly what I wanted to know. "The meeting is a setup. He plans to take Princess Cordelia and use her as blackmail against you. He wants me to take her."

I should have guessed. That must be why he wanted Eric to create a distraction, so the others would leave Dee unguarded while I met with him. It made complete sense given what I knew of Eastam's way of thinking, but then, so would a million other things. The sheer scope of what he could be capable of made him impossible to predict.

Knowing the game gave us a huge advantage we hadn't had before, and I couldn't overestimate my gratitude towards my friend for giving it to us. I couldn't even begin to imagine how he had to fight against all his natural instincts to even pretend to be working for a man like Westley. Bran was the most honest, upstanding man I knew. "I understand. Thank you."

Not wanting to get him in any trouble, I turned to go but his voice stopped me. "Wait, there's something else. The dark-skinned woman is working with Eastam. I'm not sure what she wants with Arthur, but it's all a setup too."

Dark-skinned woman? The words were a complete mystery to me, I had no idea what he meant. I hadn't seen anyone like that here in

Lassaria, but perhaps Arthur would know more. I would check with him as soon as we got back to the inn.

Again, we didn't have the time to discuss it in more detail so I simply thanked him again. "I'll speak about it with the others. Lady Elodie is here, by the way. She has been worried for you."

His head immediately swivelled around the room, seeking her out, and I winced at the sudden movement, wondering how it would look to the men watching him. Perhaps I shouldn't have said that, but I had only been thinking that if our situations were reversed, I would be desperate to hear something of Dee.

"Where is she?" he asked breathlessly, his eyes still scanning the room.

Of course he wouldn't recognize her in her current state of dress. "By the back wall, at a table with Eric. She and Dee are wearing men's clothes."

His eyes widened as he caught sight of them and he looked genuinely speechless for a moment. "Is she okay with that?" he finally asked, his voice full of concern. "And why is she with Eric?"

"Everything okay here?" Before I had a chance to answer, one of the men who had entered with Bran had come up behind him as we'd been talking and gave me a hard look. I bowed my head, trying to hide my face. I didn't recognize him, but if he worked for Eastam, he might know me.

Bran had a response ready, as usual. He had always been quick on his feet. "This 'gentleman' tried to get his order in ahead of me, but we've worked it out, haven't we?"

He gave me a hard look which, if I didn't know any better, would have been genuinely intimidating.

"Yes, sir," I muttered, taking a step back. "It's all yours."

Bran grabbed the drinks off the counter of the serving hatch and made his way back to his own table with the other man, who cast one last suspicious look in my direction before turning away.

That was too close. Exhaling in relief, I put in an order of my own to continue the charade and then returned to my table with another set of drinks even though the first ones had barely been touched.

"Did you get what you needed?" Eric asked curiously as I took my seat back next to Dee.

Her blue eyes also looked up at me curiously and a flash of desire ran through me. She really did look ridiculously enticing in her current getup, though I couldn't explain why. The reaction of my body to it completely confused me.

"I know what he's asked Bran to do, which makes what he asked you to do make a lot more sense too."

"What's the problem, then?" Dee asked, picking up on the things I left unsaid just as she always did. She could read me so well.

"He talked about a woman who's working for Eastam and has something to do with Arthur, but I have no idea what he means. I haven't seen any woman around."

To my surprise, Dee turned slightly pale at my words. "A woman with Arthur? She's working for Westley?"

I nodded. "That's what he said. It should be fairly easy to identify her, he said she had dark skin and there aren't many people like that around."

We only had a handful in Silatria and I hadn't seen any in Lassaria since we'd arrived. They were more common abroad, at the courts of other kings I'd visited alongside my father.

This time, Eric repeated my words incredulously. "Dark skin?"

I nodded again, wondering if I needed to speak more clearly. "Yes. Why? Have you seen someone?"

"I have," he confirmed. "Just before you arrived, a woman like that dined at the inn where we stayed. I spoke with her briefly but as far as I know, Arthur had no contact with her."

Without waiting for any further discussion, Dee got to her feet.

"What are you doing?" I asked, glancing around to make sure she hadn't attracted any unwanted attention. Thankfully, everyone else seemed too focused on their own conversation and drink to notice her sudden movement.

"Arthur has been meeting with a woman privately," she explained to me in hushed tones. "That's what he's been busy with in the evenings. He seemed to think it might be something romantic, but if what Bran's saying is true..."

"Then she might be dangerous," I filled in as I stood up too. "Let's go."

Eric looked down regretfully at his half-empty drink. "It can't wait a few more minutes?"

My temper began to rise at his selfishness, but Dee put a hand on my arm to calm me, sensing I needed it. "It'll be quicker if it's just the two of us," she whispered to me, and I couldn't argue with that. With an apologetic smile, she turned back to her friend. "Lodee, are you okay to come back to the inn with Eric if Cass and I leave now?"

Elodie looked surprised at the suggestion, but not nearly as much as Eric did. His cheeks even turned slightly pink, strangely. "That's fine," he quickly agreed. "I will bring her back safely."

"You better." Dee's narrowed eyes made it clear she meant it before we both headed towards the door, fighting the urge to look over at Bran again before we left.

As soon as we were outside, Dee broke into a jog. "Be careful," I called out as I hurried to keep up with her. "You're not used to running in boots like those."

"I have to get to him," she told me as she continued to run, not heeding my warning at all. "He could be in danger, Cass. I have to get there before he gets hurt."

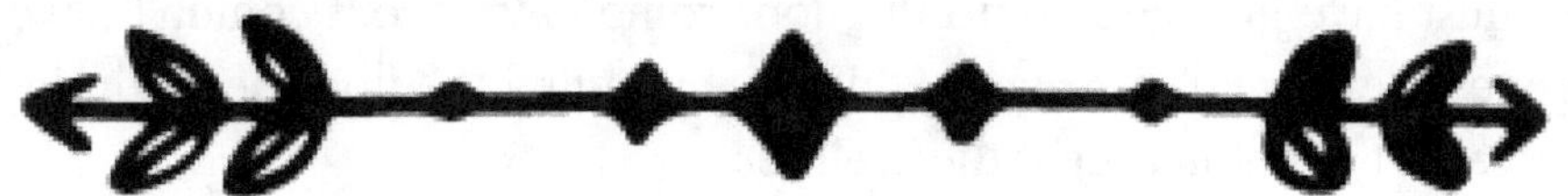

~**Arthur**~

My heart ached for Zara as I watched her process the news I'd just given her.

I couldn't begin to guess what she must be thinking. How was she supposed to feel when I'd just told her that the mission she'd dedicated nearly half her life to had essentially been pointless?

All the time she'd spent looking for her father, all the sacrifices she must have made just to survive let alone to travel around lands completely foreign to her, these were things I could barely even imagine. And the whole time, her father had been safe and sound back with her family, probably heartbroken about being separated from her in the same way she had been worried about him.

"Do you know where my home is?" she asked me, her voice quiet and a lost, haunted expression on her face that I hadn't seen there before. She suddenly looked so much younger, and far more vulnerable. It only made the aching in my chest worse. "I don't even remember the name. I thought when I found him, he would know where to go. Do you know where the ship took him?"

"My father doesn't say," I explained, holding up the letter in my hand. It only contained the specific information I had asked for with no extra details. "But he may know if I ask. I will reply to him right now, I just need a quill and my seal…"

My hand went instinctively to my finger as I mentioned the seal, but it only found bare skin there. I had forgotten I'd taken the ring off to dance with Zara.

Turning away from her, I moved towards the table where I had put it, but to my dismay, the wooden surface appeared completely empty. My ring had vanished.

Ice cold disbelief washed over me as I blinked in surprise. It couldn't just have disappeared. Panic began to fill me, but I tried to keep calm. It must have just fallen onto the floor somehow since it couldn't have gone anywhere else. Squatting down, I scanned the floor beneath the table, but I couldn't see it there either.

Feeling more ill by the second, I pushed myself up and turned back around, scanning the room without any real sense of what I expected to find. This couldn't be happening. That ring formed the legal proof of my identity, and in the wrong hands, anyone could pretend to be me and cause a great deal of damage. The fact that Eastam lurked nearby only made the idea of losing it more dangerous. What would he do if he got his hands on it? It didn't even bear thinking about.

At last, my eyes fell on Zara who stood watching me with a pained expression on her face. Different from the hurt and confusion that had just been there, the expression she wore now looked almost closer to shame.

With a trembling hand, she reached into a pouch I hadn't noticed, concealed within her skirts, and pulled something out, holding it out to me on the palm of her hand: my ring.

But... how? Why? What was she doing with it in her pouch?

"I'm sorry," she whispered, her voice barely audible and her eyes cast downwards.

Still completely confused, I reached out and took the ring from her palm. Her eyes closed as my fingers brushed against her skin, and when they opened again, her lashes were glistening.

"Why did you take it?" I truly didn't understand. What use could she possibly have for it? Did she think it might be valuable and plan to sell it? If she needed money, she could have simply asked me for it.

"I put my trust in the wrong person," she said, still speaking quietly, her voice sounding tight. When she raised her eyes to mine at last, they were filled with regret and sadness. "And so did you, Your Highness."

My heart sank as I realized her words referred to herself, meaning that I shouldn't have trusted her. But why not? I still couldn't see the full picture.

Before I could ask any follow-up questions, the door to my room burst open and a man came running in, out of breath. Or rather, it initially looked like a man, but on closer inspection, I realized the stranger was my sister, dressed as a man for reasons I couldn't even begin to guess at.

"Dee? What are you doing here?"

Cassian appeared at the door a moment later, also breathing heavily and dressed in very odd clothing too, although at least he still appeared to be the right gender. What on earth had I missed?

Dee focused her attention on Zara, her eyes narrowed in suspicion as she stepped between the two of us, facing Zara but speaking to me. "You can't trust her, Arthur! She's working with Westley Eastam."

No. That couldn't be true. I had no reason to doubt Dee, but I glanced over to Cassian for confirmation anyway, and bitter disappointment seemed to hollow out my stomach as he nodded at me, backing up what his wife had just said.

Dee spoke to Zara next, her voice harder than I'd ever heard it. My sister rarely lost her temper, but she had a fierce loyalty to those she loved, including me, and that came to the fore now. "I don't know what kind of game you were playing, but it ends now. He is not someone you can toy with. Arthur is far too good for someone like you."

Zara's deep, dark eyes returned to me, that same sadness still in them. "He is," she agreed softly. "I truly am sorry."

I didn't know if she meant the apology for me, or Dee, or perhaps to Cassian in advance, because in a flash, she had moved to the Silatrian prince's side at the door, bringing him to his knees with a well-timed twist of his arm and thrust to the back of his legs.

With him out of the way, Zara cast one last, fleeting look at me before running out the door.

"Stop!" Dee called out, ready to take off in pursuit, but I put an arm around her waist to hold her back, using all of my weight to keep her in place. She had always been stronger than she looked.

"Leave it, Dee."

She looked up at me in astonishment. "What are you talking about? She wanted to betray you!"

"I know." It made sense now why she wanted my ring. Westley must have asked her to get it, offering her information about her father in exchange. Thinking back over all our encounters, I could see his fingerprints now clearly. What I had attributed to fate was actually all the design of Westley Eastam, playing me like a puppet on a string to get what he wanted.

"She'll run to him now and tell him we're onto him," Dee continued, still struggling against me as Cass got back to his feet. "We have to stop her!"

"No, she won't." I knew that as surely as I knew anything. Whatever she had done, she did it because she thought Westley knew her father's location. He held it as leverage over her, and now that she knew the truth, she would be as furious with him as we were.

She wouldn't betray us to him because it didn't serve her interest, and everything she had done up to now was solely in her own self-interest. Finally, I could see that clearly.

Knowing what I did of her history, I couldn't blame her for it. I still believed the story about her father; after all, my own father had confirmed the man's presence here in Lassaria in the message he'd just sent me. I couldn't entirely blame her for doing whatever she felt would be necessary, and yet it stung anyway, like a thousand tiny pin pricks all across my skin.

How could I have been so completely fooled? As the future king, I should be able to spot those who simply wanted something from me, and yet it had never even crossed my mind with Zara. I naively believed that she was interested in me, that she felt an attraction to me like the one I felt towards her. Even if nothing could ever come of it, coming from two different worlds as we did, I honestly believed she had felt it too.

When I kissed her earlier, I could have sworn something passed between us, something deep and profound.

But now, I knew the disheartening truth: it had all been an act. None of it was real. She had wanted my seal and nothing more. I had offered her my friendship, my help, and perhaps even more, and all the while, she had only wanted to betray me to my enemy.

Disappointment flowed through my veins, disappointment in her but even more in myself, ashamed of how easily I had let my guard down. Perhaps I should count myself lucky that she had only wanted the seal. I had given her countless opportunities to harm me if that had been her intent, and based on the way she had just incapacitated Cassian, I had no doubt she could have done me real damage if she wanted to.

Dee helped Cass back to his feet, checking for injury. He seemed alright other than perhaps being embarrassed about a woman having got the drop on him, and when she had satisfied herself on that count, she came back over to me. "Are you okay?"

I really didn't know how to answer that. In reality, nothing had changed: Zara hadn't taken my seal, so whatever plan Eastam had for it couldn't go ahead. I would have to be extra cautious now that I knew he wanted it and that he potentially knew its location on my ring; Zara may have already shared that information with him.

We were no worse off than we had been, and yet, I felt I had lost something anyway. The sense of anticipation leading up to the time spent with Zara, the way she made me laugh and intrigued me with her stories about her home, they had been a welcome addition to my life, and now they were wiped away, gone not only from my future but the memory of them also tainted in the past.

As my disappointment continued to swirl inside me, I couldn't help thinking it would have been better if we had never met. At least then I wouldn't have known what I had been missing.

CHAPTER THIRTEEN

~Bran~

From the corner of my eye, I watched Cass and Cordelia leave in a hurry. I assumed the urgency had something to do with the information I'd just given him, but I didn't understand why Elodie and Eric hadn't gone with them. I didn't understand why the two of them were together at all, and now they were not only at the same table, they were there alone together.

My sweet, innocent Elodie, in the middle of a dockside ale house, dressed as a man, with the biggest scoundrel in all of Silatria.

It drove me absolutely crazy.

My fingers twitched against my ale glass and my legs tensed beneath the table, ready to jump to my feet at a moment's notice if anything untoward seemed to be going on.

"Bran?" One of the men next to me gave me a funny look. "What are you staring at?"

He turned to follow my gaze so I quickly looked back down at the table. "Nothing. Sorry, I got thinking about something Eastam said and must have been staring off into space."

I had been surprised that Westley had agreed to let us come into town for the evening. I knew he'd never let me go alone, so after I saw Cass' message, I spoke to some of the other men about making a night of it.

Tomorrow promised to be a big day and who could say when they'd get another chance to have a night off? They completely agreed with me, and between the three of us, we managed to talk Eastam into it. Pulling me aside, he warned me to keep an eye on the other two and I would bet anything he'd said the same thing to both of them about me. We were all spying on each other, all ready to turn against each other to gain more favour with the man pulling the strings. That was part of his game and how he kept everyone loyal to him rather than banding together and turning on him.

A true leader would never stoop to such manipulation. My loyalty to Cassian stemmed from the mutual respect we had for each other, not because I'd been tricked into it. Eastam could never claim anyone's respect, nor did he truly care about anyone else either.

I did my best to focus back on the men in front of me, but when Eric's obnoxious laugh drifted over to us, I couldn't help looking that way again, my chest tightening as I saw Elodie blushing. What had he said to her?

The man beside me looked over in that direction again too, not failing to notice my drifting attention. "Do you know them?"

Once more, I quickly averted my eyes. "No. I thought I did but it must have been a trick of the light."

I changed the subject, asking them about what they planned to do once they had their rewards from Eastam. They both had rather small dreams, only wanting the money to make their lives a bit easier. It saddened me to know they would sell out their own prince for such a meagre profit, but there were all sorts of men in the world, I knew that well enough. Including ones who would go into any woman's bed who would have them, and who were now sitting with my fiancé.

Against my will, my eyes returned to the table where Elodie and Eric were still talking. As she spoke, he appeared rapt, which came as no surprise to me. She was a natural born storyteller and wonderful to listen to. How I wished I could be the one listening to her now.

"You've clearly got a problem with that guy," the man next to me pointed out as he caught me staring once again. When he took a harder look at the table, his brow furrowed. "Wait, isn't that the prince who came to see Eastam earlier today?"

Damn it. I really hadn't meant to give Eric away, and I definitely didn't want them looking any closer at his companion. Although from this distance she appeared to be a young man, if they got any closer, they would soon see the pale complexion and beautiful pink lips that could only belong to a woman as lovely as Elodie.

"That's what I wondered, but it isn't," I lied. "It does look like him though. That's why he got my attention. I'll go grab another round."

The words spilled out of my mouth in a tumble as I tried to convince them not to get up and investigate. Returning to the serving hatch, I knew they would be watching me so I forced myself to keep my head straight and not look over in Elodie's direction though I could still see her in my peripheral vision.

As I put in our order, Eric and Elodie got to their feet and my heart beat faster as they moved towards me. Would she actually come to speak with me? I knew what a bad idea that would be, but I wanted her to do it anyway. I wanted to talk to her more than anything.

To my disappointment, they moved past me, heading towards the door, but before they could reach it, the men I had been sitting with stood up to block their path. Eric quickly stepped in front of Elodie, shielding her from their view.

"This feels like a pretty big coincidence," one of my colleagues said, his eyes narrowed as he looked between me and Eric. "That you'd happen to be here the same time we are. Almost feels like a setup."

Eric held his head up imperiously, as only a prince could. "I don't know who you are or what you're talking about. I came here for a drink, nothing more."

"Then why can't he keep his eyes off you?" the other man grunted, gesturing over at me. "Are you passing information between you? Scheming behind Eastam's back?"

He'd come far too close to the truth for comfort so I stepped in to try to defuse the situation. "Trust me, this man and I are not friends."

Eric glared over at me. "That's true. I don't fraternize with sanctimonious men who don't know their place."

The animosity in his voice sounded real enough, as it should. We had very little love lost between us.

"I don't like it," the first man said to the other. "I think we should take them all back to Eastam and let him sort it out."

Panic flashed through me, sharp and cold. The idea of Elodie anywhere near that monster made my skin crawl, and I would never let it happen. "You've been around Eastam far too long. You're getting paranoid."

"I've been around him long enough to know when something's suspicious," he growled back at me. "Now, are you going to come along quietly or not?"

Eric and I exchanged glances, for once completely on the same page. "Not," we both replied at the same time, each throwing ourselves at one of the men.

Chaos erupted in the small room as we crashed into one of the nearby tables, sending the mugs of ale flying. Other men soon joined the fight, some pulling at me, some urging me on. I tried to find Elodie amongst the crowd but there were too many people and I had lost sight of her.

So many men joined the fight that I soon lost contact with the man I had been fighting in the first place. Disentangling myself from the crowd, I could see that Eric continued to attack the other of Eastam's men, his fist connecting squarely with the man's jaw, sending spit and blood flying across the room.

At last, I spotted Elodie, pressed against the wall, as far back from the action as she could get, and as quickly as I could without making it too obvious, I made my way over to her. "Are you alright?"

These were the first proper words I had spoken to her in a month, and though they weren't much, the way her eyes brightened as I spoke them filled my whole body with warmth. "I'm fine," she assured me. "But you're bleeding."

I raised my hand to my lips and, sure enough, my fingers were smeared red as I pulled them away. I hadn't realized, and it didn't matter as much as her safety anyway. "You need to get out of here. Go just outside the door and I will send Eric out as soon as I can."

Her face clearly registered her dismay. "You're not coming?"

I wished I could, more than anything, but if I left with them now, Westley would know he'd been discovered and he would simply disappear. If we were to have any chance of flushing him out and bringing him to justice, I had to play along a little longer.

"Not just yet, but soon, my lady. As soon as I can."

I hoped that she could see in my eyes just how sincerely I meant it, and it seemed she could for she offered me her sweet, tentative smile. "I will be counting the minutes."

I wished I had said it like that. She had a far better way with words than I did.

"What do we have here?" The man's voice took me completely by surprise as he came up from behind me. Eastam's man, the one I'd been fighting, sidled up next to me and a disgusting, lecherous look crossed his face when he got a full look at Elodie. "You've been holding out on us, Bran. Is that what you were trying to sneak away for? You could have just told us and we could all have a turn."

My blood boiled at the insinuation and I turned to punch him again but he hit me first, clearly anticipating my reaction. I hit the ground hard, my vision slightly blurred from the blow to the side of my head.

Through my daze, I could see him move towards Elodie and my heart seemed to stop beating as he grabbed her arm and pulled her towards the door.

Stumbling to my feet in a blind panic, I raced after them, pushing my way through the crowd until the cooling night air hit my face. They were still in sight, thank goodness, and as I raced towards them, the man suddenly stumbled, dropping Elodic's arm.

"Elodie?" I called out, wanting to make them both aware of my presence.

Her face collapsed in relief as she saw me, but my eyes were drawn to the figure on the ground who pulled a small knife out of his stomach in disbelief. "You stabbed me!" the man snarled at her.

Had she really? Despite my shock, pride also filled me that she had defended herself.

"Here, allow me," I offered, taking the knife from his hand and then quickly sinking it into him again, into his chest this time. Dragging him into a nearby alley, I finished him off as fast as I could. Explaining his absence to Eastam would be tricky, but I had no alternative. He had seen far too much, not to mention that his intentions towards Elodie were worthy of such an end on their own.

"Elodie?" Another voice called out in panic, and we returned to the street to find Eric frantically scanning the area.

I called him over to us and quickly told him what just happened. "Take her back to the inn. Keep her safe."

"I will," he assured me. "Come along, my lady."

Elodie gave me one last soft, sweet smile before they hurried off together, and I returned to the ale house, looking for the other of Eastam's men. He appeared to have a broken nose courtesy of Eric's fist, but appeared otherwise unharmed.

"Are you happy now?" I growled at him. "Eastam's probably going to be furious that we attacked the prince, and our companion is dead on the street. One of the drunkards got carried away."

The man's face paled as he realized just how out of hand things had gotten. "It wasn't my idea. The other man started it."

I expected him to say that. Everyone only cared about covering their own ass. "That's what we tell Eastam then. Deal?"

He quickly agreed and we stepped outside again, leaving the ale house in far worse shape than we'd found it. As we made our way back to the farmhouse, I could only hope that the information I'd given Cass would be enough for him to come up with a plan. Hopefully by tomorrow, they could capture Eastam for good and this would all be over.

And Elodie and I could be together once again. If my lip hadn't been bloodied earlier, I might not have been able to stop myself from kissing her, no matter where we were or who could see.

The next time we met, I knew for sure that I wouldn't.

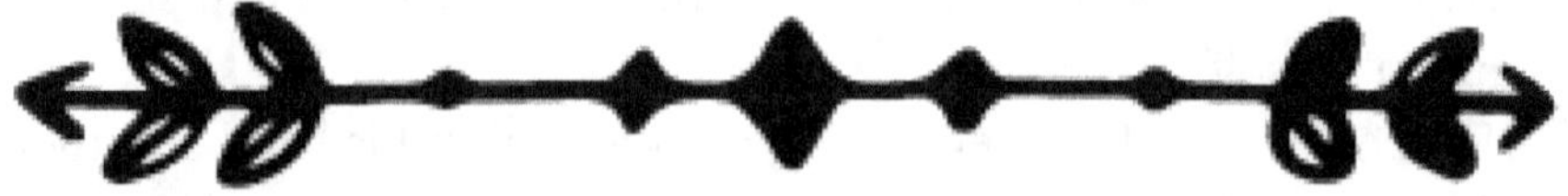

~Cordelia~

Cass winced as he held onto his arm, the one that the woman had twisted, while closing the door to Arthur's room. Her skill had been impressive, but as worried as I might be for Cass' arm, my concern for my brother outweighed it. How could he let the woman leave when I had just told him about her working for Westley Eastam? Why did he think she wouldn't be running straight back to Eastam now? What did he know that I didn't?

What exactly had gone on between them?

"Her name is Zara," Arthur told us as he sank down onto the bed, his fingers playing with the ring on his other hand. "That's what she told me, at least, but I think that much is true."

"How did you come across her?" I asked as I sat down next to him. I wanted to know the whole story from the beginning.

A brief smile flashed across his face, no doubt a reaction to his memory of the moment in question. "I walked in on her half-naked in my room."

Cass' eyebrows raised in surprise, a mirror reflection of my own. "Excuse me?"

The smile reappeared on Arthur's face at our stunned reaction, but I could see the sadness in it too. "I thought there had been a mix-up between our rooms, but I suppose it must have been a set-up. She knew I would find her there. She must have been waiting for me."

"She seduced you?" Cass asked, taking what Arthur had said to its logical conclusion.

Rather than agreeing, Arthur looked surprised and perhaps a bit offended. "No, of course not. I simply traded rooms with her."

The small room we had found him in when we first arrived came back to me, suddenly making a lot more sense. "And then what?"

"Then I ran into her again, by accident, I thought, but I suppose it must have been planned. She didn't seem to be digging for information or anything. Our conversation seemed like just that: conversation. I had no idea that she wanted anything from me."

He said that, and yet he hadn't seemed surprised when I outed her just a moment ago. Something else must have happened in the meantime.

"And you had dinner with her last night?" I prompted him, still trying to understand the full picture.

"Yes. That's when she told me why she came to Lassaria in the first place." As briefly as possible, Arthur filled us in on Zara's story about her father. Even knowing that she was working for our enemy, I couldn't help feeling a pang of sympathy for her as Arthur relayed the terrible story.

"So where does Eastam fit into all of this?" Cass asked, obviously seeing the same gaps in the narrative that I did.

Arthur grimaced. "His father bought Zara's father. The senior Eastam, that is. Zara must have learned that somehow and come to find him. My guess is that he offered to give her the information she wanted in return for her assistance with his scheme. Our quarrels with Eastam are of no importance to her. She only cares about her father."

It still didn't make sense to me. "Then what is stopping her from telling Eastam everything now to get that information?"

"He doesn't have it," Arthur replied bluntly. "I got a message from the king explaining that her father returned to his home years ago. Westley lied to Zara, manipulating her the same way he does everyone else. I wish she hadn't fallen for it."

The regret in his voice couldn't be missed, but something else lingered there too, something I hadn't heard in my brother's tone before. "You really care for her, don't you?"

When his eyes met mine, I knew the answer even before he spoke it. "I thought there was something real between us."

My chest tightened in sympathy for him, though I couldn't even really imagine how he felt. When I found out that Cass had pretended to be someone else, I couldn't have been happier, but for Arthur, the situation was completely reversed. He *wanted* her to be the woman she had seemed, and now he had to accept that person had never existed.

"But what did she want from you?" Cass asked, still focused on the practical side of things. "What did Eastam want her to do?"

"He wanted to get my royal seal," he told us, and Cass' eyes immediately widened. He knew as well as I did exactly what kind of power that seal could confer. The idea of Westley getting his hands on it could hardly be more terrifying.

"Thank God she didn't get it then," I breathed, but Arthur only shook his head.

"Actually, she did. I fell for her act completely and she took it from me."

"What?" Now, the fact that he let her escape seemed even more unbelievable. How could he be so blasé about it?

"She gave it back," he quickly added, seeing the worried expressions on our faces. "That happened just before you came in. I told her what I'd learned from the castle and she returned the seal to me. She must have realized that Eastam had been playing her all along, which is why I don't believe she will tell him any of this. She must be furious with him."

At last, things were making a tiny bit of sense. "So, she could have left with it but chose not to?"

"I suppose she could have," he agreed. "Though it wouldn't have done her any good if she no longer wanted to help Eastam. I think she gave it back simply because it did her no good anymore."

The bitter disappointment in his words tore at my heart, especially since I didn't know if I believed them. Now that my thoughts had started to settle, I remembered the look she had given him before she left and the way she apologized. I recognized something in her expression that perhaps only another woman could.

"Maybe she gave it back because she did feel something for you in the end, whether she originally meant to or not," I suggested. After all, I knew how easy it could be to fall for someone your head knew you shouldn't. Sometimes the heart did what it wanted, regardless of logic.

The flash of hope in his eyes told me just how much he wanted that to be true, but he quickly closed it off again. "It doesn't matter. We'll never see her again, I'm sure of that."

At that precise moment, a knock at the door interrupted us and Arthur and I both looked at each other warily. It couldn't be her... could it?

Cass got up to open the door, but when he stepped back, Eric and Elodie walked in rather than Zara, and Arthur's pain was pushed to the back of my mind as I took in their appearance. Eric's face had been scratched and bruised and there appeared to be blood on Elodie's hand.

"What happened?" I exclaimed, rushing over to her and examining her hand for a wound. I couldn't see one though; someone else's blood stained her skin rather than hers.

"Your man almost blew his cover," Eric grumbled to Cass. "And nearly exposed Lady Elodie in the process."

"Bran did that?" Although Cass spoke the words, I felt equally surprised. Bran had done such a good job of protecting us last night when we were spying on him, I couldn't believe he would have intentionally endangered Elodie for anything.

"Are you okay?" I asked her quietly and, surprising me again, she nodded firmly.

"I defended myself until Bran could get there."

Defended herself? From what? Obviously, we had missed something else. No one could complain about this night being short of action.

"But Bran is still uncompromised in the end?" Cass asked Eric, pressing him for more information on Bran's current situation.

"I think so. He returned to Eastam, in any case."

With that settled, and now that we were all reunited, Cass filled us all in on what Bran had told him at the ale house and what he thought it meant. "They want to take Dee because they believe I'll do anything to protect her from harm."

"Are they wrong?" I challenged him with a teasing smile.

His heated expression in return flooded my whole body with warmth. "They're completely right, which is why we can't let them take you. But we *can* use what we know to turn the tables and set our own trap. This time, we'll be the ones in control."

I definitely liked the sound of that. "What do you have in mind?"

The twinkle in his eyes turned more mischievous. "I think it's time that you pretend to be someone else."

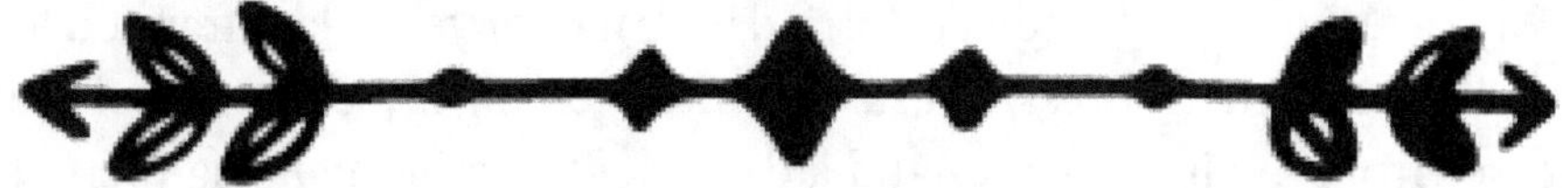

~Zara~

Tears pricked at my eyes as I ran out of the inn and out into the darkened streets of the town. Nothing had made me cry in a very long time but I felt dangerously close right now. I also had no idea where I should go, only that I couldn't stay at the inn any longer. The threat of imprisonment or worse for attempted treason against the crown prince was a powerful deterrent, but even more than that, the look on Arthur's face made me run.

The look that told me he had figured it all out. The look completely devoid of the respect his eyes had previously held for me. I hadn't had any idea how much that respect meant to me until it had gone.

Nothing remained for me here, no way I could make amends to him for how I had deceived and misled him. Though it felt like my heart broke apart a little more with each step, I knew I had to cut my losses and go. Perhaps someday he could forgive me, but I couldn't wait for that day to arrive. Now that I knew my father had gone home, I had no reason to stay. Even if I still didn't know exactly where to find my home, I had learned enough over the years to know the general direction: over the sea, far south of here. Perhaps if I simply headed in that direction, talking to people as I went, I could eventually find my way there.

Arthur had said he would try to find out for me, but that was before he knew what I'd done. That offer must have evaporated in the moment he'd learned the truth. I had no reason to think otherwise.

But as my thoughts began to clear, I realized one other man might know, one other person I could ask before I left this kingdom behind me for good: the man who hadn't told me a word of truth in all the time I'd known him, back when I still had something to lose.

Now, I knew better. Now, I knew that I could threaten Westley Eastam all I wanted and he could do nothing to me in return since he had nothing I needed. I intended to do just that.

My saif, the special blade I'd carried with me for years, lay strapped to my skin beneath my dress, as usual, so after helping myself to one of the horses from the inn's stables and a dark cloak I found hanging there, I set off down the road towards the farmhouse where I had been taken to meet with Eastam earlier today. An innate sense of direction had always been one of my gifts; I could find my way back to almost anywhere I had ever been. I could probably even make my way back to the castle of the prince who had originally separated me from my father, if I wanted to.

It was only my real home I didn't know how to get back to.

As the farmhouse appeared in the distance, I dismounted and tied the horse to a nearby tree, approaching the rest of the way on foot. There had been men standing guard outside earlier and, sure enough, as I got closer, I could see them still there. There were only a few of them so the rest of the men must be inside, but that didn't worry me. They wouldn't be expecting me, so I had the element of surprise on my side, and I felt no guilt over the idea of cutting down any man who chose to work for a man like Westley Eastam.

Moving stealthily through the shadows, pulling the cloak tight around myself to avoid drawing any attention, I made my way to the unguarded rear of the house. Two shuttered windows gave me a choice of entry options and I crept up to the first one, pulling it open just a crack to get a look at the situation inside.

Westley sat at a table, talking to two men: the red-haired one who had spoken to me earlier and another shorter, heavyset man. The short man appeared visibly nervous about whatever they were talking about while the red-haired man seemed calmer. Westley's expression gave away nothing, as always.

Just as I was trying to decide how best to take the other two out, leaving Westley alone at my mercy, he spoke to them, loud enough for me to hear.

"The cost of that man's service to me will be deducted from your own earnings. So long as nothing else goes wrong, I will allow you both to live. Is that clear?" Both men nodded and he dismissed them, sighing heavily once they were out the door and looking over towards the window, towards me. "Apparently, after all this time, people still think I'm an idiot."

My blood froze in my veins at his words. Were they directed to me? How could he possibly know I was here?

A moment later, however, another man stepped forward from the shadows in the corner of the room, just as well concealed as I had been. I had seen him with Eastam before but never spoken to him directly.

"You think Cassian's man is double crossing you?"

Westley sighed again, getting to his feet and moving closer to the window. I ducked down beneath the windowsill to ensure I couldn't be seen. Luckily, his words were still clear through the opened shutter.

"I'm certain of it. I let them go tonight as a test, and he failed. The one who died must have seen something so he killed him."

I had no idea what they were talking about, and the longer I stayed here, the greater the chance that I would be discovered. Drawing my blade from beneath my clothes, I prepared to make my move.

"What will you do?" the other man asked, also moving closer to the window. That worked to my benefit: the closer they were to each other, the easier it would be for me to attack them both.

"I still need him to get Cordelia, but after that, he's expendable. I'll have someone take him out as soon as she's in hand."

"Zara could do it," Westley's companion suggested.

The sound of my name froze me in place once again as I waited to see what Westley's reply would be.

"No, I need her on Arthur. She'll have the seal for me tomorrow, and when everyone's out looking for Cordelia, she can kill him."

Kill him? The thought of any kind of harm coming to Arthur made me feel physically sick, let alone the idea of being the one to do it.

"Isn't that dangerous?" the man pointed out. "What if it comes back to you?"

"It won't. She'll be taking the blame for the whole thing. I'll make sure she's caught red-handed, and who's going to believe the word of someone like her over me?"

That bastard! Not only had he withheld the truth of what happened to my father from me, he planned to use me to do his dirty work and make me his scapegoat. I knew he had few morals, but the depths of his deceit surprised even me.

My hand tightened on the handle of my blade as I tried to calm the fire in my veins. I needed to be calm to ensure I made no mistakes. Anger only clouded the vision; my grandfather had taught me that.

"And if she won't do it?"

"She will," Westley replied coolly and confidently. "She's desperate enough to do anything I ask of her, that's why she's so valuable to me. But should something happen and she can't, then I have others I can call upon. Blood is going to flow tomorrow, a lot of it, and when it's over, my claim to the throne will be more secure than ever. Tomorrow is the day I've been waiting for, for a very long time."

"Hey!"

The exclamation of surprise came not from inside the room but from outside, from the side of the building where the red-haired man had just appeared. As our eyes met, his widened in surprise, looking from me to the blade in my hand to the slightly opened window.

Immediately, Westley and the other man inside stopped talking, obviously having heard him, and they quickly pulled the window shutter firmly closed.

No! I had lost my chance and frustration raced through me, frustration mostly with myself. I should have moved as soon as I had the opportunity but I let myself be distracted by everything that had happened, and now, I had let myself be caught.

Pushing myself to my feet, I held the blade out in front of me so the man could see it and spoke to him in a low voice. "I don't want to hurt you. Let me leave and I won't have to."

His eyes flitted once again between the blade and the now-closed window. "Were you going to attack Eastam?" He also kept his voice quiet, apparently not wanting to be overheard any more than I did. "Perhaps I can help you."

I wished I could believe that, but I knew what kind of men worked for Eastam, men who were just as twisted as him. Men who would say one thing and do another, and push everyone else down so they could get ahead.

"It's too late," I told him bitterly. "But if you can hold your tongue about seeing me here, I will let you live."

He swallowed as my blade glinted in the moonlight. "Don't be hasty, my lady. We might be on the same side."

No one was on my side. The closest person had been Arthur and I had destroyed whatever trust existed between us. But now, after what I just heard, I knew that no matter how painful or awkward it might be, I had to return to him. I had to tell him how much danger he was in, even if it meant risking whatever punishment he might want to bestow upon me for my deception.

I owed him that much.

"I guess we will see tomorrow who's on whose side," I told the man in front of me. "Watch your back."

Before he could say anything else, I took off in a sprint in the opposite direction, keeping to the shadows as I made my way back to my horse. Soon, I made it back to the inn, darker and quieter now that most people had retired for the night.

Going inside would be too dangerous, but I knew which window led to Arthur's room. I could see the dim glow of candlelight coming from between the slats of his shutter as I crept up to it, but no sound came from within. It seemed he had not yet gone to sleep and had no company. I could ask for nothing better.

Tentatively, I knocked on the shutters and then backed away against the wall, just in case there were others with him. It took a moment for him to react, no doubt confused about where the noise came from, but eventually, he pushed the shutters open. "Hello? Is someone there?"

The sound of his voice found its way straight to my heart, but I forced myself to take a deep breath and step out into the light. Arthur's lips parted in surprise and disbelief as he saw me.

"Zara?"

The question almost made me laugh. Who else would it be, looking like me, at this time of night? But I knew he asked it because of his shock at seeing me, so I simply nodded.

"I need to speak with you, Your Highness. It is a matter of life and death."

CHAPTER FOURTEEN

~**Arthur**~

It seemed my eyes were playing tricks on me. When I told Dee we'd never see Zara again, I had been completely convinced of it. She had no reason to come back. The mission she'd been sent on had been a set-up, and without that mission, she wouldn't have come into my life in the first place.

Dee said she thought Zara might feel something more for me, but she saw the whole situation through a protective older sister's eyes. Her words were meant to ease the sting I felt, just as she'd always tried to do when we were younger, though now my wounds were emotional rather than scrapes on my hands and knees.

So, I half believed I had dreamed up the vision of Zara outside my window until she spoke, telling me she needed to talk to me, calling me 'Your Highness' in that charming accent of hers, and I knew it must be real. Elodie was the storyteller amongst us, not me; my imagination had always been far more limited.

"You should not open the window when you don't know who is there," she scolded me, even though she had knocked on it. "There are people who want to hurt you. You must take more care."

"People other than you, you mean?"

The words burst out of me, pushed out by my hurt and disappointment and I saw their sting as they landed against Zara's skin. However, she did not deny them or hide from them; she looked me straight in the eye instead. "Yes, people other than me. May I come in? It would be better if we are not overheard."

She wanted to come in through the window? There were good reasons I should say no, more than a few reasons why I shouldn't trust her, but I had to admit that her return intrigued me. Perhaps I could get some information out of her about why Westley wanted my seal and exactly what he intended to do with it.

"You can come in, but you must stay at the table. I will be armed."

To prove my point, I turned my back on her, grabbing my sword from its spot under the bed, and turned back around just in time to see her pull herself in through the open window, her skirt up around her hips so it didn't get caught, her bare legs perfectly formed beneath the layers of fabric.

With that brief glimpse, I had now seen nearly all of her, but this time, I didn't think she meant the display to be seductive. She was merely being practical.

Zara closed the shutters behind her and took a seat at the table as I had instructed while I remained at my bed, the sword in my hand in case she should try anything. Her eyes drifted to the blade with a hint of regret, but it soon passed and she seemed to steel herself, looking me straight in the eye once again.

"I have just been to see Eastam. I meant to confront him over the lies he told but I did not have a chance. Instead, I overheard him plotting against you. He means to kill you, Arth... Your Highness." She stopped herself from saying my name, understanding as well as I did that such a level of intimacy between us had been lost.

"It is no surprise that Eastam wants me dead," I couldn't help pointing out. "He wants my throne. It would be the easiest way for him to take it."

"Yes, but this is more than theoretical. He said he means to kill you tomorrow while he is meeting with the other prince."

That *was* news to me. Eastam certainly had a lot of plans for to-morrow: his meeting with Cassian, Eric creating a distraction, Bran kidnapping Dee, and now this.

It fit in what I knew of his operations: sowing chaos and pitting people against each other. I had no reason to think Zara's words were untrue, but I still couldn't guess at her motive in sharing them with me. With no alternate way to find out, I asked her directly.

"Why are you telling me this?"

Her lips tightened at my cool tone. "I do not wish to see you dead, Your Highness. Whatever else you may think of me, I hope you can believe that."

I truly didn't know what to believe. "But what is in it for you? Do you expect me to get more information for you?"

She cast her eyes downward. "No. I expect nothing further from you. You have already done far more for me than anyone else has, far more than I had any right to expect. Perhaps you can simply think of this information as my payment to you for the efforts you undertook on my behalf."

"I didn't do it for any payment, Zara."

She winced as I said her name, as if it pained her to hear me say it. "I know, but I am in your debt anyway. There is more I can share with you too. I will tell you everything I heard."

She went on to do just that, repeating the conversation as well as she remembered it and explaining her encounter with the 'red-haired man', whom I knew immediately must be Bran. I had to stifle a groan as she recounted how he had offered to help her attack Eastam but she did not trust him. If they had worked together, it might have made our path considerably easier, but it didn't surprise me that she wouldn't have taken him at his word. In her world, no one could be trusted.

And now, it appeared Bran's life hung in the balance too, but who had Eastam been speaking to? Zara described him to me, but her description could match half the men in the kingdom. He had no defining features like Bran's height or red hair.

"I know where they are staying tonight," she told me. "I could lead you there, if you like."

For a long moment, I considered it. The offer certainly held some appeal. Our numbers were small, but with the element of surprise, we might be able to overpower Westley and take him down. However, he would have familiarized himself with his temporary location; he would know the escape routes and have a backup plan. He always did. If we tipped him off and lost him now, who knew when we'd get another chance?

No, in the end, I decided it would be better to let his scenario play out and let him think he had the upper hand before we beat him at his own game.

I therefore declined her offer but asked her about her plans instead. "What will you do now?"

The muscles in her cheeks tightened as she thought it over. "If I disappear, he will send someone else to do the job, so it would be better for you if I stay and make him believe I am still on his side. I could work with you to ensure he is not successful."

That would indeed be a big advantage for us, but I didn't know what she had in mind. "He will expect you to have my seal, won't he?"

Zara nodded. "Yes, but he does not know what it looks like. I did not tell him about your ring. If you give me something else to give to him in its place, I will make him believe it is real."

My heart beat slightly faster as I considered how that might work. It sounded like she sincerely wanted to help us. "That may be dangerous for you if he uncovers the deception."

She gave me a sad, almost wistful look. "I can be very convincing, Your Highness."

Indeed she could.

"Zara..." There were so many things I wanted to say to her right now, so many things I might not ever get another chance to say, but the words seemed to stick in my throat. Most of all, I wanted her to know that I did not despise her, no matter what she might think, and I tried to find the words to express that. "I understand why you did what you did. I wish you hadn't trusted him, but I can understand why you thought you must."

To my surprise, tears gathered in the corners of her eyes. Even when she had told me the story about her father, she had not cried, but now, my words seemed to bring forth her emotion. "Your Highness..."

"Arthur," I cut her off, correcting her once again. It seemed pointless to pretend she had not called me by my name before, and it would do no harm for her to do it again now.

However, my correction only seemed to upset her more, making her eyes turn more red. "I know you have no reason to believe me, but I truly am sorry. At first, I thought you were merely another prince like the others I have known before, like the man who separated me from my father in the first place. I did not feel bad about deceiving that kind of man. And by the time I began to learn you were not, when you showed me what kind of man you truly are, I was in too deep. I thought that I needed Eastam's help, but I would not have killed you for it, not even if I still thought he could lead me to my father. Not after what we have been through together."

I wanted to believe her. I wanted it more than I could say, but she had fooled me so completely before. How could I ever trust her on a personal level again?

"You intended to seduce me on the night we met, didn't you?" I asked, once again blurting the words out before I had fully thought them through.

She did not deny it. "I did. It is the easiest way to get most men to let their guard down. You were different."

"Is it something you have done often? Taken a man to your bed to get what you want?" I sounded like a jealous lover now, I heard it myself, but I wanted to know what had led her to this point, what she had been forced to do to survive.

Once again, she did not hide the truth from me. "Yes. The first time, I was still very young, probably no more than fourteen, and starving. A farmer's son came across me on the road, half-dead from hunger, and told me he would feed me if I let him have his use of me. It seemed to me a fair trade."

My chest tightened at the idea that she could think so little of her own worth, but then, on the other hand, I had never starved before. I could not say for certain what I would do in that situation.

"After the first few times, it became easier. I can think of other things as it happens. I must confess, I do not understand quite why men are so obsessed with it. I can only assume it feels different to them than it does for me."

"I wouldn't know." I meant the words to be in my head, but somehow, they came out of my mouth instead and Zara looked up at me in genuine surprise.

"Do you mean you have never...?"

She did not finish the sentence but she didn't have to. We both knew what she meant.

"No, I haven't." I saw no reason to lie to her, even if I had never confessed it to anyone else before.

"Why not?" She sounded completely bewildered. "There must be many women who love you and would like to please you."

"Love?" I repeated the word rather ironically. "Most women see only my crown. They are interested in what they might gain from me, not in me as my own man."

"Just as I tried to use you." Her words were soft and full of self-recrimination before she gave me a small smile. "I apologize for being a poor representation of my gender."

I couldn't help scanning her body, remembering what she had looked like with her dress open and the sight of her legs as she climbed in the window tonight. "Actually, I think you are a rather fine representation."

For a moment neither of us spoke, our eyes searching each other's from across the room. It felt like we were on the edge of something significant, something still fuzzy and undefined.

Before I could decide what it might be, Zara got to her feet. "I should go back to my room and check in with my chaperone. I don't want Eastam to be suspicious. Do you have something you could give me to pass as your seal?"

It took a few minutes but at last I settled on a small wooden knob on the top of my bedpost. Breaking it off, I used my knife to carve a design into the bottom, which, while not perfect, should be passable. Hopefully, it would be enough to temporarily convince Eastam of its legitimacy.

As I handed it to her, our fingers brushed against each other, giving me the same spark of excitement I had felt earlier when we'd kissed. From the way she reacted, I felt certain she noticed it too.

Perhaps Dee had been right after all. Perhaps something real did exist between us, something that shouldn't have grown but found a way anyway, like a flower among the thorns of Eastam's scheming.

"I will see you tomorrow, Arthur," Zara whispered to me, her dark eyes looking up at me from beneath her lashes, almost shyly. "Please take care until then."

"And you."

I let her out of my room, through the door this time, and once she had gone, I took a deep breath before getting ready for bed and extinguishing the candles.

It seemed, one way or another, after tomorrow, things would never be the same again.

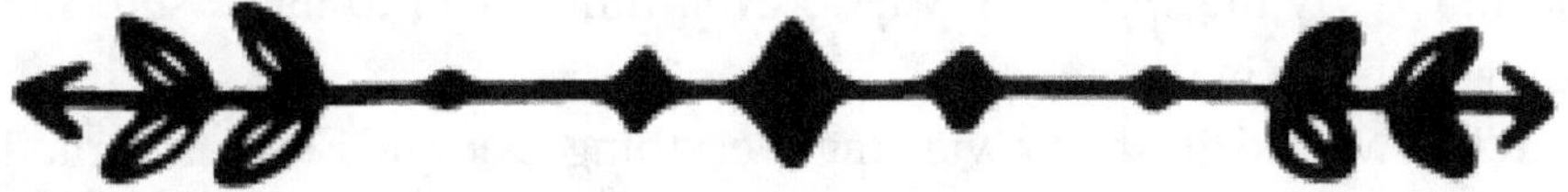

~Cassian~

The next morning, the five of us were back together in Arthur's room, making our final plans. Dee and Elodie sat next to each other at the table, Eric sat on the bed and Arthur and I both stood, both of us too full of adrenaline to sit still.

Arthur's news about Zara returning last night had surprised us all, and even more so when he shared what she told him. When he said they were planning to kill Bran after he'd taken Dee, Elodie turned frighteningly pale and Dee quickly put an arm around her.

"Don't worry," my wife assured her friend. "Now that I know, I can warn him. I could even try to give him a weapon so he can defend himself."

Appreciation for her quick thinking filled me, as always. "That's a great idea, Dee, but are we certain Zara can be trusted?"

I directed that question at Arthur specifically. We couldn't afford to make any mistakes right now. Everything came down to what happened today: this day would see Westley's defeat or ours, not to mention all the lives that now seemed to be at stake. So far, Westley had threatened Arthur and Bran specifically, not to mention 'everyone I cared for' if I didn't comply with his orders.

Everything hung in the balance.

"I trust her," he replied simply before turning to his sister. "I sent another message to our father last night, after Zara left, to see if I could find out where her home is. She doesn't know I've done it though. If I am unable to..."

He let the sentence remain unfinished. Everyone knew speaking of your own death could bring bad luck, and we didn't need to tempt fate today.

Dee nodded at him, understanding what he wanted without him having to say the words. "I will do everything I can to make sure she knows what is in the message."

When we had finished reviewing everything, Dee and Elodie returned to their room to get Dee ready to play her part while Eric and I went to my room to await Westley's message. Eastam had said he would send me information on where to meet him today and I had no doubt he knew exactly which room to find me in.

"You're certain of your role?" I asked my brother when we were alone.

His lips tightened into his habitual pout. "I'm not an idiot, Cass. I understand what you need me to do."

"I don't think you're an idiot. It's not about you, Eric, it's about me. It makes me feel better to hear it reviewed and to know we haven't missed anything. Please, humour me."

Though he still looked suspicious, he did as I asked. "Once you go to the meeting with Westley, I distract the other men like Eastam told me too, telling them that Eastam's been spotted down at the docks. We'll all leave together, but I will break away and return to Lady Elodie who will be waiting for me in the stables. When Bran comes for Cordelia, we'll follow them."

Originally, I only intended for Eric to follow Dee, but when Elodie heard that she played no part in the plan, she put her foot down, and to my surprise, my brother backed her up.

"I need your eyes on Dee," I tried to explain to him at the time. "She is the most precious thing in the world to me, Eric, and I need you to keep her safe. If you're also worried about keeping Lady Elodie safe, your attention might be too divided."

"Lady Elodie can keep herself safe," he told me firmly, while Elodie looked both surprised by and proud of his support. "And she would never let anything happen to Cordelia. Instead of just having my eyes on her, you'll have two pairs. I promise, it won't be a problem."

When Dee joined their cause, I knew I had no choice, so I gave in and agreed. Hopefully, I had made the right call.

Eric continued to review the plan, as I'd requested. "Arthur will go to the docks with the others where Zara will be waiting for him. She will pretend to kill him, letting both Eastam's men and our men think he's dead while she secretly brings him to your location."

That all sounded right. It felt like it could work. It really felt like this might be the day everything turned in our favour, as long as we hadn't missed anything.

A moment later, we heard the knock on the door, followed by a message being pressed into my hand, a message bearing Eastam's seal.

Time to put our plan into action.

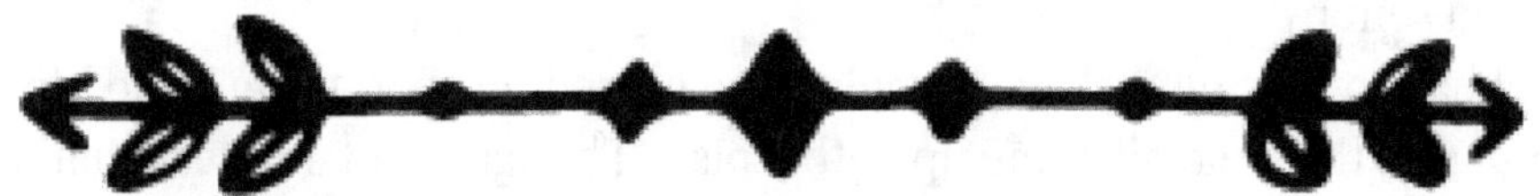

~Bran~

Although Westley seemed to have accepted our story last night about how and why his man had been killed, I still felt uneasy about it, and so did the other man who had been with me at the alehouse. He and I had been paired together for today, which mustn't be an accident. I also noticed he carried a knife, though he had told me he had no weapon. He'd concealed the knife within his boot, and he kept reaching down to make sure he hadn't lost it, which had tipped me off.

My best guess was that Westley had told him to kill me as soon as we had Cordelia, and then, most likely, someone else would be sent to kill him afterwards.

Eastam left no loose ends and offered no forgiveness for messing up, and last night, we messed up.

It hadn't been my only blunder last night either. I'd also messed up when I came across the dark-skinned woman crouching behind the farmhouse window. I hadn't realized who lurked in the shadows when I shouted out at her; I only saw a cloaked figure in the darkness. Once I recognized her and saw the blade in her hand, I realized she must be there for Eastam and I tried to offer my assistance. From everything I'd seen of her so far, I had no doubt she could deal with him, probably more effectively than any of the rest of us.

But I'd blown it by startling her, and so she ran. Though frustrating, the encounter still gave me some hope. Something must have happened to turn her against Eastam and I would much rather have her working against Eastam than for him. Even if she wasn't directly on our side, the enemy of our enemy was still our friend.

For now, Eastam had told me that something would happen to cause the men to leave the inn, leaving Cordelia alone and unguarded. When they had gone, I should go to her and lure her away, claiming to have been sent by Cass himself.

I had to assume that Cass would have passed on everything I told him and that they had all come up with a plan. Though I had no idea what it might be, I stood ready to do whatever Cordelia told me to. Hopefully, it would be enough.

When we reached the town, we took up a surveillance position not far from the inn, and just as predicted, less than half an hour later, Arthur's men ran out, Arthur and Eric among them, some grabbing horses while others sprinted on foot, heading away from the inn towards the water. I couldn't see any sign of Cordelia or Elodie among the group.

Just the thought of Elodie made my chest tighten in both fear and hope. If all went well, by tonight I could be sitting with her and hearing her sweet voice as she told me exactly how she had come to be here and what she had done in the time we'd been apart. I couldn't wait to hear her stories and to see her smile at me once more.

Despite all that, I also hoped I wouldn't find her with Cordelia now. It would kill me to have to leave her behind, but I couldn't take her anywhere near Eastam. That would be far too dangerous.

When all the men had disappeared from sight, I went into the inn, the other man trailing behind me. "Wait at the door," I told him. "She won't come with me if she sees you there too."

He scowled at that but couldn't argue with the truth of my statement, so he hung back while I made my way to the room I had been told would be occupied by Cass and Cordelia.

She threw the door open a second after I knocked, pulling me inside. "Bran." Her warm smile, while not as beautiful to me as Elodie's, made a very welcome sight after such a long time apart. "It's good to see you. And you're alone, which is even better."

As pleased as I felt to see her too, her appearance confused me. "I'm not entirely alone, there's a man just outside. Why are you dressed this way, Your Highness? You almost look like..."

I trailed off as I realized this must be part of the plan, and she quickly confirmed it. "You leave that to me to worry about. But quickly, take this."

She reached into her skirts and pulled out a small, sheathed knife for me.

"Eastam's men will turn on you. You need to be prepared."

I expected as much, though how she knew it too, I couldn't guess. I took the weapon gratefully in any case.

"Are you ready to go then?" I asked once I had the knife safely hidden away.

She nodded at me firmly. "More than ready. Let's get this over with."

CHAPTER FIFTEEN

~Zara~

First thing in the morning, I sent a message to Westley telling him I had the seal. His reply didn't take long to get to me, as I expected.

I am busy today but I will send someone to pick it up and give you your next instruction. E.

Even though I already knew what he intended, my blood still boiled at his presumption. There shouldn't be any 'next instruction'. Our deal had been for me to get him the seal in exchange for my father's location. With every second, it became clearer how he had only ever intended to use me, to string me along for as long as he could before coming up with some excuse as to why he couldn't take me to my father, since I now assumed he actually had no idea where to find him.

I couldn't wait to see him in chains in Arthur's dungeon. I couldn't wait to spit in his face and squeeze his tiny bollocks in my hand until he begged for mercy.

That last thought might have given me a little too much satisfaction.

Following the message, it didn't take long until one of Eastam's henchmen arrived at my door, a man I had seen with him several times before. Large and mean-looking, with a scar down the side of his face, it felt like every time he looked at me, he pictured me without my dress on, so I had always avoided being alone with him. Today, I had no choice as he quickly entered my room, closing the door behind him.

"You have something for me?" he grunted.

I shook my head firmly. "No. I will only deliver it to Eastam himself."

Westley really underestimated my intelligence if he thought I would place the seal in anyone's hand other than his. Not to mention that I didn't have the actual seal at all. The longer Westley had with it, the more chance he would realize that I'd delivered a fake, so I would hold onto it for as long as possible.

The man's eyes narrowed at me as he took a step closer, his foul stench filling my nose. One thing I had never understood was why men in these northern lands bathed so infrequently. Back in my homeland, men washed regularly, in fragrant waters, just as the women did. Everyone smelled a lot better.

The thought of returning there filled me with both excitement and sadness, which took me by surprise. It took me a moment to pinpoint the source of the sadness, and finally I had to accept that the idea of leaving Arthur behind had caused it.

What a ridiculous thought. Even though he had been kind enough to accept my offer of working together, I knew that anything further between us would be impossible. Not after the other thing he'd told me last night: that he had never even lain with a woman before. He would marry some sweet, pale, virginal princess, not a woman like me who had literally sold herself for bread.

I had told him that so he would know exactly how far beneath him I was. Better that he know the full truth, to help extinguish the stubborn hope inside me that refused to completely die off.

The man in front of me snarled at me. "He sent me to pick up something from you. I won't leave without it."

If he thought he could intimidate me, he had been misinformed. "And I will not give it to you. Tell me where Eastam is and I will take it to him myself. Otherwise, I will leave with it now and you can tell him that you let me get away."

He took another step towards me, a menacing glint in his eye, and I quickly pulled out my blade that I always kept close at hand, stopping him in his tracks.

"Where is Eastam?"

Though I clearly had the upper hand, the man did not appreciate it. He scowled at me even as he gave me my answer. "He is meeting the Silatrian prince in the church."

In a church? The man truly had no shame at all.

"But there is something else he wants you to do, something that must be done this morning."

As he outlined my instructions to kill Arthur, I did my best to appear shocked, even though I expected nothing less. "My agreement never included murder!" I argued, as he must have anticipated I would.

"I don't know anything about that," he replied. "I am only telling you what he said."

"Well, you can pass this message back to him: I will do this for him, but that is it. If he doesn't give me the location after this, then I will kill him just as I will kill the prince."

The man took a step back from me, something in my tone of voice combined with the blade in my hand convincing him I wasn't messing around. "I will tell him. Come to the church when the prince is dead."

I nodded curtly and he went to open the door. Before he could leave, however, we heard the sound of shouts and men running down the hall outside my room. That must be my cue. Arthur would be heading towards the docks, expecting me to find him there, and I had no intention of disappointing him.

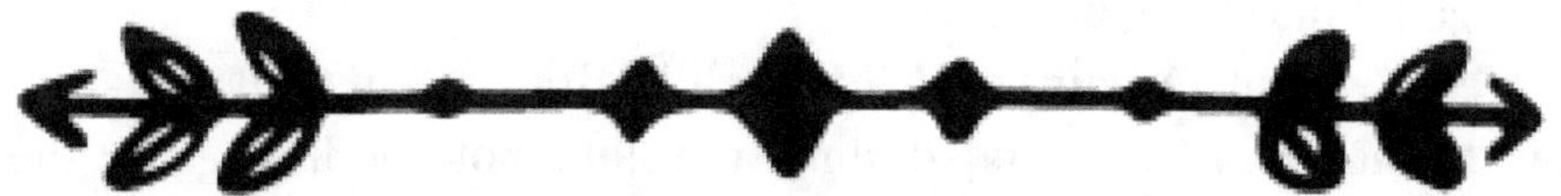

~Cordelia~

The man Bran had warned me about awaited us as we exited the inn.

"Follow me, Your Highness," he said to me. "The prince is waiting for you this way."

I recognized this as part of the charade. They wanted me to think that Cass had sent for me and that Bran had come to lead me to him, so I followed along willingly enough, hoping that Eric and Elodie were behind us, as planned. It took all my discipline not to look back to see if I could spot them, but that would have been too suspicious.

Soon, we arrived at a small stone church near the centre of town surrounded by a leafy cemetery, the whole scene quiet and almost serene until we approached a rear door and found another man waiting for us. "This is her?" the man asked Bran.

As soon as Bran nodded, the man grabbed me and placed a hand over my mouth.

Fear shot through me as the man who had brought us here grabbed a knife from his boot, but Bran had anticipated it. He already had his hand on the knife I'd given him, and before the other man could even get himself ready, Bran had slashed him across the arm, forcing him to drop his own knife before expertly slitting his throat open. The man made an unearthly gurgling sound as he dropped to the ground, his eyes still wide in surprise.

"You son of a bitch," the man holding me snarled as he released his grip on me to attack Bran. This man was stronger and more prepared than the first one, and he went for the knife in Bran's hand, attempting to grab it from him. They struggled together for a while and it seemed clear that no one had the upper hand until I reached into my skirts for my second knife, the one Cass had given me on our journey here, and plunged it into the man's back.

He cried out in pain and shock while Bran, taking advantage of his distraction, quickly ended him too, rolling both bodies against the church wall where they could be mostly hidden from view.

"Thank you for the help, Your Highness," Bran said to me, breathing heavily as he came back to where I stood, his clothes now stained with blood.

"You didn't need much of it," I pointed out. "I am both disgusted and impressed, Bran."

He gave me a grim smile. "They are not the first men I've killed in Cass' service, and I'm afraid they won't be the last. I hope, however, that they will be the last you'll have to witness."

"So, now what?" The churchyard around us was once again peaceful, birds singing in the trees above and clouds floating lazily past, not at all bothered by the bloodshed which had just taken place.

"Now, we wait," Bran replied. "We wait for Eastam's summons."

~Cassian~

I couldn't help shaking my head as I opened the heavy wooden door of the town's stone church. It made sense that Eastam would choose this location for us to meet: it had several different entry points, making it easy for him to make an escape if things went wrong. There were a hundred different hiding places inside where weapons or other people might be concealed. It couldn't be clearer that he'd laid a trap for me, but I knew I had to go along with it anyway. We all had to play our parts to bring this whole ridiculous game to an end.

"Prince Cassian."

The deep baritone voice greeted me as soon as I walked through the door, and I finally laid eyes on the man who had been plaguing my life for so long. He had tried to kill me, tried to take my throne to set up my brother as his puppet, he had planned to kill Dee and replace her with her long-lost twin sister, and a million other insane plots that had, thankfully, been unsuccessful. Most recently, he had captured Bran in order to lure me here, and now, according to my brother, he planned to ask me to abdicate my position as crown prince so that Eric would be next in line for the throne.

He planned to do that by using Dee's life as blackmail, and I had to admit, if I were faced with the choice for real, I would not hesitate. I would much rather be Dee's husband, poor and destitute, than King of Silatria without her at my side. Luckily for me, so long as our plans bore fruit, I wouldn't have to make that choice today.

As I took in Westley Eastam's appearance, I couldn't help noticing that he bore a disconcerting resemblance to Dee. They were, after all, half-siblings, but where her blue eyes sparkled with life and fun, his were cold and calculating.

"It's about time we got to have a chat," he greeted me with a smug smirk.

"I wanted to have a chat with you in my dungeon a month ago," I reminded him. "You left before we had a chance."

That answer made his smirk deepen. "Your hospitality left a lot to be desired, but we can make up for lost time now."

"What do you want, Eastam?" I was in no mood for his fake pleasantries. "What's the point of all this?"

"I want you to give up your claim to the Silatrian throne."

I laughed in feigned disbelief, though I had expected those words exactly. "You're crazy. I knew you must be, but this just proves it."

"I'm not crazy, Your Highness, nor am I joking. You *will* give it up, and you'll do it today."

"And why would I do that?" I knew what his answer would be, and I hoped that by asking him the question, I could move this along.

Luckily, it worked. "Because if you don't, your wife will meet an unfortunate end."

Eastam merely raised a hand to gesture to one of the back doors and a man appeared from nowhere, having been cleverly concealed, to pull the door open. Two figures walked over the threshold, and I took great pleasure in watching Eastam's look of surprise as he recognized Bran.

He hadn't expected Bran to be here. He thought his men would kill him, but clearly, based on the state of Bran's clothing, the other men had met their end instead.

"Here she is, Eastam," Bran said, shoving Dee towards our enemy. "But next time, I'd appreciate not having to slaughter your men to fulfill the task you've given me."

Westley blinked a couple of times in surprise before he seemed to gain control of himself again. "It appears I've misjudged you, Bran. It's not a mistake I make often, but I'm glad to be wrong. This may be the beginning of a strong collaboration between us."

Unbelievable. Westley didn't even care that Bran had killed his men; in fact, he respected him for it.

Unaware of my disgust, Eastam turned back to me. "I'm sure you understand your position now, Prince Cassian. Your man is working for me and your wife is under my control. You will give me what I want, or you will lose the woman you love. The choice is simple."

Slowly and deliberately, I began to laugh; just a small chuckle at first, letting it grow louder as Westley's look of confusion grew.

"What is funny about this to you?" he demanded, clearly not happy about not getting the reaction he wanted.

"I can't believe you've been fooled by the very same trick you tried to play on me," I explained, hoping with every fibre of my being that this plan would work.

"What trick?" Westley had begun to scowl by now. He really didn't like not being the one in control.

"This one." I pointed at Dee who stared off into space, her fingers winding around each other in a spot-on impersonation of her sister, Charlotte. "That is not my wife. It's her twin sister, the one *you* sent to me in the first place."

Westley's jaw dropped open, his eyes wide in shock as he truly looked at Dee for the first time, scrutinizing her closely. "It can't be."

"But it is," I said firmly. "And since you've got nothing left to threaten me with, I believe this conversation is over."

I drew my sword, ready to end this once and for all, but my action was quickly met with the sound of other swords being drawn around the room, making my stomach sink. He had more men here than I'd anticipated.

Though Westley still couldn't be called happy, he did seem once again in control. "I'm afraid it's not that easy, Your Highness. I wanted to get your agreement the easy way, but since you prefer the hard way, we can do that instead. I'm afraid neither of you will be walking out of here today."

~Elodie~

As Eric, Arthur and the other men disappeared in the distance, Bran and another man approached the inn, and my stomach flipped at the sight of him. Today could be the day when we finally got to see each other again properly, not just fleeting glimpses or hurried conversation. I couldn't wait to speak with him but I had to confess to being apprehensive about it too, after he looked so surprised when I used my knife on that man in the street. Although the words he spoke were kind and supportive, uncertainty lingered in his eyes that suggested he didn't know quite what to make of it. Almost as if he didn't know who I was anymore.

And I had to admit, I *had* changed in the last month, and in the last ten days especially. However, I felt the changes were for the better, and hopefully he would too.

I pressed my hand against the small book concealed within my dress, hoping for a happy ending for all of us as Eric returned to the stables, slipping in quietly beside me. "Have you seen them?"

I nodded in confirmation. "Bran has gone inside. That man by the door arrived with him, and he should be out with Dee any second..."

Before I could finish my sentence, the inn door opened and Dee and Bran appeared. We had made Dee up to look like her sister with her hair slightly askew and her dress hanging far more loosely on her than usual. At first glance, someone might simply think she looked disheveled, but anyone who had met Charlotte before would quickly see the resemblance on closer inspection. We had done a pretty good job; good enough to fool Westley Eastam, I felt certain.

As soon as Dee and the two men had gone far enough that they wouldn't immediately notice us behind them, Eric and I set out after them.

"Stay close to me, my lady," he murmured, placing his hand on my back. "We may need to duck out of sight at a moment's notice."

I did as he requested but luckily for us, nobody looked back. They all seemed intent on their destination, which turned out to be a church. When it became clear they were heading to it, Eric pulled me aside, pressing us both against the side of the closest house to the churchyard, my back to the wall while he leaned in close on me.

"What are you doing?" I whispered, shocked by his intimate proximity.

"If anyone sees us, they will assume we are lovers stealing a moment together," he explained. "They won't pay us any attention."

It did make some degree of sense, but I had never been this close to a man before. The scent and heat of him felt slightly disorienting.

From our vantage point, we could see Bran, Dee and the other man walk up to a door where another man stood waiting for them. In the next moment, everything seemed to happen at once: one man grabbed Dee while Bran and the other man attacked each other, followed by blood and shouting. I opened my mouth to call out to them, but Eric covered my mouth with his hand, holding me firmly in place. "We won't get there in time to help, and they're doing fine on their own. We have to keep our cover."

Thankfully, he was right. With Dee's help, Bran brought both men down, and I could breathe again as they both seemed to be unharmed. I leaned forward, ready for them to go inside and for us to follow, but to my surprise, they stayed where they were, simply talking to each other instead, though from this distance we couldn't make out anything they were saying.

"What are they waiting for?" I whispered to my companion when he'd removed his hand from my face.

"A sign from Eastam. He will send someone to collect Cordelia, so they'll wait for that to happen."

It seemed we would have to wait here for a while longer, and Eric seemed in no hurry to move away from me.

We waited in silence, keeping our eyes fixed on Dee and Bran, until the door opened and they were summoned inside. As soon as it closed again, Eric stepped forward. "Stay behind me at all times, Lady Elodie, until we know what the situation is."

He certainly took his duty of care of me seriously, and the thought made me smile. Eric did indeed seem to be trying his best to change. Perhaps all he had needed was someone to believe in him all along.

When we reached the church moments later, we had our first bit of luck. The door had not been completely closed behind Bran and Dee so Eric could peer inside and hear the conversation taking place there. I couldn't hear anything being said but I did hear the unmistakable sound of metal as swords were drawn from their scabbards. When Eric looked back at me, his face was grim.

"There are too many of them," he whispered to me. "The two of us would be of no help."

What did he mean? "We can't just leave them to fend for themselves!"

"We won't," he promised me. "But we do need to leave, just for a few minutes. Will you trust me, my lady?"

Despite his earnest expression, I felt torn. What if Eric only wanted to save himself and had no intention of helping Cassian, Dee or Bran? After all, he had behaved selfishly before. But if he sincerely had a plan and I didn't trust him, would he ever put his faith in anyone again?

"I trust you," I finally agreed, and his face lit up as he grabbed my hand and pulled me away.

CHAPTER SIXTEEN

~Arthur~

I felt guilty about deceiving my men as we raced towards the dock, but we couldn't take the chance that we had another mole amongst us. Eric told them that Westley had been spotted at the docks and we all took off, as planned, but while I knew the whole exercise to be a decoy, they didn't. They thought we actually had a chance of finding him and they were excited to do so. After a month of chasing the bastard around the kingdom, we were all ready for this to end.

The difference between us was, when this whole adventure finished, they would be delighted to return to the castle and their families and lives there, while for me, even if everything went our way today, life would seem a little more dull than it had been before. If we apprehended Westley at last and if my father could tell me exactly where to find Zara's home, she would have no reason to stay here even a day longer. The thought of the most fascinating woman I'd ever met getting on a ship and disappearing from my life forever left me feeling hollow inside.

But I couldn't see any other way this could end as I raced through the streets, shouting orders at my men. She said she didn't want me to die. That was something, I supposed, but not very much. She'd given me no indication that her feelings went deeper than that, and even if they did, even if she suddenly and dramatically confessed that she loved me, what then? Would my parents accept her as a suitable match for the crown prince? Would the rest of our subjects? She held no title, she had worked with Westley against me, and she had a past that could set tongues wagging throughout the kingdom.

What could I truly offer her other than being my mistress? And that, after everything she had already been through in her life, would be like a slap in the face. I wouldn't do it. I would rather her be with someone who could give her what she deserved than treat her like some kind of shameful secret.

There were a hundred different reasons why I should push her out of my mind completely and yet, as Zara's arm reached out of an alley and pulled me in close to her, so quickly that to my men it appeared that I simply disappeared, admiration for her filled me once again.

"I know where Eastam is," she told me, not wasting any time on pleasantries. "I will take you to him, but first, we need to make you look more dead."

"*More* dead?" I couldn't help repeating, teasing her while I had the opportunity. "Do I look partially dead already?"

She clearly understood I meant it as a joke, and she returned it in kind. "You all look like ghosts to me since you have no colour, but Westley will want more proof than that."

She reached down to a small sheepskin bag at her side, and when she opened it up, a foul, pungent smell immediately spilled out, making me blanch. "What is that?"

"Pig's blood." My eyebrows raised in surprise and she pressed her lips together, trying not to smile. "Don't ask."

I held my tongue and tried not to breathe either as she poured the contents over my chest and stomach.

"Now, get in."

I looked further down the alley, in the direction she pointed and saw a small handcart there. It would be a tight fit, but I might be able to squeeze in, with my limbs hanging over the sides. I did have one concern, though. "You can't pull me in this."

Her lips pursed in disapproval. "I can and I will. Hurry, Arthur. We don't know what other tricks Westley has planned."

I did as she instructed, smiling to myself at the fact that she had called me Arthur without me having to prompt her to drop the title.

The ride could hardly be called comfortable, but I did my best not to wince or react in any way, and to look as though she had, in fact, killed me, just in case any of Eastam's men happened to be watching. As she pulled the cart, Zara explained to me the other contents of the cart, impressing me with how much she had been able to put together on such short notice.

"There it is," she whispered at last, though with my eyes closed, I had no idea what 'it' might be or where we were. "Remember, wait for my signal. Until I say your name, you should remain dead."

~**Bran**~

My stomach sank as the other men emerged from the shadows, all far better armed than my small knife. Cordelia still had her knife too, tucked back within her dress, but she could hardly pull it out while pretending to be her sister. That left Cass against ten armed, trained men, and those weren't odds anyone would take.

"You're going to kill me, Eastam?" Cass asked him, buying himself time to size up the situation. "How will you explain that? My father will demand retribution."

"He would, if he were alive to do so," Westley retorted. "This very night, one of my men will be poisoning him at dinner. With you and him both out of the way, that leaves Eric as king, and we all know he will do exactly what I say."

Cass's face paled at the news that Westley intended to kill his father, but as he had no way of verifying it or of doing anything about it right now, he pushed through that to respond to the comments about Eric instead.

"You're wrong about Eric. He's not your puppet anymore."

As he said it, Cass' eyes flitted momentarily to the door, as if expecting someone to enter, but nothing happened. Westley caught the motion too and gave a dark laugh. "He really fooled you, didn't he? You thought he'd changed? That you could rely on him now? It was all an act, Cassian. No one is coming to help you."

Though it might be wiser to keep my mouth shut, I couldn't help but intervene.

"My lord, what about Princess Cordelia? She will still be alive since they fooled us with her sister here. She will know you were responsible for this and she could rally others to her side."

"The princess has no real power," he smirked, sparing a disparaging look for the woman in front of us who continued to do an amazing job of pretending she had no idea what was happening around her, though she must be panicking internally at the sight of her husband in danger. "It's a shame Cordelia's my half-sister though or I'd take her for my own wife and claim both thrones that way."

"You filthy pig," Cass growled, taking a step forwards, but the other men quickly stepped between him and Westley, blocking his path.

"That's enough," Westley sneered back at him. "Finish him. Let's get this over with."

The men both raised their swords while Cass prepared to defend himself, but before anyone could actually take a swing, the main door of the church flew open and, to everyone's surprise, a cart rolled in through it, a cart filled to overflowing with a bloodstained man.

"What is this?" Westley called out, just as the person pushing it came into view.

"Your delivery," the dark-skinned woman announced, her voice strong and hard. "One seal and one dead prince, as you requested. Now, tell me where my father is."

A dead prince? My heart sank as I recognized Arthur in the cart. Had she really killed him? I glanced over at Dee to see her reaction but, unbelievably, she remained completely in character, looking entirely unconcerned.

Everyone else looked at each other uneasily, unsure what any of this meant, but Westley seemed to understand her words and he directed one of his men to go to her.

"Where is the seal?"

She reached into a pouch at her side and pulled out some kind of wooden stamp, handing it to Eastam's man who brought it to Westley himself. I couldn't help noticing that Westley seemed reluctant to get close to the woman himself and I didn't blame him. I had seen what she could do.

"I have fulfilled the terms of our agreement," she told him firmly. "Tell me where he is, now."

"I will," he promised as, with a quick motion of his hand, several of his armed men advanced on her, one of them blocking her escape route out the door. "Once you're in prison."

To my surprise, she did not react to his threat or to the men approaching her. She merely smiled at Eastam, her eyes glinting with dark humour. "That is just what I hoped you would say."

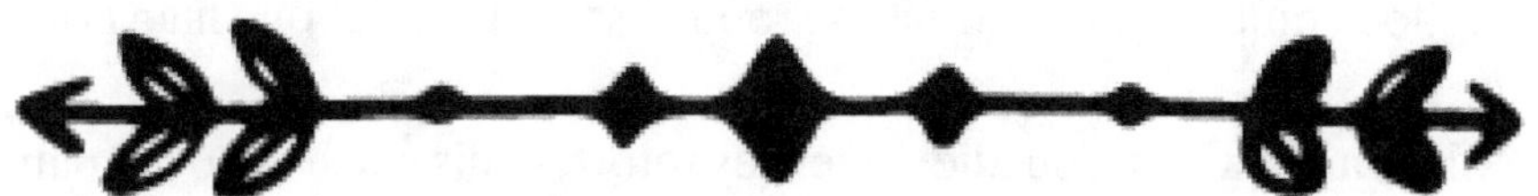

~Cordelia~

As Westley's men with their swords moved towards Cass, it took every ounce of my strength not to react. Everything in me wanted to rush to his side and help to defend him. My bow and arrows had never been missed as much as I missed them now, but Cass had insisted that bringing projectiles for an indoor meeting could cause more trouble than good. Presumably, he hadn't anticipated a full out sword fight in the middle of a church either.

Staying in character was key to our plan so that Westley believed I posed no threat and would allow me to get closer to him. At the moment, he kept his distance from all of us, but once Cass convinced him that I was Charlotte, he became less wary of me and I managed to inch slightly closer.

Just before I got where I wanted to be, the door burst open and Zara and Arthur came in. Once again, I had to force myself to look unconcerned, although this time, I felt fairly certain my brother hadn't actually been killed. I could only say fairly certain though because, while faking his death had been part of our plan, he certainly looked dead. Hopefully, nothing had gone wrong.

When Zara handed over the fake seal, Westley moved further away from me to take it and I groaned inwardly. I needed to keep him close. Twirling my hair absentmindedly, I stepped towards him again as Zara said Westley's answer was what she'd been hoping for.

A deep scowl darkened his face. He obviously didn't understand what she meant, and he hated not being the one pulling the strings. Little did he know things were about to get a whole lot worse for him.

"In that case, I will take my prince and go," Zara continued. "Isn't that right, Arthur?"

More confusion flashed across Westley's face as Arthur leapt out of the cart, coming back to life before our eyes. Gasps of astonishment and shock rang out throughout the room. "She's a witch!" one man cried out.

"She's not a witch, you idiot," Westley retorted, his voice full of disdain and anger. "Obviously, she never killed him, but we can fix that. Attack them, now!"

Arthur responded by reaching down into the cart, beneath where he had been lying, to pull out more weapons, while Zara reached beneath her skirt to retrieve a heavy, curved blade.

"Bran!" Arthur called the other man's name before tossing him a sword, leaving us now with four armed opponents against Eastam's men. Those were much better odds as swords began to clang together and the fight began in earnest.

And now, the time had come to make my move. With Westley distracted by everything else going on, I snatched the fake seal from his hands. "Pretty!" I exclaimed in Charlotte's child-like voice. "Mine."

"Give that back to me," Westley snarled, but he wasn't fast enough. I ran away, dodging merrily through the fighting men as though it were all a big game, ignoring his calls behind me. "You imbecile! Get back here."

When we reached the back of the church, far from the main action, he finally caught up with me and grabbed hold of my fist which had the seal tightly gripped within it.

"Open your hand," he ordered.

"You're mean," I replied, still in Charlotte's tone.

"You already knew that," he snarled at me, making my blood run cold. What did he mean by that? What had he done to Charlotte that she should know that about him?

As we struggled together, I dropped to the ground, covering my hands with my body so that he had no choice but to try to get beneath me, and at last, I could make my attack. Using the hold Cass had taught me, I pulled Westley's feet out from beneath him, bringing him down onto his back and quickly placing myself on top of him as I grabbed the still-bloodied knife from its hiding place in the folds of my skirt.

The flat of my blade pressed against his neck as he looked up at me in shock. "You're not Charlotte."

"Surprise."

He made an attempt to push me off, but Cass had shown me how to plant myself firmly, using my body weight as leverage, and he couldn't shift me.

I pressed the blade harder. "I will kill you, Westley, if I have to. Don't tempt me."

Cass wanted him alive to find out what happened to all the money he stole from the Silatrian treasury, but if there was even a chance that he might get away again, killing him would be preferable. He could not be allowed to escape.

"Cass!" I called for my husband to let him know I had Westley, and a few moments later, he appeared at my side.

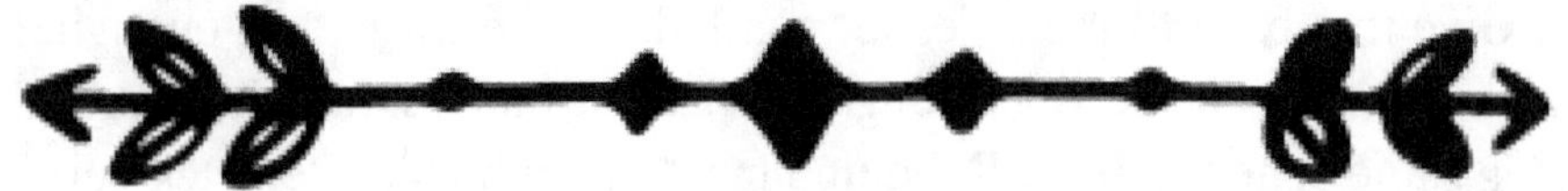

~Cassian~

All things considered, this could be going worse. Bran and I were busy disarming two men as Dee took off down the aisle with Eastam in pursuit. "Kill them all," I ordered Bran. I didn't want any more surprises, no more loose ends. Anyone who worked for Eastam had given up their right to a trial. I wanted *him* alive, but the rest were not needed.

What the hell had delayed Eric, I wondered, as I looked towards the door that Zara had left open behind her when she brought Arthur in. He should have been here by now. I would rather not believe Westley's claim that he had betrayed us once again, but I didn't know what else to think. And he had Elodie with him, which was another cause for concern. Glancing at Bran out of the corner of my eye, I knew he'd never forgive me if I had sent her off with Eric and put her in danger.

Though we were still a man short, I could see Zara and Arthur fighting together just as Bran and I were doing, back-to-back to protect against attack. Zara was incredibly impressive. She got through three men in the time it took Arthur to bring down one.

Two of the remaining men seemed to realize that their chances of success were low, and they made a bolt for the open door. Zara immediately took chase after them and I could see how much Arthur wanted to go with her, but when one of the other men blocked his path, he had no choice but to stay and fight.

"Cass!"

Dee's voice called out from the back of the church, strong and sure, and I knew before I even got there that she had been successful. Seeing her with Eastam subdued beneath her, her blade at his throat, filled me with satisfaction.

I knew he would be armed, so with Dee still on top of him, I searched his clothing to find the sword and knife concealed there, removing them from him before helping Dee up and simultaneously hauling Eastam to his feet. When I turned back around, the last of Westley's men fell to the ground on the end of Arthur's sword. Other than the two that Zara had chased after, the rest of them all lay dead or dying on the church floor.

We were going to have to do a lot of penance to make up for this later.

"You've lost, Eastam," I growled at him. Despite my pleasure at having prevailed, fury still filled me over everything he'd done, and I couldn't resist the urge to punch him square in the jaw. It hurt my hand, but from his reaction, it seemed to hurt him a lot more.

"You will pay for all your crimes against both Lassaria and Silatria," Arthur added, coming over to stand in front of Eastam, looking his half-brother straight in the eye. "And for the others you've deceived."

"Your Highness?" A new voice called out from the doorway and we all turned to find a man I had never seen before, dressed in the Lassarian court colours.

"Sir John?" Arthur seemed to recognize him, but his voice was full of surprise and confusion, and I leaned over to Dee.

"Who's that?"

"The head of my father's personal guard," she whispered back to me.

"What are you doing here?" Arthur asked the knight, obviously not expecting him.

"Your father sent me. I have orders to bring Eastam back to him once you've apprehended him. My men are standing by."

He gestured behind him and, through the doorway, I could indeed make out more men, all in guards' uniforms.

"How did you know where to find me?" Arthur asked in confusion. None of us had told anyone where we were going.

"We went to the inn but you weren't there," the man explained respectfully. "We were out making enquiries in town when someone told us they heard fighting going on at the church, so we made our way here, and here you are."

Arthur nodded, accepting that explanation at face value. "Well, you are just in time. Did my father send any other message?"

I figured he must mean the message about Zara, but John shook his head. "No, Your Highness, those were my only orders."

We all made our way outside, Bran and I holding Westley between us while Arthur spoke with his father's man. Eastam had been curiously silent since I punched him. Perhaps I had broken his jaw. That would be a bonus.

The full sight of the Lassarian soldiers outside filled me with relief. There were at least twenty of them, which should limit Eastam's possibility of escape. Even so, I didn't intend to take any chances. "I will travel with you," I said to the knight. "My wife and her brother can join us later. I want to leave immediately."

John's eyes flicked momentarily over to where Westley stood before returning to me. "Of course, Your Highness, if that's what you would like."

I turned to Dee to say goodbye to her for now, but her gaze remained fixed on the man in front of us, giving him a suspicious look. "How do you know Prince Cassian's title?"

Now that I thought about it, she had a point. I had never met this man before. How did he know who I was?

He bowed politely to Dee. "I assumed he must be your husband, Your Highness."

"Why?" Dee pressed, pointing at Bran. "I could just as easily have been married to this other man here, or my husband might not have been here at all. How did you know Cassian?"

"Because he's a traitor." Once again, the voice came from a newcomer, or in this case, someone just returning. Zara came running up the churchyard path, her blade still in her hand, dripping with blood. "He is working with Eastam. If you release Westley to this man, he will be set free. If you go with him, Your Highness, you will be killed. I saw them speaking together last night."

John's eyes went to Eastam again, just for a moment, before he tried to deny it. "That is ridiculous! I don't know who you are but I will have you arrested..."

"No, you won't," Arthur cut in. "Not when she's telling the truth."

Westley spoke up at last. "You all really don't know when to stop, do you? You could have come out of this alive if you had let him take me, but now, you won't."

With those words, all the Lassarian soldiers drew their swords, making it clear whose side they were really on and outnumbering us once again.

When would this infuriating man ever run out of lives?

CHAPTER SEVENTEEN

~Elodie~

As we reached the end of the street with the church in the distance, the crowd gathered in front of it, most of them wearing the colours of the Lassarian king, filled me with hope. Perhaps everything had worked itself out while we were away and our efforts weren't needed after all. I could see Dee, Cassian and Arthur all looking safe and sound, and my breath caught as I saw Bran too, holding onto Eastam himself. They did it! They had really caught him.

But suddenly, the Lassarian soldiers drew their weapons and so did the men on our side, and the dark-skinned woman too, and they all began to fight.

"What the hell?" Eric muttered beside me, clearly also confused by the whole spectacle, but he didn't waste any time. "Let's go! Move in now!"

A cry rose up from behind us as all the men we had found in the ale house ran forward with whatever weapons they had managed to find, taking the uniformed men in the churchyard completely by surprise.

Eric's plan had surprised me just as much when he led me away from the church earlier.

"Where are we going?" I asked him as we ran further into the town.

"The ale house we went to last night," he explained. "There will be men there, men just drunk enough to be willing to fight no matter what the battle is about."

I couldn't tell if he was serious, but he soon proved it by bursting through the door of the ale house and addressing the thirty-odd men inside, all in various stages of drunkenness.

Where I thought he might make a stirring speech about fighting for their kingdom or protecting their prince, he stuck to the very basics instead. "I need men to fight! Anyone who comes with me now will have free ale for the rest of the month."

Nearly all the men got to their feet, and Eric quickly instructed them to find whatever weapons they could. Swords or knives would be best, but any kind of blunt object would work. As quickly as they would move, Eric and I led them back to the churchyard.

"Stay back, away from the fighting," Eric instructed me as he pulled his own sword from its scabbard.

"Eric," I called and he paused, looking back at me. "How did you know this would work?"

He gave me a rueful smile. "These are my kind of people, my lady. I know their language."

Though the men Eric had found were untrained, their sheer numbers and their unpredictability evened out the fight considerably, and the men in the Lassarian colours began to fall. Among the melee, I lost track of nearly everyone's location other than Bran. His tall, red-haired head stood out among the crowd, and pride filled me as I watched him fighting bravely.

The tide soon turned in our favour, and I crept closer as the danger seemed to be passing, still concealing myself behind some of the gravestones in the churchyard. As I watched, the dark-skinned woman slit the throat of one last man so that none were left standing who wore the royal uniform.

The men who were left standing all checked with each other to make sure there weren't any life-threatening injuries when suddenly, Cassian's voice cried out above everyone else's. "Where's Eastam?"

My eyes darted around as everyone else began to frantically search, and a moment later, I saw him concealed behind another tombstone, not far from me. Our eyes met before he looked over at the exit, just behind me. To get out, he would have to go through me, and as he came towards me, I knew what I had to do.

Pulling the small knife from my dress, I called to mind everything Eric had taught me, throwing myself into Eastam's path and sinking the blade into his arm, far more effectively than I had the night I stabbed Eric in the hay. "You will not get away again. You've hurt my friends for the last time, you selfish, horrible man."

Those weren't exactly the words I had been rehearsing to speak to him, but they got my point across. His cry of pained surprise as the blade pierced his skin caught the attention of everyone else and footsteps quickly sounded in our direction.

"We'll see who walks away from here," he snarled, grabbing the knife from his arm. Before anyone could reach us, he aimed it straight at my stomach, and thrust.

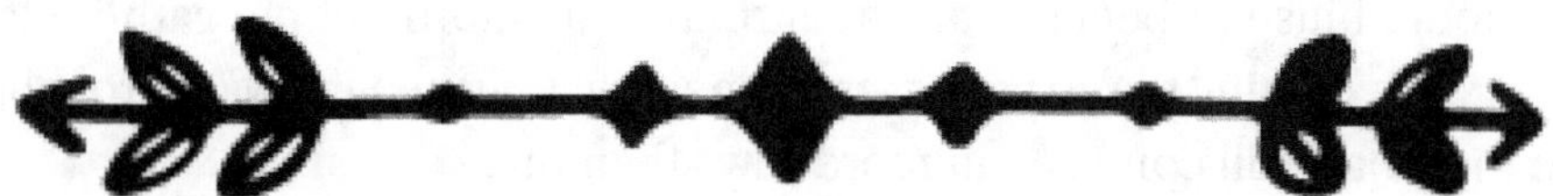

~Bran~

Time seemed to stop as Westley's arm moved, jamming the knife he'd just taken from Elodie straight into her stomach.

"No!"

The word echoed in my heart but Prince Eric shouted it out loud, right beside me as we both raced over to them.

Westley tried to pull the knife back out but it seemed to be stuck, and before he could get it, I launched myself at him, taking him down hard onto the ground, right onto a nearby grave marker.

"You son of a bitch!" With a growl, I grabbed him by his shirt and slammed the back of his head onto the hard tombstone.

"Help me get out of here," he begged, his eyes desperate. "I'll give you anything..."

"You just put your knife in the only thing in this world I want!" His head came crashing down again and this time, it knocked him out, or maybe even killed him. I wouldn't mind either way. Although he had gone limp, I picked him up once again, ready to strike another blow, but Cass' hand on my shoulder stilled me.

"That's enough, Bran. You've got him."

His sympathetic tone made me fear the worst, and I quickly dropped Eastam, his body flopping onto the ground as I turned back to Elodie. The knife still protruded from her midsection where Eastam had left it, but no blood seemed to be seeping through her dress, which confused me.

What confused me even more was the way Prince Eric had his arms around her.

"I'm so sorry," he whispered to her, his face anguished as I pulled myself to my feet. "I shouldn't have left you."

"Lodee?" Cordelia's voice sounded shaky and her face looked pale as she rushed to her friend's side. "Are you okay? How do you feel?"

Elodie blushed beneath all the attention as more people gathered, everyone craning to see what was happening. I pushed my way through to the front, still confused in more ways than one.

"Can you take it out?" she managed to whisper to Eric, though she sounded short of breath.

Though his lips tightened, he did as she requested, grabbing the handle firmly and pulling the knife free. My eyes remained on her dress, expecting to see the telltale staining as the blood pooled from the wound, but it still didn't come.

"That's better," Elodie said, placing a hand on her stomach where her dress had been torn. "It really knocked the wind out of me."

She took a step on her own and the men around us gasped, whispering amongst themselves about what kind of magic this might be. How could she have been stabbed but not be injured at all?

The dark-skinned woman figured it out first. "What is beneath your dress, my lady?"

Cordelia gasped and put her own hand on Elodie's stomach. Whatever she felt there made her face light up in relief and disbelief. "Your book?" she asked Elodie, who nodded back at her, giving Cordelia a hug.

"I'm fine, Dee. It just pushed the book into my stomach so hard, I couldn't breathe for a moment."

She had a book beneath her dress? It must have stopped the knife from reaching her skin in an unbelievable bit of luck. I had no idea what book they were talking about but right now, I didn't care. All I heard and all I cared about was that Elodie would be okay.

Eric looked overjoyed as well. "I never taught you that trick," he said, and Elodie laughed.

"No, this one is my own, Your Highness, though I didn't do it on purpose."

She smiled at him in a far more familiar way than I would have expected, her eyes shining in happiness. It seemed to take him by surprise too, and something in his expression shifted, his gaze turning more heated until he took hold of the back of her head and pulled her towards him, kissing her firmly on the mouth in front of everyone.

Hoots of approval rang out from the gathered men, half of whom seemed to be drunk, while Dee and Cass looked on in surprise, and my stomach dropped so hard I thought I might be sick.

Eric and Elodie? I knew I had been away a long time, and I had seen them together in the ale house the night before, but I had never truly believed there could be something between them. He was far too much of a scoundrel, and she far too pure.

But the way he looked at her when he held her and the look he had just given her, before their lips connected, suggested something else: he had fallen in love with her.

It was easily done, I knew that for a fact. And if he truly had, if she had captured the heart of a prince, what could I offer that could compete? I could not even promise to never leave her again, since my life would never be fully my own. I must go wherever my prince commanded me.

With a heavy heart, I backed away.

"Bran?" Cass called after me as I picked up Eastam's unconscious form.

"I'll take him back to the inn," I said without looking back. I might as well do something useful, since I didn't seem to be needed here any longer.

~**Elodie**~

I would have thought Westley Eastam trying to stab me would be the most shocking thing to happen to me on any given day.

By pure coincidence, he chose to strike me in the spot where I carried my book of stories, all the things I wrote down to remember for later to entertain Dee or, more recently, to remember to tell Bran once we were together again. So, although Eastam certainly could have done me harm had the knife gone where he meant it to go, in the end, the pages of vellum concealed beneath my dress were the only victim.

But none of that compared to the shock I got when Eric kissed me.

Nothing about it suggested a 'glad you're not dead' kiss, nor was it a sweet, respectful kiss like the ones Bran had given me.

It felt so very different and new, and took me by such surprise, that it took me a moment to stop it. Before long, however, I came back to my senses and gently but firmly pushed Eric away. "Your Highness, this is hardly appropriate."

He didn't seem to care. "I'm hardly ever appropriate, Elodie, but thanks to you, I have been trying."

He really had been making an effort, but at the moment, we needed to focus on what he had just done. "Well, you need to try harder. You can't kiss an engaged woman that way."

As soon as the words were out of my mouth, I realized that Bran must have seen that kiss too. I had been in so much shock, it hadn't crossed my mind yet, but as soon as it did, I immediately looked around, scanning the crowd for his familiar red hair.

I couldn't find him, but I did see the crowd of people watching us, and I blushed a deep red as I realized just how many people had witnessed what happened.

Eric quickly noticed the same thing. "Okay, the show is over, everyone," he announced imperiously. "Move along."

With a grumble, they began to disperse. Dee seemed reluctant to leave my side so I whispered quietly to her, "Let me have a word with Eric."

With a nod, she squeezed my hand and she and Cass went over to speak with Zara and Arthur, leaving Eric and me alone. I still didn't know where Bran had gone, but I needed to clear the air with Eric first before speaking to my fiancé anyway.

"Your Highness..." I began, but Eric shook his head.

"I think you can call me Eric now."

I shook my head right back at him. "No, I don't think so, Your Highness. We are not so intimately acquainted."

"How can you say that?" He looked genuinely bewildered and perhaps even a little hurt by my tone. "You do like me, don't you?"

"I do like you, but as a friend. As a prince. As my dear friend's brother-in-law, and nothing more than that. I am very grateful for the time we have spent together, for all that you have taught me, and to know that there is more to you than most people think. There are women who will love and respect you for that man, Your Highness, rather than the man you have presented to the world until now."

"But you are not one of them." Resignation filled his voice, accompanied by something that almost sounded like sadness, as he realized I meant my words sincerely.

"I have already given my heart to another man," I reminded him. "And I only have one heart to give."

"And where is he?" he challenged, looking around at the mostly empty churchyard.

I had no answer to that but I intended to find out. I tried to soften my next words to help Eric understand. "Your Highness, I am very flattered that you should think of me in this way, but it simply isn't meant to be. When you find the woman who is meant for you, you will know it and she will feel it too. There won't be any doubt. Even if the world conspires to make things difficult for you, somewhere in your heart, you will know the truth."

He took a deep breath as he pondered my words. "And you know this about Bran?"

I nodded with complete and utter certainty. "I do."

"In that case, I suppose you better go and find him."

He offered me a small smile and I gave him a kiss on the cheek in response. "Thank you, Your Highness, for all your help. I won't forget it."

"I won't either, my lady." He bowed his head in dismissal.

Cassian and Dee were still standing by the church door so I hurried over to them next. "Do you know where Bran is?"

Cassian nodded, not quite meeting my eye. "He took Eastam back to the inn to secure him there."

I should have guessed; he attended to duty, as usual.

"Do you want me to come with you, Lodee?" Dee's eyes were curious and I knew she wanted to know what happened with Eric and all the rest of it, but her questions would have to wait.

"No, I will go alone. I will see you for dinner later."

Waving them goodbye, I set off back to the inn to try and find my fiancé.

~**Bran**~

Arthur's men were surprised to see me when I arrived at the inn, and even more surprised to see the figure slung over my shoulder.

"What happened?" one of them asked, but I was in no mood to convey the whole long, complicated story.

"His Highness will fill you in later," I answered simply. "For now, help me to restrain him. There's no way he's getting away again."

They were all happy to oblige, just as relieved as me that we finally had Eastam in our custody. As I pulled the ropes tightly around his chest, I couldn't stop my mind from wandering to the future and what awaited me back in Silatria.

As much as I liked and respected Cass, if Elodie and Eric were together publicly, the sight of them would be too much for me to take. Even seeing Cass and Cordelia would remind me too much of what I had almost had. To the outside world, I could sometimes seem reserved and dispassionate, but privately, I felt things very keenly even if I didn't always express them, and I already knew this pain would cut me deeply and hurt for a long time.

Elodie embodied everything I had ever wanted in a wife, but perhaps I hadn't done a good enough job of convincing her of that. Prince Eric was flashier and more exciting. He wouldn't be lost for words as I sometimes found myself. Though he certainly had a scandalous past, I knew that Elodie would not hold that against him. Kind-hearted and forgiving, she always saw the best in people. That had been just one of the things I loved about her, and now it formed part of the reason I had lost her.

I didn't resent her at all for her decision, not when I only had myself to blame. Perhaps I could have resisted Cass' orders to leave on this trip in the first place and then none of this would have happened. I put my duty above my desire, and it led me here.

"Bran?"

I could almost hear her voice as I finished tying the ropes around Westley's legs. Completely secured, he could not find a way out of these bindings, or away from the three men who would be with him at all times. We would take him straight to the Lassarian court where he would have to answer to the king, his father, for all the trouble he'd caused.

I even gagged him for good measure so he couldn't try to talk his way out of things this time.

"Bran?" Elodie's voice said my name again, and this time, it sounded closer. Maybe I hadn't imagined it after all?

In the next moment, she appeared in the open doorway, her eyes scanning the room until they found me, and a hopeful smile appeared on her face, one that made absolutely no sense to me given everything I had just witnessed.

"There you are. Could I speak to you, please?"

She must be here to let me down as gently as she could. I should have known she would be thoughtful enough to tell me herself what had happened.

After ensuring the men all understood the consequences if Eastam were to disappear, I followed Elodie down the hall into the room which must be hers, trying not to think about whether Eric might have been in here with her. Her sweet eyes met mine as she came to stand in front of me, just out of arm's reach. "You must be confused about what just happened in the churchyard."

I wouldn't have chosen that word. Disappointed, yes. Saddened, certainly, but not confused. I understood it perfectly well, and I told her that now. If I could make this easier for her, I would. "Not at all, my lady. I understand that you and the prince must have spent a lot of time together recently, and I cannot fault him for recognizing what I had already seen: that you are an extraordinary woman. You deserve anything he can give you and more."

Her brow furrowed as she processed my words. "What are you talking about, Bran?"

"The prince is in love with you, isn't he?" I couldn't be much clearer than that.

"Well, yes, he thinks he is, but..."

That was all I needed to hear. "Then you must do what is best for you, my lady. I knew from the moment I met you that you were as wonderful as any princess, and it makes me glad that the whole world will see that too."

Her confusion only seemed to grow, joined by a touch of anger. "You are *glad* that Eric kissed me?"

I couldn't help grimacing at the reminder, no matter how hard I tried to maintain a neutral expression. "I am glad that you will have the life you deserve," I clarified. I didn't want to think about what might go on between them behind closed doors.

"So, I don't deserve to be with the man I love?" She crossed her arms, her head tilting to one side as she waited for my response.

I didn't understand the question. "Of course, and I understand why you would love the prince..."

This time, she cut me off before I could finish. The palm of Elodie's hand connected with my cheek, the sting of her slap taking me completely by surprise. With my own hand cradling my sore cheek, I looked down at her in shock. I had never imagined the almost timid woman I'd fallen for doing anything so forceful.

"Lady Elodie?"

"Stop with the 'my lady' and my title," she commanded, her hands on her hips as she looked me straight in the eye. "Bran, when you asked me to marry you, I thought you understood me and the kind of woman I am."

"I do," I assured her, more hurt by her accusatory tone than by the force of her hand.

"Then how could you ever think I would change my mind about something I have given my word to? I pledged my heart to you, Bran, and I meant it. I don't love the prince. I love you, you great, silly oaf!"

And with that, she reached out and pulled me down to her, bringing my lips straight onto hers.

~Elodie~

Bran tensed in surprise as I kissed him, and to be fair, it shocked me too. I had never done anything so bold in all my life, but desperate times called for desperate measures. How could he have possibly thought I would leave him for Eric? Would he have left me if our situations were reversed?

I decided to put that question to him as I pulled back from him, both of us gasping for air. "Does that mean that if a princess were to turn up and declare her love for you, I should want you to fall in love with her and be glad to see you go?"

His eyes were filled with a heat I had never seen there before. "I would never leave you, Elodie."

At least he called me by my name again. "Then why should I be any different? Do you think I don't love you the same way you love me?"

He groaned, putting his head in his hands. "I didn't mean to doubt you. We've just been apart for so long, and he kissed you, and I thought the worst. I'm so sorry, Elodie. Please, forgive me."

Of course I forgave him now that he saw the error of his assumption. I knew he had been trying to do the honourable thing by stepping aside, but he had to learn that when it came to love, honour paled next to passion. Dee had shown me that when she explained the 'punishment' she had received from Cass. Though it still puzzled me, I understood this much: we must put ourselves on the line, opening ourselves up to hurt and embarrassment, if we wanted to truly let another person in.

And I wanted nothing more than to let Bran in, fully and completely.

"I forgive you," I told him out loud. "But I would like to get this book out of my dress now. It is still uncomfortable since Westley stabbed it. Would you help me with the dress?"

I turned my back to him, partly so he could undo my dress and partly so he couldn't see the blush that spread across my cheeks. No man had ever seen me undressed before, but the one man I would trust to do it, the only one who I could imagine seeing me without feeling slightly ill, stood behind me.

For a long moment, nothing happened, and my stomach began to sink, thinking that he might refuse me. But at last, his fingers took hold of my laces and he cleared his throat gently behind me. "I would be honoured, my lady."

This time, the 'my lady' carried so much fire in his voice that I didn't mind at all that he had used my title.

The laces began to loosen and I held the front of my dress against me, keeping it in place until he had finished. As he took a step back, I turned to face him and slowly, without a word, I let the dress fall away to my waist.

Bran's mouth hung open, a shuddering breath escaping his lips as he looked at my bare chest. I looked down too so I could grab the book that had been resting against my stomach. As I pulled it away, I could see a bruise where it had been, no doubt caused by the force with which Westley had thrust the knife at me. The thought of what might have happened if the book had not been there made me shiver.

Bran's large hand closed over mine as I held the book up and together, we looked at the hole the knife had left.

"What does it contain?" he asked, looking from the book up to my eyes.

"The stories I wanted to tell you when I saw you again," I told him truthfully. "I have been looking forward to it every day."

"I have been looking forward to it too," he promised me. "But perhaps they can wait a little longer?"

He took the book from my hands and placed it on the table behind him. With his back to me, he pulled off his own shirt, revealing a firm and muscled back. When he turned around again, I could see a smattering of red hair covering his chest, like that on his head. My fingers itched to touch it and the hard muscles underneath.

I had told Dee I wouldn't want to look at him naked, but it seemed I'd been mistaken. I did want to, very much.

"I don't want to rush you, Elodie," he said as he stepped back towards me, his large frame soon taking up my whole view. "If you would like to wait, I completely respect that. But I have missed you every moment, and I've dreamt of holding you and of making love to you, and if you would like to, I would very much like to make that dream come true right now."

"Have you really thought that way about me?" I could hardly believe it.

He smiled at me, shaking his head in disbelief of his own. "You truly have no idea how wonderful you are, do you?"

My cheeks heated at the compliment but, surprising myself once again, I did not look away. "What exactly did you dream about?"

His eyes seemed to darken as he heard the agreement in my reply. I wanted to make his dream come true too.

"First, I dreamed of seeing you like this," he said as he placed his hand softly on my bruised stomach. The touch of his skin felt like the warmth of the sun, sending ripples of heat through my body and sending my heart racing. As his hand moved upwards to cup my breast, his thumb gently rubbing my peaked nipple, a sigh slipped out of my mouth. Instantly, I bit my lip in embarrassment, but Bran simply smiled at me. "Don't hold anything back, Elodie. I want to know everything you are feeling. I want to hear it all."

When he bent down to take my aching nipple into his mouth, I did as he requested, gasping in surprise. "Oh, Bran. I like that."

His lips curled into a smile with my nipple still caught gently between his teeth. "That's good, Elodie. I like it too."

My whole body felt stranger by the moment, hot and throbbing, while Bran's tongue continued to play with me. As he slipped his hands beneath the fabric of my dress to pull it over my hips, letting it fall completely to the floor, dampness gathered between my legs along with an aching want there, an incompleteness that had never troubled me before.

"You are beautiful," he whispered as he helped me step out of the dress completely and led me over to the bed.

To my surprise, having him look at me like this didn't seem so scary. Dee had been right after all: with the right person, it felt almost natural. And when he removed his breeches, getting himself completely naked too, I didn't look away either.

I did, however, start to get nervous again at the sight of him. His large cock seemed to be in proportion to the rest of him, and as I thought about where he wanted to put it, my nerves began to return.

"It's okay, Elodie," he whispered as he lay down beside me. "I won't do anything you don't want me to."

"Have you done this before?" I asked him, not sure if I should ask him now while we were naked, but wanting to know all the same.

His cheeks turned almost as red as his hair. "Once. I... um, I paid a woman to teach me what to do, so I wouldn't disappoint my wife when I met her."

That actually struck me as rather sweet in a way. "When was this?"

He gave me a sheepish smile. "Eight years ago, but I think I remember it pretty well. Will you trust me to show you?"

Since I trusted him in all things, I nodded and he kissed me again, his naked body covering mine and his hard length pressed against me. He groaned as I pressed my hips against it, and a thrill went through me at the idea that I could make him feel as good as he did to me. I wanted us both to feel the joy of our reunion and the promise of all that lay ahead of us, now that we were finally back together.

"I'm going to touch you with my fingers first," he explained, telling me in advance so he wouldn't startle me, and as his big, rough fingers began to explore between my legs, the aching there got better and worse at the same time. One spot in particular made me melt every time he touched it.

When his finger began to press inside me, discomfort did come, but he kept kissing me and touching me and soon, I forgot all about it.

"I'd like to try to fit inside you now," he whispered, removing his fingers. I immediately wanted them back, but I understood that he planned to put something much larger in their place. "If it hurts, just say so and I'll stop."

I nodded again, kissing him quickly before he pushed himself up and lined up his long, hard cock against my aching centre.

It did hurt as he began to push in, and when I told him so honestly, he stopped immediately, kissing me again and telling me how much he admired me, touching me gently until I felt comfortable enough for him to continue. When at last he told me he had gone all the way in, I could hardly believe it, and yet I utterly believed it at the same time. I had never felt so full or so complete.

"This next bit is the best part," he promised me as his hips began to move, sliding his cock in and out of me, and I couldn't argue with him. The discomfort gradually disappeared entirely until only pleasure remained, a pleasure that grew greater and deeper when I saw the awed look in his eyes as he looked down on me. The connection between our bodies mirrored the deeper connection that had already bound my heart to his, enhancing but never overwhelming it.

When his hand reached down to that special, sensitive spot again, it felt like I was going to explode. "Bran, this is... I can't..."

I didn't have the words for what I felt. There had been nothing like it in any of my stories before, and it felt so much better than I had ever imagined it. And when at last I couldn't take the pressure anymore, it suddenly all seemed to fall apart, taking me with it and washing me over with sweetness and light.

"Elodie." Bran moaned my name as his movements stilled, and I could feel him shuddering within me, his body contracting the same way mine did. "I love you."

"I love you too, Bran."

Suddenly, I had brand new stories to tell.

CHAPTER EIGHTEEN

As the crowd of men in front of the churchyard began to disperse, I could finally let myself relax. Westley had been captured, Arthur was safe, and I hoped I had done enough to redeem myself in Arthur's eyes so that he wouldn't want to imprison me for attempted treason.

Placing his hand gently on my arm, Arthur led me over to two other people, the two who had interrupted us in his room the night before. "You haven't had a chance to be properly introduced yet. Zara, this is my sister Cordelia and her husband, Prince Cassian of Silatria."

Another prince? I seemed to be surrounded by them suddenly, but it did make sense. Arthur's sister would be a princess, so who would she marry besides a prince? Princes and princesses married each other, not anyone else.

"It's a pleasure to meet you." I offered them both a tentative smile before addressing Cassian directly. "I'm sorry if I hurt your arm yesterday."

He winced at the reminder, his hand going defensively to his shoulder. "No permanent damage done, but I'm glad we ended up on the same side."

I could hardly believe he would be so forgiving. These men were certainly different from most I had met since leaving home. "I am too. What will you do with Westley now?"

"We'll be taking him back to my father's castle," Arthur answered me. "We should leave immediately. I don't want to wait around for anything else to go wrong."

I nodded even as my heart sank. Of course he must go back to his castle and back to his life. Before long, this whole time would be nothing more than a memory for him, just as it would be for me once I returned to my home, wherever that might be.

"I hoped to hear from my father before we left," he continued. "But it is not worth waiting around for, especially when we could just ask him for the information in person."

He looked straight at me as he said the words but I didn't understand. What information? And who did he mean by 'we'?

I would have to ask him. "What information, Your Highness?"

He sighed. "Please, Zara, you've just saved my life, and Cassian's, and probably everyone else's too. Would you please call me Arthur?"

Cordelia put her hand to her mouth to hide her smile while I rephrased my question. "What information, Arthur?"

"The information about where your home is."

Those were the last words I expected him to say. "What?"

"I wrote to my father to ask him, but his messenger hasn't arrived yet. It would mean a great deal to me if you came with us to the castle so we could ask him in person."

I had to be missing something. "You want me to come with you to meet with the king?"

"Yes."

"And you wrote to him before you knew for certain that I would help you today?"

"Yes." His smile, as warm and kind as always, convinced me that I did, in fact, understand him perfectly.

"You can't just set off without a destination," Cordelia interjected. "With our father's help, we'll figure out where you need to go. Please, come with us."

Tears threatened to well up as I looked around at all of their support-ive, caring expressions. These were people my father would have liked, I felt certain. They were people I liked too.

And in the end, I had no good reason to refuse. "Alright. I will go with you."

Arthur's face lit up. "Wonderful. Let's go, then."

We all walked back to the inn together, Cassian and Arthur making plans for our departure. "I'll go and find Bran," Cassian said as we stepped back through the door, but Cordelia placed a hand on his arm to stop him.

"I suspect he's with Elodie, so let's give them a few more minutes," she said, her eyes twinkling. "We'll only bother them when we're ready to go."

The names weren't familiar to me so I simply returned to my own room and gathered my few belongings before joining Arthur back at the stables where all his men were preparing to leave. More than a few curious looks were thrown my way, but Arthur ignored them all as he led me over to a horse. "You can use this one and ride next to me, if you'd like."

Did he really have to ask? I hadn't expected to even have this bit of extra time with him, but I would enjoy it while it lasted. Soon, Cordelia and Cassian joined us, along with the red-haired man and another woman who were holding hands and smiling at each other.

"I'm Bran," the man with the red hair introduced himself to me at last. "Thank you for your help today, Zara. And no hard feelings about before, I understand that Westley lied to you, as he did to so many others."

Just when I thought I couldn't be any more surprised by the good will of these men, they continued to impress me.

At last Westley himself was brought out, tied and gagged, and once again conscious. His eyes narrowed as he saw me standing next to Arthur but I simply looked away, not giving him another minute of my time. His time had clearly come to an end, and I had moved on. Arthur would make him pay for all the things he had done, and I washed my hands of him.

The ride to the Lassarian castle took the rest of the day, but it hardly seemed like any time at all. Arthur and I talked about his family, with him telling me funny stories about his younger brothers while Cordelia occasionally added a few stories of her own, including some embarrassing ones about Arthur as a boy which had us all laughing. He took the teasing in good humour, responding with stories about her that had her husband howling in laughter. Cordelia glared at Cassian and told him he would pay later for making fun of her, but he didn't seem at all bothered by that idea.

They reminded me of my parents, their love for each other clear in everything they did. As my parents crossed my mind, it made me glad to know that they had not been apart all these years after all, though it also saddened me to think that I had missed all that time with them.

As the last sunlight faded from the sky, the stone walls of the castle rose above us and my nerves started to play up as I remembered the last castle I had been in, the one where my father and I were separated in the first place. Hopefully, my experience here would be a lot more pleasant. With Arthur by my side, it seemed certain to be.

Arthur called out orders as we entered the busy courtyard, clearly in command, and it fascinated me to see him this way. Although I knew logically he had always been a prince, most of our time together had been alone. I had rarely seen the public side of him, and witnessing it only increased my admiration for him.

He didn't forget about me though. After helping me down from my horse, he offered me his arm and, together with his sister and her husband, we all walked into the great hall where the king and queen held court.

Gasps and shocked whispers quickly circulated amongst the onlookers as they caught sight of me on their prince's arm. I had encountered that kind of reaction many times before, though, so I simply held my head a little higher as Arthur's steady support never wavered.

"Good evening, Your Majesties," Arthur greeted them loudly as we approached the front of the room where his parents were seated on their large, wooden thrones. Though he spoke to the king and queen, his words were meant for everyone to hear. "We have captured the traitor, Westley Eastam."

A cheer went up through the crowd and I had to try not to smile, remembering how recently I had been on Westley's side.

"And who is this?" the king asked once the crowd had quieted, his eyes examining me curiously.

"This is Zara," Arthur introduced me simply. "She is the daughter of the man I wrote to you about. She has been looking for her father."

The look in the king's eyes changed from curiosity to sympathy, and it seemed obvious where Arthur got his compassion from. It certainly didn't seem to come from his mother, who eyed me much more suspiciously.

"I hadn't responded to your latest message yet because I hoped to get some further information from the scholars in Brathbury," the king said to Arthur, and though I didn't understand all of what he said, I got the gist of it: he didn't know where to find my home either. Before I could let the disappointment sink in, the king turned to me. "I should hear from them tomorrow. Since I'm sure you're all tired from your ride anyway, why don't you retire for the night and we can reconvene in the morning to see if we can get you the information you're looking for."

I bowed my head respectfully and with gratitude. "Thank you, Your Majesty."

"I need to speak with my father," Arthur whispered to me. "Dee will take you to a room where you can stay tonight and I'll stop by to say goodnight later if that's okay."

His thoughtfulness when he had so much of his own to deal with humbled me yet again. Bowing once more to the king and queen, I followed Cordelia and her lady-in-waiting as they took me to a very comfortable room on the castle's second floor. "Is there anything you need?" Elodie asked me. "We lived here until very recently so I know all the tricks to procuring anything you want."

"I would love to have a bath," I admitted. "If it's not too much trouble."

She assured me it would be no problem at all, and soon after they left me, three serving girls arrived with a washing basin and some lukewarm water. As I removed my clothes for them to wash me, they couldn't hide their gasps of surprise to see that my skin remained the same colour all over. I could guess exactly what the topic of conversation would be in the servant's hall when they returned, but tonight, I only found it amusing.

When they had finished, I felt much better, and after brushing my hair out, I put on the clean, white linen nightdress they had left for me, and sat down by the window, looking out over the stars shining above the Lassarian kingdom as I waited for the prince to arrive.

~Arthur~

My eyes followed Zara as she left the hall with Dee and I couldn't help thinking how beautiful she looked within the castle and how naturally she behaved here. Having her on my arm as we walked in filled me with pride, noticing how every head in the room turned in her direction, even though I had no basis to feel proud. Nothing had been decided between us besides our mutual respect.

My father had recognized that I wanted to speak to him in private, so he invited Cassian and I to join him in his receiving room with my mother following along. She never liked being left out of anything. There were people who claimed she actually ran the kingdom rather than my father, and there was some truth in it. My father rarely stood up to her when she truly wanted something.

She had a request to make of him now. "Westley Eastam has to die," she declared as soon as we were alone. "He's been allowed to make a nuisance of himself for far too long. Now that you've got him, you have to put an end to this."

My father grimaced, making it clear that no matter what Westley had done, he found it difficult to accept. At the end of the day, Westley was still his son.

"He tried to have me killed," I explained, hoping to make my father's decision easier. "He sent someone to steal my seal and kill me. No doubt he planned to use the seal to impersonate me, either to extort more money out of people or to make demands of you, or God knows what else. He wouldn't have stopped until our entire family had been wiped out."

My father nodded slowly as he took that in. "He has gone too far, there's no question. I wish he hadn't, but I can't change what's happened. He will be executed for treason."

My mother exhaled in relief. "At last."

This whole situation reminded me exactly why I had no intention of creating any bastard children of my own, though I had never experienced the temptation to risk it quite as much as I had over the last few days.

"Your Majesty, I would like to speak to Eastam tomorrow before his sentence is carried out," Cassian interjected. "He took a great deal of money from Silatria and I would like to recover any of it which remains."

"Of course," my father agreed.

"I would also like to request your fastest messengers to travel to Silatria immediately. Westley told me he intended to have my father poisoned and I need to know if it's true."

My mouth dropped open in dismay as I heard that particular threat for the first time. I hoped for Cassian's sake that it had been a bluff, but with Eastam, we could never know for certain.

"I will have them dispatched immediately," my father promised.

"In that case, I will bid you all a good night. Your Majesties. Arthur." Cassian bowed to each of us in turn and left the room, no doubt on his way to spend the night in my sister's bed. A pang of jealousy hit me as I thought about how happy they were together and how well everything had worked out. Despite my happiness for them both, I couldn't see any future quite that simple for me.

My mother seemed to be following my train of thought precisely as she gave me a critical look. "You should not have walked in with that woman on your arm as though she were your equal."

"I don't know what her rank is," I admitted freely. "And neither does she, as she's not even sure where she's from. More importantly, I don't care. She saved my life and for that, she has earned my respect."

"People will be talking of nothing else for a month," she exclaimed, obviously not satisfied with my response. "It would not matter even if she were a princess, which she clearly isn't. The colour of her skin is a sign of impurity and wickedness. You can't associate with someone like her."

She couldn't be serious. I had never heard my mother say such things before, but then, we'd never had a foreigner like Zara in our court before. Perhaps she had always thought so and simply never had a reason to express those views

My father looked at his wife with disbelief and perhaps a hint of disgust. "You don't know what you're talking about, Mathilde."

Her eyes widened in surprise at his tone. "What do you mean?"

"I mean that is superstitious nonsense and I expected better of you. Leave us. Arthur and I will speak alone."

Her mouth flapped a couple of times as she tried to decide how to respond, but in the end, she must have decided the effort wasn't worth her time, so she gave up and did as he requested, leaving my father and I by ourselves.

With a sigh, he turned to the window, looking out over the courtyard lit by torches and the darkness of our lands beyond. "I'm afraid that attitude isn't uncommon among people throughout the kingdom. It would be very hard to overcome, Arthur."

I hadn't even said anything yet about the state of my heart, but somehow, he seemed to have guessed at it anyway. "But you don't agree?" I asked him tentatively.

The corners of his mouth raised in a slightly sad smile as he kept his gaze focused outside. "I have met all kinds of men in my travels, particularly as a young prince, and I have found there is no correlation between the outer appearance and inner value of a person. Zara's father is one of the most intelligent, principled men I have ever met."

My heart beat faster at his words. "You met him? You spent time with him?"

He nodded, lost in his memories. "As I told you in my message, I released him from Eastam and arranged for him to return home, but I didn't mention that we dined together before he departed."

No, he certainly hadn't mentioned that. "What did you speak about?" I asked eagerly, hoping for some kind of information I could share with Zara. She would be glad for any news of her father, even from years ago.

"As I said, I found him very intelligent and thoughtful. We discussed the barbarity of owning and selling men, and then we moved on to discuss several other things. His reasoning and his eloquence in a language not his own truly impressed me. So did his love for his daughter and his drive to redeem himself for abandoning her, though it hadn't happened through any fault of his own."

My heart sank as I began to piece things together. "He intended to search for her?"

My father nodded once again. "He planned to go home and assemble a fighting force to return to the king who had taken her. He would fight for her if he had to, but it sounds like that would have been in vain."

It certainly would have been since Zara had escaped from that palace long before then. How long had her father been searching for her? Had they both been looking for each other all this time?

"I am glad to know she is alive and well," he continued, turning to look at me at last. "I do know that he held an important position in the Munisian empire, I simply can't remember which city he called home. Hopefully, the scholars I have contacted will be able to find the answer, but if her father is still alive and still in the same position, his daughter could potentially be of a status to consider forming an alliance with."

My head spun as I tried to make sense of all of that information. I had heard of the Munisian empire, naturally. They were a large and powerful territory far to the south of us, across the sea, and they did not generally trade or engage with kingdoms as far away as we were.

Did he really mean what I thought he did when he spoke of an alliance? I was almost afraid to ask.

My father's expression softened as he watched the emotions play out across my face. "I have never seen you look at a woman the way you look at her, Arthur. She is not the Lassarian noblewoman we had discussed for you, but perhaps, in a way, that's better. It will stop any of the local families from thinking they are better than the rest simply because you chose their daughter to marry. After what happened with the Eastams, we don't need anyone else becoming too convinced of their own importance. Besides, I know from my own experience that marrying the most suitable match does not always lead to the happiest marriage."

It truly shocked me to hear these words coming out of my father's mouth. "But you forced Dee to marry the Silatrian prince whether she wanted to or not." Luckily, it had worked out in the end, but it just as easily might not have.

He grimaced again. "It's different with daughters, I'm afraid. We needed an alliance with Silatria and Dee could buy that for us. In your case, depending on the situation at Zara's home, she may actually be a more beneficial bride to you than anyone here."

I had not even really dared to hope for such a thing, so to have him giving it to me as an option now went beyond my wildest imaginings. "What about my mother and the others who think like her?"

He gave me a wry smile. "I'm not saying it would be easy. It will be for you to decide if it's worth it, but I wanted you to know it might be a possibility."

That gave me a lot to think about, especially since I still didn't even know if Zara had any interest in me as a husband.

"Here's my suggestion," my father continued. "You can travel with her to her home to meet with her father and the Munisian emperor. If you can reach an agreement and if, after the time spent together on the journey, you still wish to marry her, then you have my blessing. If not, at least you will have one last great adventure before you need to start taking on some of my duties here. What do you think?"

I thought it sounded like a dream, but I couldn't find the words to tell him so. "Thank you, Your Majesty," was all I said instead, but he seemed to hear in my voice how much it meant to me.

"You're welcome, Arthur. Now, go and get some rest. Tomorrow will be a busy day."

CHAPTER NINETEEN

The knock on my door was so tentative that I almost didn't hear it. "Is someone there?" I called out from my spot by the window.

A moment later, the door opened to reveal Arthur, still wearing his riding clothes, and he blushed adorably as he saw me in my nightdress. "I'm sorry, I didn't realize you were ready for bed. I'll come back in the morning."

"No, please!" The words came out louder than I meant them to, making me wince, but I didn't want him to go at all. "I just bathed and didn't want to put my dress back on. It's fine with me if it doesn't make you uncomfortable."

He hesitated a moment at the door while I held my breath, truly not knowing which way he would decide. At last, he took a step inside and closed the door behind him while I exhaled in relief. I had so much I wanted to say to him before I left tomorrow and I knew I wouldn't be able to sleep at all if I didn't get it out now.

"I hope the room is suitable?" he asked as he stepped closer to me, looking almost nervously around the large stone-walled room with its curtained bed.

I had to laugh. "Arthur, I have slept on the floor of barns before. I slept in the street when I had to. You have put me up in a castle, and I can assure you that it is more than okay."

Sympathy crossed his face at the reminder of my past and he came closer still, taking a seat on the opposite side of the window bench, our knees nearly touching across the narrow space as the candles in the room cast shadows which danced across his face.

"What do you remember of your home?" he asked me curiously. "How did it compare to this?"

I took another look around the room as I tried to decide how to answer that. The stone walls, tapestries and heavy linens were beautiful, but imposing and cold. "Everything felt warmer," I replied honestly, to his amusement. "There were a lot of flowers, plants, and fountains. Tiles on the floor kept it cool in the daytime. I remember running on them in my bare feet."

He smiled with affection as I described it to him. "I would like to see it for myself."

That thought made me smile too, remembering my daydream about how everyone would stop and stare at the pale man in their midst. It could never be more than a daydream, I knew, but to my surprise, Arthur's expression turned more serious.

"I mean it, Zara. I would like to accompany you to your home, if you would allow me. I would not feel right about sending you off without knowing what you will find when you arrive."

That wouldn't be possible, and I tried not to get my hopes up. "You must have other responsibilities here. The journey will not be short."

"I know that, but I have spoken to my father and he believes it might be beneficial for Lassaria to secure a trade agreement with your empire. He has agreed to let me go and see if I can negotiate one."

Very little he could have said would have surprised me more and hope rose inside me, that stubborn, persistent hope that refused to die off, that hope which whispered that Arthur might actually care for me in a different way than he cared for others.

"I won't force you to accommodate me if you'd prefer to go alone," he quickly added. "If you'd rather I didn't come, just say so."

Did he truly think my silence meant I didn't want him to come? How could I explain to him all the thoughts and emotions swirling through my head and my heart?

"Arthur, I would be honoured to have you join me, but more than that, I would be glad for your company. I have enjoyed the time we have spent together, very much, and the idea of it coming to an end has been weighing heavily on me."

Hope sparked in his eyes, mirroring the hope inside me. "I don't like the idea either, Zara. I would much rather spend more time with you and get to know you more intimately." His eyes went wide as he heard the words come out of his mouth, and he hastened to clarify them. "I mean: better. I'd like to get to know you better, and more deeply and..."

He groaned as he managed to make it sound worse and I began to laugh, amused by his embarrassment, by his innocence, by his sweetness. This could not be an act. He truly was as good as he seemed.

He smiled too as he realized he hadn't offended me and, summoning all my courage, I leaned forward, bridging the distance between us, and kissed him full on the lips.

I knew the risk I took in doing it. In my homeland, women could be executed for kissing a prince without permission, but I had little fear of that here. I feared much more that he would tell me that I had misunderstood his intentions and that he did not feel attracted to me in the same way I did to him. Even so, the possibility of the alternative, that he actually wanted this too, enticed me enough to overrule my fear.

And to my great relief and joy, he did not push me away. His hand came gently to my face instead, cupping my cheek as our lips pressed together. Further emboldened, I rose to my feet, keeping my lips on his, and sat down on his lap. He groaned as my bottom found his cock, already hardening within his breeches.

As he obviously didn't have much experience, I took the lead, opening my mouth and letting my tongue play against his lips until he tentatively parted them, letting me in.

I had kissed many men this way before, but it felt entirely new. Each part of my body sparked with excitement, feeling alive and fully in the moment as I never had before. And as much as I felt aware of my own body, I felt more aware of him too: of the muscles of his thighs beneath me, of the stubble on his chin against my face, of the strong smell of him, of horses and leather and sun. It felt like I had been drinking though I hadn't. It felt like falling and drowning and flying all at the same time.

"Zara." Groaning my name, he gently pushed me back, off his lap and the growing bulge there. "This is wonderful but I think I should go. I don't want to do anything we will regret."

I couldn't imagine anything we could do that I would regret, but I wanted to know what he meant. "Why would you regret it? Why have you never been with a woman?"

Although embarrassment flashed in his eyes, he answered me truthfully. "I don't want to have children with anyone other than my wife. You have seen for yourself all the trouble it can cause."

Was that the only problem? "There are ways that we can enjoy each other without making children, Arthur."

"There are?" The innocence and sweetness of his question made me melt all over again.

"There are," I confirmed. "Would you like me to show you one of them now?"

~**Arthur**~

My heart already raced from Zara's kiss but her words set it galloping even faster. I truly had no idea what she had in mind, but one thing had at last become clear to me: she did desire me. She felt this attraction just the same as I did; her kiss had left me in no doubt of it.

I hadn't shared everything with her that my father had said about her potentially being a suitable match for me for two reasons: first, because I still hadn't been clear if she had any interest in me that way, and second, because I didn't want to get her hopes up if she did want it too but it turned out not to be true. If her father had been disgraced or lost his position somehow, it would change things. As much as I wanted her, I understood the way the world worked.

And so, I did not want to take advantage of her while I still didn't know for sure what I could offer her, nor did I want to risk getting her pregnant, as I told her truthfully. But when she said there were ways around it, I knew without question that I wanted to find out what she meant.

"Do you trust me, Arthur?" she asked, smiling her beautiful smile at me, and I didn't have to think about my answer for a second.

"I trust you."

Perhaps my reasoning wouldn't hold up if cold logic were applied to it, since only one day ago, I discovered she had deceived me from the moment we met. But after everything we'd been through and how she had come through for me today, I trusted her more than I trusted most of the people I had met in my life. She would not hurt me on purpose; of that, I could be certain.

Still smiling at me, her hands went to the strings of my breeches as my heart thudded almost painfully within my chest. When she had loosened them, she encouraged me to stand up, and when I did, my legs trembling beneath me, she pulled the breeches down, freeing my already stiff cock from within them.

No woman had ever seen me like this before, and no woman had ever touched me, but a moment later, she did just that, her small, dark hand wrapping around my swollen length as a rush of need and pleasure ran through me.

Her mouth found mine again as her hand began to move against me, stroking me firmly, and finally, I began to understand. I had done this to myself before, though the priests advised against it, but I had never thought of another person doing it to me. It seemed I truly did have a lot to learn, but with Zara as my guide, it shouldn't take me long to catch up.

I couldn't decide which sensation to focus on: her sweet lips and tongue that played with mine or her hand caressing me, making me harder by the second. In the end, both of them combined to nearly overwhelm me. She broke the kiss for just a moment to spit into her hand, making my cock naturally slick, and as her hand went faster and faster, my head fell back, my whole body surrendering itself to her and the pleasure she could give me. The pressure began to build inside me, stronger and faster than it ever had on my own, and a moment later, I called out her name as satisfaction washed over me, my cock pumping harmlessly within her grasp.

When I managed to open my eyes again, the sight of her wiping the evidence of my arousal from her hand greeted me, and I stared at her in awe and amazement. "That was incredible."

She gave a wide smile, looking pleased with my praise. "That was only the beginning, Arthur."

I certainly hoped so. "Are there ways I can make you feel that way too? Ways that won't give you a baby, I mean?"

She nodded slowly. "I think so. Other men have tried, but I suspect you might have more luck. Perhaps it is something we can work on when we are on the ship together."

The idea of being alone with her for weeks as we travelled together suddenly seemed more appealing than ever.

"But for now, you should go to bed, Arthur," she told me, placing one more sweet kiss on my lips. "I will see you in the morning."

As much as I would like to stay, I knew she had my own interests at heart. If I stayed any longer, there would be talk, if the rumours hadn't started already. Retying my breeches, I went to the door of the room, but I couldn't help glancing back at her one last time before I left, getting one last glimpse of her beautiful face to tide me over until the morning. I could hardly believe that she might be my future after all, a future that had never seemed so full of promise to me before.

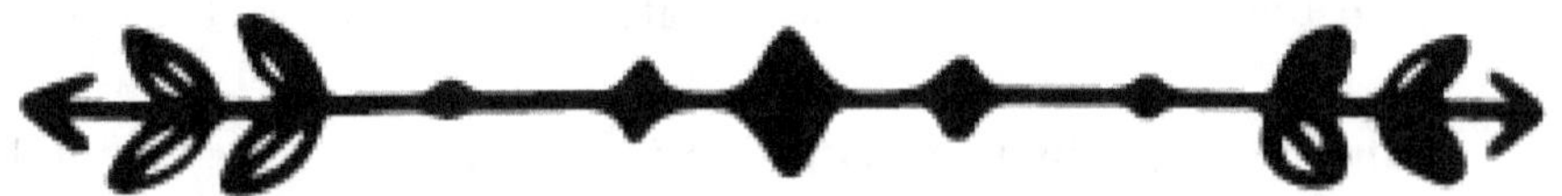

~Cassian~

Early the next morning, Dee and I returned to the great hall. Arthur and Zara were already there, but my eyes kept watching the door, waiting for the king to appear. Although he had agreed to my request and sent out messengers to Silatria to warn my father and check on the situation there, I still felt restless and knew that would continue until I could see the state of things for myself.

Completely in tune with me, Dee picked up on my agitation as soon as we woke up. "Do you want to go back today?"

"I do," I admitted. Realistically, I knew my presence wouldn't make any difference if the message had already got through, but I would feel better about it anyway.

"Then we'll leave as soon as we can," she promised me. "Just you, me, and William for backup. We'll move faster with a small group. Bran, Elodie, Matthew and Eric can follow when they're ready."

She couldn't quite hide her smile as she mentioned Bran and Elodie, and it made me smile too despite my worry. Elodie and Dee had whispered together half the ride back to the castle yesterday so I suspected something had happened. My suspicions were confirmed when Dee told me Bran would share Elodie's room for the night. It seemed Eric's surprising kiss had spurred my old friend into action, and I couldn't be happier for the both of them, though the fact that Eric had kissed Elodie in the first place still confused me.

Dee and I spent the night in her childhood bedroom. It intrigued me to imagine her there as a young girl, especially after some of the stories Arthur had shared with us on our journey, but I couldn't deny that I much preferred the woman she had become. The present and the future were all that concerned me now.

Eric had already arrived in the great hall too, and when he saw me, he came straight over. "Cass, I've been thinking that perhaps I should speak to Eastam instead of you."

He inhaled, bracing himself for an argument from me, but I stuck to one curious word: "Why?"

Cautiously, he explained his reasoning to me. "He knows you'll never give him anything, so he has no reason to tell you where the money is. With me, he still believes he can manipulate me. If I can get him to believe that I will help him escape, he might confide in me. It's our best chance."

I could see the logic in it. After threatening Dee, Eastam would have to know I would never give him an inch, but Eric could conceivably be more pliable. Eastam thought so, and so had I until very recently. However, Eric had proven himself to me over the last few days, and I was willing to keep giving him the opportunity to do so.

"Alright. I will leave this in your hands then, Eric. Dee and I are going to return to Silatria straight away, so you can report back to me when you have the information."

Something close to pride flashed across his face before quickly being tempered with discomfort. "Actually, if you don't mind, I will send the information to you when I have it, but I would rather not return home immediately."

He hadn't said a word about this before. "When will you be back?"

His eyes drifted across the room to where Bran and Elodie had just entered, arm-in-arm. "Perhaps in a few months."

"Months?" Each word surprised me more. "Where will you go? What will you do?"

A grimace crossed his face. "I'm not entirely sure, but perhaps there are some trade negotiations I could take on? I just need some space, Cass. Please."

Before I could ask what he wanted space from, the king and queen entered and everyone in the room turned to bow. As they took their seats, the king's advisor called the seven of us over: me and Dee, Arthur and Zara, Bran, Elodie and Eric.

"I have received the information about where Zara's father went after he left here," the king explained to us all. "It is the seat of the Emperor of the Munisian empire. Arthur will be leading a small expedition to return Zara to her homeland and to meet with the emperor there on behalf of Lassaria. I hope that the trip will lead to new opportunities for us all."

He gave Arthur a wry look that seemed to indicate some kind of inside information between them, confirmed by Arthur's answering smile.

Meanwhile, Eric turned to me in excitement. "This is perfect. I could go with them and see what opportunities there might be between the empire and Silatria."

His desire not to return home still felt completely out of the blue for me. "And it's got nothing to do with going to a country full of women you haven't slept with yet?"

He winced but didn't try to defend himself. "Honestly, no. Not this time. Trust me: I need this, and it will be good for Silatria too."

A couple of weeks ago, I certainly wouldn't have trusted him with something of this nature, but things had shifted. He had really come through for us with Westley, and a diplomatic mission fell within the range of responsibilities that the second son of the kingdom *should* be involved in. I couldn't see many faults with the idea, especially since it seemed to be what he wanted. "If Arthur is happy for you to go, then it's fine with me, once you've got the information from Eastam."

"Of course," he quickly agreed. "Thank you, Cass."

He went to Arthur to begin making plans while Dee and I told her parents and Bran and Elodie of our own plans.

"I hope your father is well," the king said. "You have whatever support of mine that you need."

"Thank you, Your Majesty."

We took our leave and Dee and I quickly packed up, gathered William and headed out along the road to Silatria at a full gallop.

The sun had started to dip below the tops of the trees that evening when a messenger reached us, coming in the opposite direction. Dee recognized him as one of her father's men and flagged him down.

"You have news from the Silatrian court?" she asked, jumping off her horse to go and take any message he might be carrying from him.

The man also dismounted, more slowly, and spoke to Dee in a quiet voice, too quiet for me to hear. But though I couldn't make out what he said, I could see her hand fly to her mouth at whatever words the man spoke, and I saw the glint of the setting sun off the metal as he opened up his side bag and pulled out the golden circlet.

A golden crown.

My father's crown.

My limbs seemed heavy and unfamiliar as I slid off my own horse, stumbling clumsily to the ground to make my way over to them. Dee's bright blue eyes, normally so full of joy, held only sympathy and concern as she looked over at me.

"I'm so sorry, Cass."

Truthfully, I knew what had happened as soon as I saw the crown, but her words confirmed it, and my knees buckled beneath me as I dropped down onto them, right in the middle of the dirt road we were travelling.

My father was actually dead. It had been no bluff; Eastam had killed him, and the last memory he had of me would be how I had abandoned my duty to chase after my wife and adventure one last time.

My training had only just begun and now, I would get no more of it. Ready or not, the responsibility of the crown and the entire kingdom now rested entirely in my hands.

My eyes on the ground, I saw Dee's feet appear in front of me. For a moment, I thought she had come to comfort me, but as I looked up, I saw that she held the crown in her hands, holding it out in front of her until it rested just above me.

"Long live the king," she whispered as she placed it on my head.

~**Cordelia**~

We found a nearby farmhouse where we could spend the night since the sun had started to set and we no longer had the same sense of urgency we had when we set out. We did still need to go to Silatria, with Cass now the king, but we didn't have to rush. Nothing could be done to help his father.

If my own father hadn't already condemned Westley to death, Cass would have done it now. He would have happily ended Eastam's life himself given the chance. I could barely believe the amount of destruction one man had caused, but if we hadn't gone after him, if Cass and Elodie and I hadn't made the trip, Westley might not have been captured and he might have inflicted even more damage on both my family and Cass'.

I shared that thought with Cass that night when I could see his guilt getting the better of him over the way he had left, without even a personal word of goodbye, only a note to tell his father he would return soon.

"He would be proud of you," I assured my husband, my king, who lay with disarming vulnerability in my arms in the small farm owner's bed. "He knew what a good man you are. You will honour him by being the best king you can, and I will be beside you the whole time. You are ready for this, Sean."

My use of his false name made him smile, but sadness still filled his eyes as he looked into mine. "I will have to be Cassian for good now. Sean's time is over."

I didn't want to make light of the responsibility he now bore, but I also disagreed that it had to be his whole life. "In public, perhaps. Between us, he will always have a place."

Once we entered Silatria, we took our time returning to the castle. In every town we passed, William went ahead to spread the news that the new king and queen were passing through, and all the townspeople turned out to pay their respects. It had been a long time since Silatria had a queen. Cass and Eric's mother had died when Eric was very young and though people were saddened by the loss of their king, they were also curious and supportive towards Cass. They wanted him to succeed, just as I did.

By the time we reached the castle, a messenger sent by Eric already awaited us. By promising Westley he would help him escape his death sentence at the last minute, Eric had discovered the location of what remained of the money stolen from the Silatrian treasury. It didn't cover half of what had been taken, but some was better than none.

Apparently, my half-brother really believed he would live to try his luck again another day. I wondered if it would only be when the ax came down that he would realize that luck had finally run out.

Cass met with his father's advisors late into the evening while I waited for him in my bedroom, as long as I could, until I couldn't wait anymore. Throwing my formal robe over my nightdress and pulling on some slippers, I headed towards the door of my rooms.

"Your Majesty?" The new title caught me by surprise as my guard at the door stepped in front of me. "Is there something you need?"

"I need to see the king." I would prefer not to have to explain myself, but when his job consisted of keeping me safe, I could hardly blame him for doing it.

"I will send a message to him to come and see you," he suggested.

"No, I am going to see him now. You may come with me if you like, but I will go myself."

Seeing my determination, he acquiesced, and he and one other man accompanied me down to the king's private receiving room. I could hear murmurs from the other side as we approached but I knocked on the door anyway. The guard on the other side appeared taken aback by my presence as he opened the door to me.

I spoke loudly enough that everyone inside could hear me. "I would like to speak to His Majesty."

"Dee?" A moment later, Cass appeared, his eyes full of concern. "Is everything alright?"

I hadn't meant to worry him. "It's fine. I just need a moment of your time."

I raised my eyebrows at him, trying to get my meaning across without speaking the words aloud and he seemed to catch my drift, turning to the others in the room. "We'll reconvene in the morning."

Grumbling and mentions of how much work they still had to do met his announcement, but one look from Cass sufficed to send them on their way. My husband instructed his guard to wait outside with my two men, ensuring that we were not disturbed.

As soon as the door closed behind them, Cass' arms encircled me. "Thank you. I thought they were never going to stop talking."

I knew he only half meant it. These discussions were important, but so was taking some time for him to rest and process everything that had happened. After returning his embrace, I slipped from his arms and took a look around the room. Though I had been in here with the late king before, I had never paid much attention to it. Now that Cass would be working here, I wanted to know it well.

"Have you sat on it yet?" I asked him first, pointing to the throne beneath its canopy at the end of the room. Not as grand as the one in the great hall, it still impressed with its sturdiness and elaborative carving, designed to convey power and inspire servitude amongst those who were granted permission to speak to the king here.

His lips tightened as he looked over to it too. "Not yet. It feels strange, like it doesn't belong to me."

"That's only because you haven't claimed it yet. Go and sit on it now."

His eyes scanned my face, checking how serious I was, and I held his gaze steadily, letting him know I would be beside him every step of the way. Taking a deep breath, he walked over and slowly and cautiously lowered himself onto the large wooden chair. Its high back forced him to sit up straight as he spread his arms over the carved armrests.

"Well?" I asked when he didn't say anything.

He grimaced again. "Do I look like as much of an imposter as I feel?"

I would never have used that word. "You look strong and powerful. In control."

His eyebrows raised in surprise as he held his head higher. "Really?"

I nodded truthfully. "And very sexy too."

A grin spread across his face, his body relaxing even more. "I'm not sure that's what I'm going for when it comes to my subjects."

"No?" I couldn't help teasing him as I walked over to him and dropped down to my knees submissively in front of him, forcing him to spread his legs to make room for me. "You don't want me to find you sexy, Your Majesty?"

A groan sounded from the back of his throat. "You're hardly any subject, Dee."

"That's good, since I would hate to think you would let just any subject do this."

Reaching up, my heart racing in the anticipation that always accompanied being intimate with him, I ran my hands up his breeches to his groin, pressing against the already-hardening length beneath them. Cass groaned again as I ran my hand across it firmly, pressing down with just the amount of pressure that he liked.

Looking back up at him, I gave him a teasing wink. "I think you would look even better sitting on this throne with your breeches off."

I didn't have to ask him twice. Cass had them pulled off almost before I could blink, pulling up his shirt too so that I could see and touch him freely.

Though I had hardly gone a night without seeing it in the last month, the sight of his cock, straining and growing for me, never failed to excite me. And when I lifted it gently and brought it to my lips, my king moaned just like any other man in the kingdom would in the same situation.

"I love you, Dee." He whispered the words as his hands gathered my hair back, leaving me free to concentrate on the task in front of me: tasting every inch of him, licking and kissing him, pressing my tongue hard against him and then flicking it, feather soft, as it twitched in my grasp.

I had only just taken him into my mouth fully when he pulled me back by the hair, gently but firmly. "No, not like that. I want you to sit here with me. Sit on me on the throne, my queen."

Excitement and desire raced through me as I hurried to obey, getting to my feet and lifting my skirt. Taking Cass' hand as he helped me onto his lap, I slid my legs beneath the armrests so that I straddled him while he sat upright. His strong hands raised my hips as I lifted his cock into place, and slowly and perfectly, he pulled me down onto it, letting it fill me as our bodies combined into one, fitting together as perfectly as always.

"Cass." I moaned his name in pleasure before addressing him by his title just as he had done to me. "Is that what you wanted, Your Majesty?"

Passion flared in his eyes, as I hoped. "This is what I always want, Dee. Tonight, and tomorrow, and every night for the rest of our lives."

It took us a moment to find a rhythm. My feet didn't quite reach the ground, so I couldn't get the leverage to ride him as I wanted, but Cass wouldn't let that stop us.

"Hold on," he instructed, placing my hands on the throne's armrests. With his hands, he lifted me by my hips, suspending me in midair as his hips thrust up, driving his cock deep into me, hard and fast.

"Oh, yes!" For a moment, my mind flashed back to the first time we had made love, back in the cold, damp cave, and how I had asked him if he knew any other ways to make love besides on the floor and against a wall. A month later, he still had new things to show me, and I hoped we would never run out of things to discover together.

His hips moved faster, his back pressed hard into the back of the throne to support him. "No one has ever had a sexier queen, Dee. Never one so smart and brave and perfect. I'm so lucky to have you."

"I'm lucky too," I managed to stutter as my climax built inside me. The controlled king on his throne, the passionate lover, the playful Sean, my husband combined all these men and more, and I would never get tired of discovering new sides of him.

My arms began to tremble as he thrust into me, over and over, as I climbed higher into the heights of my pleasure, and when Cass released inside me, I gave way too, collapsing down onto him and onto his throne as we rode out the wave of bliss together.

A few moments passed with nothing but the sound of our heavy breathing and the feel of our still-joined bodies. Cass' hand stroked my head as it lay against his shoulder.

"You know, Dee," he said, breaking the silence. "Now that I'm king, the whole kingdom will be expecting an heir. We will need to do our best."

That had actually already crossed my mind. "What do you think we were just doing?"

His chest rumbled beneath me as he laughed. "We'd made a good start, but I think we might need to do it again tonight, just to be sure. And maybe in the morning for good measure."

"I am at your service, Your Majesty."

His arms tightened around me once more. "And I am at yours, Dee. Always."

~Elodie~

Bran and I were still at the Lassarian court when the messenger arrived with the news that King Philip of Silatria had died. The messenger told us that he had encountered Cassian and Dee on the road so they already knew and were proceeding straight home so Cassian could take on his new role and reassure the kingdom of the stability of the crown.

The messenger also carried a personal message from Cassian for his brother. Eric's face turned pale and drawn as he read it, and my heart went out to him. Turning to Bran, I asked him to grant me leave to speak to the prince.

"He won't try to kiss you again, will he?" Bran grumbled, shooting a suspicious look in Eric's direction.

I tried not to smile as I answered him honestly. "I don't think so, but if he does, I know how to defend myself."

That earned me a smile in return. "I know you do. I will go and make arrangements for our departure. We should leave first thing in the morning, Cass will need all the help he can get."

We parted as I made my way over to Eric, who shoved the note from his brother into his pouch. "I'm so sorry for your loss, Your Highness. Are you alright?"

Eric must not have seen me approaching for he startled at the sound of my voice before quickly arranging his face into a neutral expression. "Yes, my lady, I'm fine."

He obviously wasn't. "Well, I am shaken up by this news and I could use some fresh air. Would you walk with me in the garden for a while?"

It couldn't be clearer from the way his lips tightened that he wanted to refuse, but in the end, his good manners won out. He really had changed for the better in the last week. "Very well."

We walked together out into the courtyard and then through the small hidden door in the wall that Dee and I had always used to escape from the castle when we wanted a bit of freedom. When *Dee* wanted freedom, to be more accurate; usually, I just went along for the ride.

"Will you return to Silatria with us tomorrow, Your Highness?" I asked him as we stepped out into the hedged rows of the king's formal garden. "Your brother will be in need of your help more than ever."

"That is what he says," Eric replied, gesturing at the pouch which held his brother's letter. "But we had just agreed that I would go with Arthur to the Munisian empire once Eastam is taken care of, and I still intend to do so."

My heart sank at the stubborn edge to his tone. "But if His Highness... I mean, His Majesty... needs you..."

"Cass doesn't need me," Eric said, cutting me off. "He thinks that in my upset about our father, I'll spiral out of control again. He wants me there so he can keep an eye on me, but going on this trip is the best way I can honour my father. He always spoke of making a deal with the Munisian emperor, but it is notoriously hard to get an audience with him. With Zara as a way in, I can do what my father never did. I can make him and my brother proud."

It all came back to his feelings of inadequacy, it seemed. "You have already made a good start," I pointed out. "I know that Prince Cassian... or King Cassian, rather... acknowledges and appreciates your help in capturing Westley Eastam. I heard him say so to Dee."

That news did seem to make Eric happy, but only for a moment. His mood soured again almost immediately. "It is my fault that my father is dead."

"What?" That came completely out of the blue, and I didn't understand what he meant. "How is it your fault?"

"Eastam told me he meant to harm him, but with so much else going on, I forgot to mention it to Cass. If I had said something..."

"When did he tell you?" I cut him off, trying to understand the timeline in my head.

"What?"

"When did Eastam tell you this?"

Eric thought about it for a moment. "When I met with him the day before we captured him."

I had figured as much. "So, even if you had told Cassian then, there's no way a messenger could have reached Silatria in time."

That thought seemed to take him by surprise. "I suppose not." He fell silent for a moment, thinking things over before he continued. "But if I hadn't helped Westley in the first place, he might not have had contacts within the Silatrian court who could carry out this work for him."

There may be some truth in that, but casting blame seemed pointless now. "Westley Eastam would have found a way to cause trouble no matter who helped him. You have taken responsibility for your mistakes and vowed to do better. There is nothing more you can do, Eric. We can't change the past, no matter how much we may like to."

I thought he might be offended by my blunt summary, but to my surprise, he smiled. "You called me Eric rather than Your Highness."

Had I? My own impropriety made me blush. "I'm so sorry, Your Highness, I didn't mean to…"

"It's okay, Elodie," he said, leaving off my title as well. "I don't mind. I would like to be more than 'Your Highness' to you. I understand you have chosen to marry Bran, and I respect your choice, but I would still like to be friends. I could use someone like you in my life, someone who will tell me things as they are rather than trying to flatter me or get something from me."

My turn had come to feel flattered. Besides Dee, I had very few friends. My duty always came first, and other women often found me boring, I knew. "It would be my honour, Your High… Eric."

I changed my address to him mid-word as he pursed his lips at me, and when I said his name instead, he smiled.

"Good. Then as my friend, Elodie, I would like you to tell my brother when you get home that I thank him for his invitation, I send my condolences and sympathy, but I still intend to travel with Arthur. I will be in touch with him when I can."

"You're sure that's what you want to do?"

He nodded, his jaw setting as he looked into the distance. "I've never been more sure of anything. I can't quite explain it, but I feel like this is something I'm meant to do. Something important will come from this journey, I know it."

"I hope so. Good luck, Eric." We parted amicably as I returned to Bran. I had never expected to have a prince's admiration, but as flattering as it might be, my heart had never wavered.

CHAPTER TWENTY

~Bran~

Two weeks later

The day before the whole kingdom turned out for the coronation of the new King and Queen of Silatria, a much smaller group gathered in the royal chapel. Our new monarchs sat on their thrones as I stood at the front next to the priest, with my parents and a few of my comrades from my time in the prince's service filling out the pews, as my beautiful Elodie entered and walked towards me down the aisle.

I could hardly believe such a wonderful woman had agreed to be mine. She was nothing less than a dream come true.

She entered the church accompanied by Cordelia's sister, Charlotte, who had gotten so excited at the news of a wedding that my sweet fiancée couldn't bear to tell her that it had nothing to do with her. They therefore walked in side-by-side, with Charlotte in a beautiful dress that matched Elodie's, smiling in delight, thinking that this day belonged to her. It didn't matter to me. There couldn't be a more perfect reminder of Elodie's character: kind-hearted, humble and generous, and I loved her all the more for it.

The priest kept the ceremony mercifully brief. Neither Elodie or I particularly liked being the centre of attention, and I had never been good with words. We made our vows to each other and the priest blessed us, followed by a blessing from the king himself. My friend placed his hand over mine and Elodie's clasped ones, and gave us both a warm smile.

"I am sure that I will attend many weddings as King of Silatria, but it's my great pleasure that my first one should be the wedding of a couple so deserving of the happiness they have found in each other. I wish you both long life, love, and good health."

"And lots of babies," the queen piped up from her seat, making Elodie blush adorably.

We had dinner afterwards with our small party of attendees. It couldn't be any further from the pomp and ceremony of Cass and Cordelia's wedding, but this suited us far better. And when the time came for us to retire to our new chambers, the ones Cass had given me for my status as a newly-married advisor to the king, Elodie blushed again at the whistles that followed us out of the room, even though we had spent nearly every night together since that afternoon in the inn when we first made love.

So far, we had stuck to the mechanics that I had been taught by the woman I hired as a young man, but for tonight, I had asked Cass for some advice on how to make it special. Speaking about something so intimate, even to my best friend, felt unnatural to me, but he didn't seem embarrassed at all and happily gave me his advice.

When he told me what he would do, I couldn't help looking at him in surprise. "And she will enjoy that?"

Cass grinned at me, looking far more like the carefree young prince I used to know than the serious king of the last couple of weeks. "She will love it. I guarantee it."

Taking his word, once I had helped Elodie out of her wedding dress and took a moment to admire her lithe, beautiful form once more, I led her to our new bed, laid her down and knelt at her feet, gently spreading her legs open as I kissed my way up them.

She squirmed and giggled at the gentle scratch of my beard on her delicate skin, but as I approached her core, Elodie gasped and clamped her legs closed again. "Bran, what are you doing?"

If it had a name, Cass hadn't mentioned it when he gave me his instructions. I stuck to the basics instead. "I would like to kiss you, Elodie."

"There?" The word came out in a squeak.

"It will feel nice," I promised, hoping that would be true. As soon as the words were out of my mouth, I worried that they might set her expectations too high, so I figured I might as well be honest with her. "I haven't done it before, but I was told you would like it."

"This is... normal?" Her muscles began to relax as I kissed her legs once more.

"Now that we are married, I think anything we choose to do that we both enjoy is normal for us. And it is only us that matters, right? If you don't like it, we don't have to do it again, but we can at least try."

Tentatively, she agreed and opened her legs for me once more. As I lowered my face to her intimate entrance, the scent of her, warm and wet and waiting for me, nearly overwhelmed me, as did the trust she placed in me. It made me want to worship her in every way, including this one.

My first taste of her felt like an explosion of pleasure on my tongue. Cass told me to take my time, to see what she responded to and what she liked, so I tried to do just that. And though her face initially flushed a bright red, gradually it faded to simply a warm glow, and her legs spread even wider, inviting me in deeper.

"Does it feel good?" I asked, my lips brushing against her most sensitive spot.

"Yes," she admitted, sounding both embarrassed and delighted at the same time. "I didn't know you could do that."

"I think we both still have a lot to learn," I agreed before flicking my tongue across her once more, loving the way she writhed above me as I did. "But we have the rest of our lives to learn it."

It took a bit of experimentation but eventually I found the combination of touches that worked for her best, and when she cried out my name as her body shook, it might have been the proudest I had ever felt in my life.

"I love you, Elodie," I whispered to her as I took my more usual position above her, sinking my impatient cock into her and feeling the evidence of her arousal all around me.

"I love you, Bran," she told me in reply, her arms wrapping around me. "You are the hero in my story."

I would always try to be. And even if our story didn't end up being as thrilling as the ones she created out of thin air, it would always be ours and I looked forward to every single chapter.

~**Eric**~

The day of my brother's coronation happened to fall on the same day as Westley Eastam's execution. I sent Cass a message of support and congratulations, but I needed to stay and witness Eastam's death for myself, to make certain there were no tricks and no mistakes. This man had wreaked havoc on all our lives for far too long, and the time had come to put an end to it.

I knew a lot of the blame for that havoc fell on my shoulders too, no matter what anyone said. If I hadn't been taken in by his flattery and his false promises, he wouldn't have got himself so deep into my father's court, deep enough to get someone in the kitchen to poison my father's food and to pay off his official taster, the man whose very job consisted of ensuring the king's food hadn't been tampered with. The scoundrel had eaten from a part of the meal he knew to be fine, knowing full well that my father would die when he ate the rest, all because Eastam had promised him immunity and a new title when I took over as king.

Cass had found all that out and had the men involved put to death, and now, I would make sure that the mastermind behind it all met the same end. We had recovered some of the funds he'd stolen and uncovered more of his network too, though I would bet we hadn't rooted out all of it. The vines of his manipulation spread far and deep, but once we cut the head off, once we literally cut *his* head off, all his rotten plans would wither and die with him.

Then I could finally move forward and try to be the better man that Elodie believed I could be.

Until I met her, I truly believed that romantic love was a myth, something people invented to make themselves feel special. I thought it simply a name they put on lust combined with shared goals for the future. But after spending time with her, after getting to know her as a person and not merely as a body, as I did with most women, I felt something I never had before.

She made me want to be better. Her smile, her laughter, and especially her approval took on an importance that no other person had ever had in my life before, and I had been so certain she must feel the same way. It couldn't be possible for something that strong to be completely one-sided, could it?

Apparently, it could. She didn't love me, she loved that overbearing, sanctimonious giant who served my brother. And I had to believe that love existed, because I could think of no other logical explanation for why she would choose him over me. I was young and healthy, good-looking, powerful and wealthy. Knowing I was a catch, I had never chased anyone before. They came to me and they willingly took what I gave them: usually a quick rut between the sheets and nothing more.

But now, having had a brief glimpse of what could be, I wanted more than that. I wanted someone to look at me the way that Elodie looked at Bran or the way that Cordelia looked at Cass. Or even the way that Zara looked at Arthur, though I knew things were far from settled with them.

Love did exist after all, and I had just as much right to it as anyone else did. At least, I hoped I did. What if I had already missed my chance while pretending none of it mattered?

I shook my head at those thoughts as I made my way down to the dungeon. It did me no good to sound like a sniveling little boy rather than the Prince of Silatria. As heir to the throne now, until Cass had a son, I needed to act my age.

Westley had just finished his breakfast as I walked up to his cell. It would be his last meal, though he still didn't believe it. He still thought I intended to release him, but I had come to let him know that his hopes were all in vain. He would die today, whether he accepted it or not.

His expression brightened as he caught sight of me. "It's about time. They'll be here any minute to take me up, you're cutting it pretty close."

"Not as close as you'll be cutting it."

His brow furrowed as he tried to make sense of my words. "What is that supposed to mean?"

I kept my tone neutral but my message firm. "It means that you've bet on the wrong horse. Did you honestly think you could kill my father and I would still help you?"

That only made him more confused. "But you're closer to the throne now. It's what you always wanted. When you get me out of here, we can take out Cassian too…"

My control broke as I reached through the iron bars of his cell to grab him by the throat. "I don't want the throne and I don't want my brother dead. I'm not like you, Eastam, and I'm not your puppet either. You've pulled your last string. It ends now."

As the sound of soldiers' boots sounded on the stone steps behind me, I released him and his face grew pale as he realized I was not joking. These were the king's men, ready to take him up to the execution site.

"I want to speak to my father, the king," he tried next. "I have a right to be heard…"

"You gave up any rights you had a long time ago." That came from Arthur, who stepped out from among the soldiers. "The king has personally signed your death warrant. You're out of excuses, Westley. Take him."

The soldiers quickly obeyed his order as the dungeon master undid the heavy lock on the cell door. They pulled Westley from his cell and marched him up the stairs while Arthur and I followed behind, nodding to each other in grim acknowledgement.

A bright and sunny day awaited us above ground, and I winced as the sunshine hit my face. A crowd had gathered on the green hill in front of the castle, whispering in anticipation, ready for the entertainment a public execution always brought.

The soldiers led Westley up the small platform to where the executioner stood with his ax and a wooden block, and the doomed man's disbelieving eyes searched the crowd, looking for a way out. Arthur and I stood just below the platform, right at the front, needing to see this for ourselves before we would be satisfied.

"Any final words?" Arthur asked, his voice hard and cold. I knew from the time we had spent together that the Lassarian prince didn't have a cruel bone in his body. For him to be this devoid of emotion, the person on the receiving end had to really deserve it, and no one deserved it more than Eastam.

And the idiot couldn't resist making one more attempt to bribe his way out of his fate. He ignored Arthur and turned directly to the executioner instead. "I can give you anything you want if you let me go..."

I shook my head in disbelief. "You have nothing left to give, Westley. We've taken it all. Your parents have fled the kingdom in disgrace and your sister, Arabella, is still a servant at the Silatrian court. You have ruined your entire family, and now you will die."

"But I do have to thank you for one thing," Arthur added, and both Westley and I raised my eyebrows at him in surprise. What could he possibly want to thank him for?

From the crowd, Zara stepped forward to stand beside Arthur, her eyes just as hard as Arthur's as she stared up at Westley and answered the unspoken question. "Without your scheming, I might never have met the prince and found out where my home is. By next month, I will be back there with the sun warm on my skin, while you will be cold in the ground."

The soldiers holding Eastam pushed him forward, holding the struggling man down so his head rested on the block, and as the executioner raised his ax, Zara looked away, but Arthur and I kept our eyes on him. The blade sung as it flew through the air, hitting the block with a sickening thud. It took a second blow for Westley's head to completely detach from his body, and only then did the tension in my own body fully relax.

"It's over," Arthur said beside me, echoing my own thoughts exactly as we turned away, back towards the castle. "We can finally move forward."

That was exactly what I intended to do. "What time do we set out?"

"Within the hour. The ships are waiting for us at the port. We'll stay at the inn overnight and set sail first thing in the morning."

The next part of my life would begin tomorrow, then. No more sitting on the sidelines and letting others make decisions for me. This time, I would find my own way.

This time, I would write my own story.

~THE END~

IF YOU ENJOYED THIS...

The adventure continues in Munisia in the third book in the series, *Princess in Hiding.*

MORE FROM THE AUTHOR

<u>Contemporary Romance – 18+</u>

Callahan Series
A Matter of Time
A Piece of Land
A Change of Heart
A Work of Art

Christmas in the City Series
Mistletoe Mistake
Candy Cane Challenge
Tinsel Temptation
Gingerbread Gamble

A Set of Three

Charity Case

Hired Lover

<u>Contemporary Romance – New Adult/Clean</u>

It Figures duet
It Figures
Figuring It Out

<u>Historical Romance – 18+</u>

Lady in Waiting Series
Lady in Waiting
King in Training
Princess in Hiding

<u>Paranormal Romance – 18+</u>

Cold Lake Pack Series
The Curse and the Prophecy
The Spell and the Legacy
The Dream and the Destiny

Mismatched Mates Series
Mismatched Mates
Misguided Motives
Mistaken Meanings

Serena's Story
The Alpha's Second Chance
The Returned Mate
The Vampire's Consort

Sacrifice Series
Blood Donor
Life Giver

Paranormal Romance – New Adult/Clean

The Alpha's Prey

KEEP IN TOUCH

My Patreon account has daily updates from my works-in-progress,
bonus chapters and more – join me there to comment and read along
as my next books are being written:
www.patreon.com/melodytyden

You can find and follow me on Facebook at:

facebook.com/melodytyden

Join the Facebook group Melody's Romance Corner for fun games,
interaction with the author and exclusive news and excerpts.

You can also sign up to my newsletter at www.melodytyden.com for
all the latest news.

9 781739 708870